To Bed the Bar
Girls Who Dare, Book 9

By Emma V. Leech

Published by Emma V. Leech.

Copyright (c) Emma V. Leech 2020

Cover Art: Victoria Cooper

ASIN No.: B082MQRLX4

ISBN No.: 9798638803957

All rights reserved. Without limiting the rights under copyright reserved above, no part of this publication may be reproduced, stored in or introduced into a retrieval system, or transmitted, in any form, or by any means (electronic, mechanical, photocopying, recording, or otherwise) without the prior written permission of both the copyright owner and the above publisher of this book. This is a work of fiction. Names, characters, places, brands, media, and incidents are either the product of the author's imagination or are used fictitiously. The author acknowledges the trademarked status and trademark owners of various products referenced in this work of fiction, which have been used without permission. The publication/use of these trademarks is not authorised, associated with, or sponsored by the trademark owners. The ebook version and print version are licensed for your personal enjoyment only. The ebook version may not be re-sold or given away to other people. If you would like to share the ebook with another person, please purchase an additional copy for each person you share it with. No identification with actual persons (living or deceased), places, buildings, and products is inferred.

Table of Contents

Members of the Peculiar Ladies' Book Club	1
Chapter 1	3
Chapter 2	12
Chapter 3	23
Chapter 4	40
Chapter 5	55
Chapter 6	66
Chapter 7	78
Chapter 8	90
Chapter 9	101
Chapter 10	109
Chapter 11	125
Chapter 12	142
Chapter 13	154
Chapter 14	166
Chapter 15	175
Chapter 16	189
Chapter 17	202
Chapter 18	218
Chapter 19	230
Chapter 20	239
To Ride with the Knight	259
Want more Emma?	261
About Me!	262

Other Works by Emma V. Leech	264
Audio Books!	268
The Rogue	270
Dying for a Duke	272
The Key to Erebus	274
The Dark Prince	276
Acknowledgements	278

Members of the Peculiar Ladies' Book Club

Prunella Adolphus, Duchess of Bedwin – first peculiar lady and secretly Miss Terry, author of *The Dark History of a Damned Duke*.

Mrs Alice Hunt (née Dowding)–Not as shy as she once was. Recently married to Matilda's brother, the notorious Nathanial Hunt, owner of *Hunter's*, the exclusive gambling club.

Lady Aashini Cavendish (Lucia de Feria) – a beauty. A foreigner. Recently happily, and scandalously, married to Silas Anson, Viscount Cavendish.

Mrs Kitty Baxter (née Connolly) – quiet and watchful, until she isn't. Recently eloped to marry childhood sweetheart, Mr Luke Baxter.

Lady Harriet St Clair (née Stanhope) Countess of St Clair – serious, studious, intelligent. Prim. Wearer of spectacles. Finally married to the Earl of St Clair.

Bonnie Cadogan – (née Campbell) still too outspoken and forever in a scrape alongside her husband, Jerome Cadogan.

Ruth Anderson– (née Stone) heiress and daughter of a wealthy merchant living peacefully in Scotland after having tamed a wild Highlander.

Minerva de Beauvoir (née Butler) - Prue's cousin. Clever and resourceful, madly in love with her brilliant husband.

Jemima Fernside – pretty and penniless.

Lady Helena Adolphus – vivacious, managing, unexpected.

Matilda Hunt – blonde and lovely and ruined in a scandal that was none of her making.

Chapter 1

Dearest Bonnie,

I am in such a lather I cannot tell you. Minerva came home today in a flurry and I am worried out of my wits. She was seen at Mr de Beauvoir's house by Mrs Tate, of all women! She swears that de Beauvoir has silenced her for now and, praise be, he has told Minerva he will see my brother tonight to ask for her hand in marriage. The problem is, she does not seem pleased about it. She won't talk to me and there is nothing I can do. I cannot beg Robert to accept the proposal until after it happens, for she has sworn me to secrecy, and I must go to a stupid musicale this evening, and you know how I detest keeping still for any length of time. I shall spend the entire evening sat upon thorns in a misery of anxiety. I only pray there will be a happy resolution by the time I get home.

—*Excerpt of a letter from Lady Helena Adolphus to Mrs Bonnie Cadogan.*

25th January 1815. Briar Cottage, Mitcham Village, Sussex.

The cottage was everything Jemima had dreamed of, but far more spacious than she had been expecting. When first she'd seen it, the thatched roof had been in shocking disrepair, the whitewashed walls were flaking, and the woodwork was in a sorry state. Early this morning, she had left Matilda's comfortable town house full of apprehension, but now her heart swelled at the sight of her pretty new home. It had been years since she'd lived in anything but sparsely furnished rented rooms. Of late, those rooms had been damp and dingy and so cold in the winter that it was a wonder her poor aunt hadn't succumbed sooner than she had. In comparison, this was a dream come true. The thick new thatch settled heavily like a cosy hat upon half-timbered walls of brick and freshly painted lime mortar. Some hardworking soul had brought the tangle of weeds and dead briar that had been the garden back into meticulous order, and the neatly pruned limbs of rose bushes were visible, stark and vulnerable on such a freezing afternoon. Box hedges bordered the front, meeting at the gate and cut with military precision, while the handkerchief-sized lawn on each side of the path perfectly trimmed.

"He's made a fine job of it," Mrs Attwood remarked with approval.

Jemima turned to regard her companion. She still didn't know quite what to make of Mrs Attwood. Originally from Yorkshire, she was a woman in her early fifties, with a good figure. She was elegantly dressed in a dark pink velvet carriage dress with ebony buttons, and matching bonnet with stylish black and pink ribbons. It was a remarkably frivolous outfit for a woman Jemima thought rather intimidating. Her hair a rich mahogany, though shot through with white, was still thick and lustrous. A handsome woman rather than beautiful, her dark eyes missed nothing, and she had a brisk, no-nonsense manner, which was daunting to one who'd been brought up by her fragile maiden aunt. Though Jemima could not complain that Mrs Attwood had been anything but respectful to her, she was plainly spoken and had put Jemima to the blush several times already. This was the first time she'd ever referred directly to the fact that Lord Rothborn was paying Jemima for her company, however. Or that he was responsible for her new home, all the work that had been done to it, and the entirety of the contents, not to mention every stitch Jemima was wearing. Though all work had been overseen by Jemima's man of business—Mr Briggs, ostensibly using the legacy she'd been left by her aunt—Mrs Attwood knew the truth. Jemima's aunt had died without a penny to her name, and Jemima had been desperate enough to accept the baron's scandalous proposal.

Mrs Attwood had been employed by Baron Rothborn as Jemima's companion, there to lend her respectability, when they both knew Jemima was anything but respectable. Not anymore.

"Yes," Jemima agreed, a little of the pleasure she felt dimming as she remembered how she would pay for the privilege of living in this lovely home. "A very fine job."

"Well, let us get inside and out of this wind. I'm fair nithered and in dire need of a cup of tea. Bessie, leave that," Mrs Attwood said, waving a hand at their maid of all works, who was struggling to hoist an overstuffed carpet bag. "The men will bring the bags in. Go and get the kettle unpacked and make us a brew."

The girl, originally employed by the baron at The Priory, cast wide, anxious eyes at Mrs Attwood and scurried away to the back door, where the men were carrying the luggage. Jemima gave herself a shake, reminding herself she was the lady of the house, and that she ought to stir herself into getting things done.

"Come along, then," she said, striving to sound calm and in control as she took Mrs Attwood's arm and walked up the neat paved path to the front door.

Happily, the cottage had no near neighbours, being a good five-minute walk from the village proper. However, Jemima didn't doubt that curtains had been twitching as her carriage had come through, and it was only a matter of time before the first of the villagers descended upon her. She needed to be ready for them.

Not only for them.

That made her heart skip, which was most unsettling, and Jemima concentrated on retrieving the heavy door key from her reticule. They stepped through the shiny black painted front door into a tiled hallway, which led directly through the house to the back door, and out to the garden. On either side of the hallway, at the front, was a good sized room: a formal receiving room on the right, and a comfortable parlour on the left. Beyond that was to be found the dining room and staircase, and then the kitchen and scullery. There were four bedrooms, and two small garret rooms.

Jemima went first to the sitting room, finding it impossible to hide her eagerness.

"Oh!"

Despite the circumstances, she could not hold back her delight when she saw the transformation inside. Though she had chosen all the furniture herself and had dreamed of how it all might look, to see it before her gave her a little thrill of pleasure.

A fire blazed merrily in the large fireplace, and the room was blessedly warm after the chill wind outside. The walls were freshly painted white, the oak floorboards scrubbed, and the dreadfully extravagant rug she'd bought was thick and luxurious beneath her kid half-boots. One thing she had to say for the baron, he was no nip cheese. He had encouraged her to furnish her new home with every comfort, insisting that she buy quality and never balking at the bills. As she looked around, however, she noticed items that she had not bought, small items of décor that she had thought too frivolous to spend the man's money on. These included a pair of elegant china candleholders on the mantelpiece, beside two porcelain figurines. A lump rose to her throat as she also noticed several lovely framed watercolours, and that the recessed arches on either side of the fireplace had been fitted with shelves and filled with books. Jemima moved closer, finding the titles blurred, forcing her to blink hard as she discovered a wonderful selection of novels and poetry. Good heavens. How thoughtful he was. A rush of warmth surged through her and she scolded herself for it. That way lay danger.

Jemima knew her own weaknesses. She knew she had a heart only too susceptible to romance, too easily led into tender feelings.

As a girl, she had often lost herself in romantic poetry or tales of heroes who rescued their lady loves from wicked villains. Too long she had dreamed of her own knight in shining armour, of *the one* who would fall instantly in love with her and carry her away from all her troubles. Reality had crushed her dreams and brought her back to earth with such a painful jolt that she could not allow herself to indulge in such fancies again. The baron had made his position very clear. He could not offer her that. He wanted an intelligent companion to alleviate his solitude, and a woman to… to….

A blush swept over her and Jemima stood closer to the fire, hoping Mrs Attwood would attribute her heightened colour to her proximity to the flames.

"Well, this is splendid," the woman said with obvious approval.

Jemima turned to find her companion stripping off her gloves and untying the ribbons on her bonnet. She put the gloves in the bonnet and set them down on an elegant chair upholstered in cream damask silk.

"You have excellent taste, Miss Fernside, though I could tell that the first time I looked upon you. I think we shall be very comfortable here. Such a perfect location, too. Private enough not to be overlooked by the gossips, and yet so convenient for the village."

Jemima's scalding cheeks burned hotter and the lady tsked, shaking her head. She moved forward, taking Jemima's hands in her own. It was such an intimate, friendly gesture from a woman she barely knew that Jemima was too startled to react.

"Why don't we call a spade a spade, my dear? You'll be more comfortable with me if you do. You are to be the baron's mistress. There's no getting away from it."

Jemima gasped and moved to tug her hands free, shocked by this forthright manner of speech. Mrs Attwood held on tight.

"No," she said, her dark eyes intent. "You'll hear me. There's no shame in surviving, Miss Fernside. We all do what we must, and those who would condemn us can go to the devil if you ask me. Better a good man's mistress than to serve an army on your back. You chose right, and you'll find no condemnation from me, nor that little maid neither. She talks of yon baron like he's God almighty and he's told her to keep mum. You're safe here, with us, and I'll not have you come home by way of the weeping cross once you've done what you must and there's no turning back. You've made your bed, so you may as well enjoy the comforts of the mattress. At least he's a handsome devil, so it ought be no hardship."

Jemima stared at her, robbed of speech for a long moment. Then she drew in an unsteady breath and let it out again in something resembling laughter. She gave a slight nod, the most she could manage, and the hands that held hers tightened slightly.

Mrs Attwood gave her a warm, approving smile.

"That's the way, lass. Now, let's have a look at the rest of the place, shall we?"

***

Solo Weston, the sixth Baron Rothborn, took out his pocket watch and checked it against the mantel clock in his study. Ten minutes before five o'clock. Miss Fernside ought to have arrived some time midmorning. He limped to the window, cursing the cold, wet weather that made his blasted leg so damned painful. Outside, a dismal day greeted him. Nothing but drizzle, with a low misty cloud that clung to the treetops and offered a sodden outlook upon the ancient and beautiful gardens that surrounded The Priory. The view from every window of the building was picturesque, and though Solo was biased, even now on such a miserable day as this, it was still the loveliest place in all of England.

It was also inconvenient, draughty, horribly expensive, and more demanding than any mistress. He went to the chair behind his desk and sat heavily, kneading the knotted muscles in his thigh with one hand, and wondering if it would be beyond the pale for him to call upon Miss Fernside today. Surely he ought to give her a day or two to settle in?

Yes. Two days would be prudent.

Except… perhaps two days was too long. He did not wish to insult the lady, or for her to believe him indifferent to her arrival. So, tomorrow, then.

He reached for the book he'd been reading, taking out the bookmark and finding his place. It was less than five minutes before he gave up, realising he'd read the same paragraph three times without comprehending a word. The devil take it. He'd call on her today, now, before it got dark. Just briefly. Just to see she had everything she needed. He'd not stop. Not take up her time. He'd simply reassure himself all was as it ought to be, and arrange a time to call again when she was settled. Decided upon this plan of action, he headed for the front door.

The staff who remained at The Priory had worked there all their lives, as had their parents before them. Not that there were many. When the previous baron, Solo's father, had died, they had shut up the house whilst the son was away at war. On his return, half mad with grief and pain, it had been more than he could bear to have people around him. He had asked only those who'd known him since childhood to return, those who could be trusted not to gossip about the wreck of a man who had come home to lick his wounds in private. The most important of those was Mrs Norrell, the cook and housekeeper. Previously, The Priory would have had an army of staff, the kitchens alone bristling with people, but Solo could not stand the scrutiny of strangers and, with only him in residence, it seemed pointless. So Mrs Norrell ruled the roost with only a handful of staff under her dictatorial command. She was a tiny woman who barely reached higher than Solo's elbow, was as wide as she was tall, and ruled The Priory in a manner the Iron Duke would have approved of.

She tsked and shook her head as she came across Solo in the great hall, shrugging into his heavy greatcoat and picking up his hat.

"'Twill do that leg of yours no good to be out in this cold, my lord. You'd do best to sit by the fire. The lady will still be there tomorrow, when the rain has gone."

Solo turned an icy expression upon the woman, which didn't have the least effect, as he'd known it wouldn't. Having once been his nurse, she well remembered changing his clouts and smacking his arse for cheeking her. It was hard to act the high and mighty lord of the manor before a woman who had tanned his hide and sung him to sleep as a snot-nosed boy.

"Mrs Norrell, I know you find this hard to remember, but I am a grown man and in complete charge of my own mind and person."

"Aye, and with less sense than you was born with," she said, with an impatient huff. "Ah, well. Do as you will; you always did. I'll have water heated and ready for when you get back and commence blustering about your poor leg."

Solo opened his mouth to object. He *never* blustered— let alone about his leg, confound the woman! —but Mrs Norrell had stalked off back to her sacred domain in the kitchen.

"Interfering old termagant," Solo muttered as he put on his hat and headed for the door.

"I heard that," Mrs Norrell yelled, before the door that led to the kitchens banged shut.

Hell and the devil, the blasted woman had the hearing of a bat! There was something supernatural about her, he was certain of it. Solo was not the least bit fanciful. He did not believe in ghosts, despite some of the odd things that had happened in The Priory. There was always a reasonable explanation for such things, even if he couldn't think of one himself. Yet Mrs Norrell had an uncanny knack for knowing things, for knowing *him*. He'd never outmanoeuvred her as a boy, and it was beyond humiliating to discover nothing had changed. As Lieutenant Colonel of the 15th King's Dragoons, he was known for his brilliant military strategy, and yet his blasted housekeeper ran rings around him.

Still muttering, Solo pulled on his gloves, retrieved his cane from where he'd set it down, and headed out into the cold.

Chapter 2

Dear Robert,

Please forgive me for all the trouble I have caused you. I must point out, however, that it is <u>I alone</u> who have caused the trouble. Prue knew nothing of my plans outside of the fact I was infatuated with Mr de Beauvoir, and poor Inigo — Mr de Beauvoir — did his very best to make me behave myself, but it was no good.

I think perhaps I fell in love with him the very first time we met last summer, at least a little, and it's been growing worse with every week that passes. I love him quite dreadfully, you see, but I'm afraid I behaved very badly and pursued him despite his best efforts to dissuade me. That being the case, I cannot allow you to hold him responsible for what has happened.

—Excerpt of a letter from Miss Minerva Butler to His Grace, Robert Adolphus, Duke of Bedwin.

25th January 1815. Briar Cottage, Mitcham Village, Sussex.

By half past four, the bulk of the unpacking had been done. The men who had accompanied the cart loaded with Mrs Attwood's and Jemima's belongings were thanked with tea and cakes and some extra coin, and sent on their way. Jemima was helping Bessie unpack the last of her many new dresses when Mrs Attwood knocked and came in.

"What a lovely room," she said, looking around the elegant bedroom with approval. "It will have a wonderfully sunny aspect, if ever the sun deigns to show itself again."

"Thank you," Jemima replied, getting up from the floor and shaking out the wrinkles in her skirts. "I hope your own room is to your satisfaction?"

"Satisfaction?" Mrs Attwood said with a tinkling laugh. "Good heavens, child. I never had such a beautiful room in my life. Grander, perhaps," she said with a naughty wink. "But never so beautiful. You have impeccable taste."

Jemima blushed with pleasure. She'd always loved choosing fabric and colours, but it had been a long time she been able to indulge her love for pretty things, not when it had become a choice between paying the rent and putting food on the table. It hadn't always been so, but the last years weighed heavy and seemed to diminish any lighter memories that had come before.

"I'm so happy you are pleased."

She might have said more, except a knock at the door sounded and Jemima looked up in surprise. Surely the neighbours wouldn't come calling on the very day she'd arrived. She glanced at Mrs Attwood, who returned a knowing look.

"That was the back door," the woman said, smiling now. "So we know who it will be. I didn't think he'd be able to wait until tomorrow to see you. Such a gent, too, waiting to be seen in when the weather is so poor. Many a man in his position would barge in, as he does in fact own the place. I'll see him settled in the parlour while you change your dress for something pretty for him. Hurry, now."

Jemima stared at her, suddenly panic struck as Mrs Attwood bustled to the door.

"B-But," she stammered. All at once, as anxiety coiled in her stomach and twisted her guts into a knot, she wanted to be back in the miserable little flat she'd been struggling to keep hold of these past months.

"Good heavens!" Mrs Attwood said, laughing as she came back and gave Jemima a swift hug. "He's not going to ravish you in your front room, dear. I expect he's just anxious to see you are well settled, and eager to see you again. Stop looking like a virgin sacrifice, or you'll make the poor man feel like a monster."

With that, she hurried out and Jemima took herself in hand. Of course, Mrs Attwood was quite correct. She was being a complete ninny. It wasn't as if she didn't understand the agreement she'd entered into. She must stop being so dreadfully silly.

"Bessie, get me that blue and white striped gown, the last one we put away. Do hurry, we mustn't keep the baron waiting."

Bessie paled and lunged for the wardrobe. "Oh, indeed not, miss. A stickler for punctuality, he is, what with being a military fellow. Can't abide waiting for people, nor for his dinner neither."

"Oh. Is he bad tempered, then?" Jemima asked fretfully as Bessie wrestled her out of the frock she was wearing with ruthless efficiency.

"Oh, bellows like a lion, he does, what and things don't go how he likes 'em. Still, 'tis often his leg what pains him and puts him out o' temper, so we don't pay it no mind, what with him being such a war hero. My, the stories they tell of his heroics, especially at that *Sagoohny* place in Spain, where he was so badly hurt. 'Tis a wonder he came home as whole as he did, not that it weren't wretched bad when he first came back, but he's a good master, kind an' all, so we don't mind a bit o' bluster. 'Tis like a north wind, miss, and soon blows itself out, and then he's meek as a kitten."

Bessie, who had hardly spoken two words to Jemima before this lengthy exposition, suddenly realised her nerves had led her into chattering, and she blushed crimson.

"Beg pardon, miss," she said, casting Jemima nervous glances as she lifted the new gown. "I didn't mean to rattle on so. Tongue like a fiddlestick, Mrs Norrell says, not that I gossip, miss, for I don't. Not never. Only as you're to be... as you are... what with... well, I thought you'd like to know a bit about him," she said desperately, before tugging the dress over Jemima's head.

Once Jemima was clear of the voluminous fabric, she let out a breath. Bessie hadn't exactly soothed her nerves, but she wasn't entirely surprised by her description of Lord Rothborn either. Much of what Bessie had said had been apparent from their first meeting, and her estimation of his better nature had grown from the thought with which he had added items to make the house welcoming to her. The baron was a good man at heart, tempers aside, and those Jemima would learn to manage.

Bessie was just putting the finishing touches to her hair when Mrs Attwood came back.

"He's settled in the parlour, waiting for you," she said, giving Jemima a critical once over. She nodded with approval. "Lovely. He'll not know what hit him when he sees you in that frock. In fine twig, I must say. Now, have a little nip of brandy for your nerves."

She proffered a small silver hip flask and Jemima took it with a frown.

"I've never—" she began, but Mrs Attwood waved away her protests.

"'Tis good for what ails you. Just a few sips and you'll not blush and stammer quite so much, though I suspect he'll not mind that. A gentleman likes to feel protective of a little innocent, but we don't want him feeling like a brute for stealing your virtue, or some such nonsense if you overdo it."

Jemima didn't even blush this time, beginning to appreciate her companion's rather forthright way of speaking. Far better that than some farcical pretence that everything was perfectly as it ought to be. She upended the flask, taking three large swallows, and then choked as the liquor burned its way down her throat.

"Good heavens!" she gasped, wide-eyed.

"Well, it's not lemonade! I said sip it, not swig it down." Mrs Attwood laughed and tugged her to her feet. "Off you go, then, and remember to smile."

Jemima almost tripped down the stairs in her haste, slowing at the last step as the brandy bloomed into a puddle of warmth in her belly and eased into her veins. Oh, yes, she could see what Mrs Attwood meant now. Taking a deep breath, she gave herself a moment to gather her nerve, and headed for the parlour.

***

Solo stood by the fire. The room was exceptionally elegant, and he felt a flush of pride in Miss Fernside for having arranged it so stylishly. Not for the first time, he considered his good fortune and wondered if his memory was playing tricks on him. Surely she could not have been as exquisite as he remembered. It had perhaps been a trick of the light that had given her skin that luminosity, the cold that made the blush of colour at her cheeks so sweet, and perhaps she'd used rouge to make her lips that inviting soft pink. He experienced a qualm as he wondered if she might have lulled him into a false sense of security. If she was beautiful, she was likely expensive, and the restraint she'd shown in furnishing this house was the calm before the storm. Perhaps she'd demand diamonds and trips to the opera and the theatre. The diamonds he could manage, perhaps, if he must, but the idea of the opera or the theatre made him hot and uncomfortable. The noise and the throngs of people would be more than his nerves could stand. Not to mention how awkward it would be, to be in the company of all those he used to spend time with when he was so changed... no. No, that would never do.

He took out his pocket watch and scowled at it. What was taking so long? Was she having second thoughts? Perhaps she'd escaped out of the back door whilst he was waiting.

Anticipation made his heart hammer in his chest and he told himself to stop being such a damned fool. He shifted his position, taking the weight from his damaged leg as it spasmed, protesting at standing for so long. Damn thing had a mind of its own, and a deranged mind at that, contrary article. It didn't like it if he sat still, but complained if he walked about too much. It was bad-tempered in wet weather, yet if he sat by the fire it wanted him to get up and move. Honestly, it was like being attached to a fractious child.

He huffed, irritated, and glowered at the watch, willing the hands to move and tempted to give it a little shake. The door opened, he glanced up, and almost dropped the watch as his gaze fell upon Miss Fernside.

Good God.

His memory *had* been at fault. She was far more beautiful than he'd been prepared for. He clutched the watch so tightly in his hand that it was a wonder he didn't crush it, and stared as she closed the door gently behind her and curtseyed. As she rose, as elegant as a dancer, she noted the watch he held and his heart kicked in his chest at the fierce blush that bloomed over her skin. By heavens, he'd seen nothing so lovely in all his days. His mouth went dry and any sensible thought vanished, likely never to be seen again. He was hot and unsettled and out of sorts. He'd wanted a comfortable companion, a woman to converse with and to bed, and he'd… he'd…. How would he ever hold on to her? If any man of higher rank or fortune discovered this exquisite creature was his, they'd give her a far better offer and he'd lose her. The idea made him feel ill.

"I do b-beg your pardon, my lord," she said in her soft, musical voice. "I wanted to look my best for you, but I ought not have kept you waiting for so long."

Waiting? Had he been waiting? Time had been suspended and he was trapped in some world in between one heartbeat and the next. He couldn't speak and saw the anxiety in her gaze as she stared at him with growing concern.

"P-Please forgive me. It won't happen again. I promise."

Solo tried to put the watch away and almost dropped the wretched thing, concentrating on fumbling it into his pocket and adjusting the chain to give himself a moment.

"I didn't mind," he said, his voice sounding too loud, too strident in this elegant room, with this woman who was all delicate limbs, so very fragile, like a fairy queen.

Lines from a Shakespearean sonnet came to mind and he had to bite his tongue to stop the words from tumbling out as if he was some lovesick swain.

If I could write the beauty of your eyes
and in fresh numbers number all your graces,
The age to come would say, 'This poet lies;
Such heavenly touches ne'er touch'd earthly faces.

"Waiting," he added, before realising he'd paused too long to add the clarification. "I didn't mind waiting," he repeated, cursing himself.

God, what a damned buffoon.

"May I offer you some tea?" she asked, daring to come a few steps closer.

"No," he said, with a brisk shake of his head, and then wanted to take it back.

If he took tea with her, he could draw the visit out and stay longer. Too late now. Blasted idiot. He dared look at her again, to see her hands were knotted together, the slender fingers white. Poor little creature was scared witless. Damn his eyes, he was a mannerless brute.

He cleared his throat, attempting to keep his voice gentle. "I hope that everything is to your satisfaction, Miss Fernside?"

At that, her soft lips curved into a dazzling smile which knocked the air from his lungs. It was like falling from a great height and hitting the ground with a thud. He felt dazed, disorientated. Good grief, a smile like that should have a five minute warning go off ahead of time so a fellow could prepare himself for the impact.

"Oh, my lord," she said, the warmth of her words soothing him like a cleansing balm. "It is quite perfect. I've never…. My goodness, I feel the need to pinch myself whenever I look about me, for I cannot believe I shall truly live here. Your kindness as well, in taking such care to make it a home for me. I… I am so very grateful to you for everything."

"Kindness?" he queried, unable to look away, trying desperately not to stare at her mouth.

"Why, yes," she said, moving a few steps closer.

If she came any nearer, he'd be able to reach out and touch her, to pull her into his arms and kiss that soft mouth, to feel her warmth through her gown, to put his hands upon that tiny waist.

"The watercolour paintings, and the books and ornaments and, oh, a dozen little touches that have made such a difference. It was so good of you."

Solo swallowed, trying to hold on to the thread of the conversation.

"Nothing of consequence," he muttered, frowning. "You must remove anything that doesn't suit. You have turned this rather humble abode into something of refinement and elegance, and I should hate to be responsible for spoiling it."

"Oh, no!" she said at once. "Good heavens, no. Your additions have been wonderful, perfect, and I should like you to feel at home here." She hesitated, two high spots of colour burning on her cheeks as she lowered her gaze. "After all, it… it is to be your home too, after a fashion."

Solo clenched his fists as the desire to lay his hands on her became overwhelming. If he stayed a moment more, he would do something reprehensible and forget she was a lady. A wicked voice in the back of his head told him she was no longer a lady, that he'd paid for her, paid for every stitch she was wearing and for the roof over her head. He had rights. He silenced it, sickened and revolted. *Miserable bastard.* He wasn't fit to be in the same room with her. If not for circumstances, she'd not even look in his direction. What use was he to a young beauty like her? A broken down old soldier too many years her senior. God, it was disgusting.

"I'd better be on my way," he said, not looking at her, stalking to the door and trying his best to hide his limp. Mrs Norrell had been right, damn her, the cold had only aggravated the pain.

"Oh, but… my lord?"

He turned, caught by the pleading in her voice.

"I… I hope I have not displeased you?"

"Displeased me?" he repeated, astonished. "Whatever put that maggoty idea in your head?"

The demand was somewhat testy, but he was so taken aback he could not help his tone.

"Well you seem… you…. Are you angry with me?"

She blinked at him, her grey eyes wary, and he noticed her eyelashes were long and thick, and several shades darker blonde than her hair. He wondered if the hidden curls beneath her gown, those nestled in the secret place between her thighs, were that same dark gold shade, and felt a wash of colour creep up the back of his neck at indulging such a wicked thought when she was obviously distressed.

"No." He shook his head and tried to remember he was a gentleman, damn it. "It's my fault. Abominably rude. Ought to have given you time to settle in. Didn't want to intrude. Just to see all was as it ought to be. Shan't keep you. Off now."

This eloquent little speech made him feel an utter imbecile and he took himself off, barely stopping to snatch up his coat and hat from Bessie and hauling his protesting leg back out into the cold.

***

Jemima jumped as the back door slammed shut and gave Bessie a doubtful look.

"Is he always like that?"

Bessie pursed her lips and shrugged. "Yes, though he seemed touchier than usual. He's a troublesome one, though, Miss. Not what you'd call an even temper, unless he's got his head in a book. Never knew a fellow to read like he does. If he sits down with a book, he'll stay quiet as a lamb and not get up again for hours. Ain't natural, in my view. Can't be good for his brain. Handsome fellow like that, filling his head with words. He might be lame, but he's still a fine strong man. Better ways to fill his time, I should think."

Jemima's eyes widened and Bessie obviously realised what she'd said, her expression one of mortification.

"Beg pardon, miss. Must see to the supper," she murmured and scurried back to the kitchen, head down.

Jemima put her hand to her mouth and stifled a giggle. There was no point in not seeing the funny side of the situation. She stared at the back door for a long moment, wishing Rothborn hadn't disappeared so quickly. Had he been anxious, as nervous as she'd been, in fact? She rather thought he had, which made her own worries ease a little. He was every bit as abrupt as she remembered, but that good, kind man had been obvious too. She smiled, feeling perhaps that she could manage Lord Rothborn well enough, given time.

Mrs Attwood and Jemima ate their supper in the kitchen, all of them being too tired to worry about formality, though Bessie was horrified by this turn of events.

"We shall have to get more staff," Jemima said. "Poor Bessie will be worn to a thread. Yet who can we trust not to gossip?"

"Oh, that's easy, miss," Bessie said, handing Jemima a bowl of thick soup. "My ma is a wonderful cook. Only plain, mind, nothing fancy, but she's a hard worker and can turn her hand to most things. She already knows where I work, and who for, and she don't hold with gossip. I think you'd like her."

Jemima nodded, relieved by the simplicity of the idea. "I'm sure I would, Bessie. That sounds wonderful. I shall speak to Lord Rothborn about it."

Bessie beamed at her and they ate in companionable silence.

Jemima left Mrs Attwood enjoying a tot of brandy and chatting quite contentedly with Bessie and giving the girl advice about how to get her beau to hurry up and propose to her. It had been a strange day and Jemima was worn out, the excitement and stresses catching up with her. Making her way along the corridor, candle aloft, she almost jumped out of her skin at a knock at the front door. For a brief moment she panicked, wondering if the baron had returned, expecting to stay the night, but quickly realised she was being idiotic. For one thing, he'd never come to the front door in such circumstances.

Hurrying forward, she opened the door and exclaimed in surprise as she discovered a young woman shivering in the darkness.

"Minerva!" she said, astonished.

"Oh, Jemima," Minerva sniffed, and promptly burst into tears.

Chapter 3

Inigo,

Is it true you are friendly with Bedwin? For God's sake put in a good word for me. The devil despises me, but I need a damned blue blood to get my new project off the ground. Do an old friend a favour, will you?

By the by, I have no idea if you are one for investments but steer clear of anything involving a Mr David Burton. I never liked the bastard, but recent investigations have proven he's worse than I could have imagined. He approached me for financing years ago, but I didn't trust him, and you know my instincts are rarely wrong. I'd always wondered at his golden touch with those damned mills and now I know how he turned such a vast fortune in so short a time. I know I made my own name in the same period, but then I'm exceptional and he's mediocre. I'd ruin a greedy aristo without a second thought, but to make money off the weak and vulnerable is another matter.

He's about to go down in spectacular fashion, so don't touch him or anything he's involved with.

—Excerpt of a letter from Mr Gabriel Knight to Mr Inigo de Beauvoir.

26th January 1815. Briar Cottage, Mitcham Village, Sussex.

Jemima gave a soft knock on the door of the spare bedroom, and waited for a response before turning the handle. Minerva was sitting up in bed while Bessie stoked the fire back to life and ensured Miss Butler had everything she needed.

"Thank you, Bessie," Jemima said with a smile as the girl bobbed a curtsey and promised to be back with some breakfast soon. "That girl is a marvel."

"She's sweet," Minerva agreed, her blue eyes too large against her pale face.

She'd clearly been crying, and Jemima's heart ached for her. Minerva had been too wretched and exhausted to explain herself last night, and so Jemima had gently steered her into one of the guest rooms and said they'd speak in the morning when she'd had some rest.

"She's a Trojan is what she is," Jemima remarked, laughing a little as she sat down on the edge of the bed. "Now then, I think you'd best tell me what the trouble is."

Jemima watched, still astonished the young woman had come to her. Although they were friends, Minerva had always been far closer to Helena, Bonnie, and Ruth than Jemima. Indeed, Jemima had missed out on the way many of the women's friendships had grown. As the finances had dwindled away to nothing, she had faded from society.

"I'm so sorry to land myself on your doorstep, Jemima," Minerva said, wringing her hands together. "Only I panicked. I needed somewhere to go to give myself a little time, and Matilda gave me your address yesterday morning. When I found it in my reticule, I just… well, it seemed like the ideal place to come to."

"Well, I'm very glad you did." Jemima gave her hand a reassuring pat. "But why? What were you running from?"

Minerva plunged into a halting story about her affair with a Mr de Beauvoir, about being seen by the scandalous Mrs Tate, and her lover's determination to do the honourable thing.

"Don't you wish to marry him, though?"

"Of course!" Minerva exclaimed, before blowing her nose noisily into a lace edged hanky. "But not because he *has* to."

Jemima nodded, understanding completely. How awful to have a man forced into marrying you. One would never be free of the sense of obligation, of having become a burden. Still, as compassionate as she was to Minerva's plight, her arrival had certain…. complications.

"I'm so sorry, Jemima. The last thing I want to do is cut up your peace. I shall leave tomorrow, I swear. I won't bring scandal to your door."

Despite herself, Jemima chuckled.

"Ah, as to that," she said ruefully. "Min, darling. There is something I must tell you, and… and I'm afraid you might not think well of me once you know. In fact, you may wish to leave at once and never speak to me again."

"Good heavens!" Minerva exclaimed. "I should think not! After you've been so very kind, I should be a poor excuse for a friend to act in so shabby a fashion. What on earth could you have done to consider I would be so hen hearted?"

Jemima plucked fretfully at the belt on her dressing gown, feeling the colour rise to her face. "Do you swear not to tell a soul?" she asked, unable to meet Minerva's eyes. "I… I couldn't bear it if the others knew how far I have fallen."

She dared a glance up to find a spectacular pair of blue eyes regarding her with a mixture of fascination and alarm. "Jem, you do realise I have run away from my lover because I won't marry him? I am ruined and about to become the scandal of the century, and I know that not one of the Peculiar Ladies would turn their backs on me. Not one of them. Why on earth should you think—"

"Because it isn't the s-same!" Jemima burst out, surprised by the force of emotion that made her throat tight. She took a breath, putting her chin up. "My aunt did not leave me any money. She left only doctor's bills I couldn't pay. I was desperate."

Minerva frowned, glancing about her. "Then... this house...?"

"The house, the furniture, my clothes, the food we eat... all of it is p-paid for by a man. B-By... Lord Rothborn. I am a kept woman, Minerva. He pays me for my company. I am his mistress, though not because I am in love with him, but for money. I am little better than a w-wh—"

"Don't you dare!" Minerva said, pressing her fingers to Jemima's trembling lips. "Don't say such a thing. I forbid it. Besides which, what options are there are for women to earn their keep? If there's one thing I have learned from Inigo, it's that the only real difference between men and women is a lack of education and opportunity. If women were educated properly and given opportunities to earn a respectable living, things would be different. As it is, we are usually destined to be either wives or whores, and that is a man's word and not one we should use. Especially when no one gives us the chance to be anything else."

Jemima blinked, a little taken aback but also relieved. She'd confessed all, and Minerva hadn't looked at her in disgust, hadn't shunned her. Perhaps she had wronged her friends by believing she would lose their good opinion? Still, it was not something she wished to advertise.

"Thank you, Minerva. I think I should like to meet your Mr de Beauvoir. He sounds like an interesting man."

"Oh, he is," Minerva said with a wistful sigh. "He's quite marvellous and I'm hopelessly in love with him."

Jemima hugged her friend, murmuring reassurances, and then left her alone to indulge in a good cry.

To Bed the Baron

***

Today, he would not act like a blasted imbecile, Solo assured himself as he made his way along the path to Miss Fernside's back door. The rain had abated, thank heaven, and though the sky was an unprepossessing shade of grey, he hoped it would leave off until after he returned home. He'd forced himself not to turn up on her doorstep at the crack of dawn, despite the temptation to do so, nor even by late morning. Hopefully, she would invite him to take afternoon tea with her, and this time he'd not be such a blithering idiot as last night and refuse. Somehow, he had to steer them past this awkwardness and encourage a sense of intimacy. She was, after all, to be his mistress. The trouble was, even thinking about that had him as tongue tied as a small boy in trouble with the house master. What the devil was wrong with him? Once upon a time he'd fancied himself as something of a charmer. He'd always had an easy way with women and he'd never been short of female companionship. Apparently, the skill had been lost somewhere between getting shot in the leg and jilted by his fiancée. Not that he blamed his fiancée one bit. He'd promised to bring her brother, his closest friend, back home safely....

Pain lanced through his thigh and he stumbled, grabbing hold of a tree branch before he landed face first on the sodden ground. *Damn.* He took a breath, trying to force back the wave of guilt and misery that threatened to tow him back down into the darkness. It had held him there for such a long time, mostly because he knew that was where he deserved to be. He had failed. He had failed Barnaby and he had failed Hyacinth. Just as he had failed all the men under his command when he'd been declared unfit for service.

Stop it, he commanded himself. Not today. Perhaps he did not deserve the companionship and comfort he hoped to gain from Miss Fernside, but she deserved his protection. She deserved to be comfortable and well treated, and that at least he could offer.

Bessie greeted him warmly and he wondered once more what he'd ever done to earn such loyalty. In truth, though her family had always worked at The Priory, he barely remembered her. She'd served in Mrs Norrell's kingdom below stairs since his return, but the girl seemed to regard him with a slavish devotion that was as much as a balm to his battered ego as it was undeserved.

"Is Miss Fernside at liberty to see me?" he asked, moving towards the heat of the stove.

He knew he had every right to walk in as though he owned the place, because he did, but he would never treat Miss Fernside with such a wanton lack of respect. Besides which, if they were to keep their affair a secret, he would be foolish to risk finding her with one of their neighbours. They were bound to start calling upon her soon, if they'd not already begun.

"Well, she's had the world and his wife this morning," Bessie remarked, confirming his suspicions. "But now there is only Miss Butler."

"Miss Butler?" he repeated, frowning. Wasn't that Inigo's lady love? "When did she arrive?"

He hoped she had no intention of overstaying her welcome and had only come to wish her friend well in her new home.

"Oh, last night, my lord. Not long after you'd gone. In something of an upset, too, poor thing."

"Last night?" he said, incredulous, and then groaned.

Inigo, you stupid bastard. The silly sod had messed it all up, just as Solo had feared he would.

"I'll go and tell her you're here, my lord. I know she'll wish to speak with you. Might I see you comfortable in receiving room first?"

"No, no." He waved the suggestion away. "I'll wait here until you send for me."

Bessie bobbed a curtsey and hurried away, returning a few minutes later. "Miss Butler has just gone out for a walk with Mrs

Attwood, my lord. So you'll find Miss Fernside in the parlour, waiting for you."

Solo nodded and made his way through the house. He paused before the parlour door, reminding himself he'd not be an idiot this time, and went in.

"Good afternoon, my lord."

His mouth went dry and his palms began to sweat. Well, not being an idiot was going swimmingly so far. Really, though, it was a lot to ask of a fellow who'd been celibate for so long when presented with such a vision of loveliness. He cleared his throat.

"I trust you are not too fatigued after yesterday's exertions. I understand you've been inundated with visitors this morning, too?"

She smiled at him, though this time he was ready for it and only felt mildly dazed by the onslaught.

"Indeed, no. I am quite well, and everyone has been very kind, so very… welcoming."

She faltered a little, her gaze sliding away from his, and he realised how awkward her position was. She had been raised a lady, yet her new position was tenuous. No doubt she would like to make friends with her neighbours and enjoy what society there was to be had in Mitcham, yet if they were to discover the truth of her life here….

He felt a sudden weight in his chest, regret that he could not offer her something better, something honourable, but he had made a vow as amends for his guilt, and that he could not forget. No matter if he wanted to.

"I understand you had an unexpected visitor last night," he said, hoping to turn the subject.

She looked at him in surprise, and he smiled.

"Bessie is somewhat in awe of my magnificence," he said sheepishly. "If you don't wish for her to tell me something, you must go to some lengths, I fear. She's marvellously loyal, though why I haven't the faintest idea."

Her laughter, when it came, was warm and rich and curled about him.

"Oh, I know the answer to that. You are a handsome war hero, strong and brave, though she fears you read more than is healthy for you. Filling your head with so many words is a worry to her."

Solo flushed, torn between amusement, horror, and delight in her finding him handsome. In the end guilt won the day, creeping up from out of the dark as it always did. He'd always been uncomfortable with being called a hero when he was anything but. He'd been shot, sent away from the front line, leaving Barnaby alone. Barnaby had never been what one would have considered an exemplary soldier. In fact, he was ill-suited to the life. He ought to have been a poet or a scholar, for war sickened him, and though he was brave, he was also foolish. Solo had kept him out of trouble as best he could, until Sahagun and the bullet which had left him lame. Poor Barnaby had died needlessly while Solo was flat on his back. His fault. It had been his fault.

"Have I said something wrong?"

Cursing, Solo realised he'd lost time, falling into his memories as sometimes happened when the darkness tried to get a hold of him.

"No," he said, shaking his head. His voice sounded odd, hoarse and too abrupt. "I'm no hero, Miss Fernside. There are hundreds, thousands of fellows more deserving of the title."

"Oh, but my lord—"

"No!" he snapped and then hated himself for the way she jumped in alarm. "Forgive me."

"There's nothing to forgive," she said, though she sounded perplexed.

Solo ran a hand through his hair, furious and wishing himself to the devil. "I…" Oh, what was the use? "Good afternoon, Miss Fernside."

He turned back to the door, resolved not to burden her any further for one day, but before he could reach for the handle her slender hand grasped at his sleeve.

"Don't go," she said.

Solo paused, staring first at the elegant fingers on the dark blue fabric of his coat, and then at wide grey eyes the colour of the storm-laden sky outside.

"Don't run away again, my lord. I promise you I am not such a feeble creature as to be routed by a sharp word or two. I am sorry if I upset you, and will endeavour not to do so again, but you must give me a chance to learn what pleases you and what does not."

He let out an uneven breath, utterly wretched. He was making a complete hash of this and she was so…. God, she was more than he could have believed. Faced with his appalling behaviour, she was all kindness and understanding. It only made him feel ever more the brute.

"I am afraid I warned you I was not a sympathetic companion," he said, resigned to the fact she must hate him.

The smile she returned did not seem to suggest anything of the sort, though perhaps she was simply adept at hiding her true feelings.

"Indeed, you told me you were abrupt and had no warm feelings to offer, so I was well prepared. However, I think you are too severe. Perhaps you are abrupt, but you have offered me no insult. The only slights you have spoken have been to your own detriment. Please, won't you sit down and take tea with me? I'm sure this cold weather must make your leg ache, and that is bound to make you cross."

Solo stared at her in surprise, shocked that she'd referred to his injury at all. Most ladies chose to ignore it, to pretend that it was not there. He knew they did it to make him feel better, but somehow Miss Fernside's direct manner was refreshing, comforting even, and her care for his well-being soothed his frayed nerves a little.

He allowed her to steer him to a chair by the fire and ring for tea. The fire crackled cheerfully, the heat a relief as he massaged the taut muscle in his thigh. Solo watched her as she poured the tea, the ritual elegant and practised. She looked every inch a lady, the kind any man would be proud to call his wife. Yet here she was, debasing herself with him. Melancholy settled over him and he took the teacup from her with a muttered word of thanks and stared into the fire.

"I fear I am failing you."

He didn't know how long he'd been staring into the flames when her soft voice reached him. Solo blinked, regarding her with confusion. She had sunk to her knees on the carpet before him, swathes of blue satin billowing around her, making her look like a lovely nymph rising from crystal waters. He was so horribly unworthy of her.

"My job is to please you, to make you comfortable and at ease," she said, giving him such a forlorn smile his heart was pierced with regret. "I only seem to do the opposite. I pray I will do better. I shall try."

"The fault is not yours, I assure you," he said. He set down the cup and saucer, wishing he had something to offer this beautiful creature. She was vibrant and alive and so very lovely, and he wanted to protect her from the harshness to be found in the world. All he'd achieved so far was to bring it into her front parlour. "I'm afraid you see now what a wretched bargain you have struck."

He could not hide the bitterness in his words, though he avoided her gaze, not wishing to see the realisation in her eyes.

He started in shock as a soft hand curled about his own, and gazed at her in astonishment as she lifted it to her face. She held it there, and Solo stared into those storm cloud eyes with his heart pounding. He watched, his breath held captive in his lungs, unable to move or breathe as he registered the satin texture of her skin beneath his fingers, and then she turned her face into his hand and pressed a tender kiss against his palm. Solo sucked in a breath, the soft sound as audible as gunfire in the quiet room.

She released his hand and he felt the loss of contact with a shaft of regret, wishing he'd stretched the moment out. Her eyes were cast down now, hidden beneath a thick sweep of dark gold lashes.

"Have I given you a disgust of me now?" she asked, her words breathless and uncertain. "I am afraid I do not understand how it is you wish me to behave. I am to be your mistress, after all, but—"

"No," he said, his voice urgent with the need to reassure her. "How could I be disgusted? You have been… you *are* perfection."

She peered up at him and he was struck by the glimmer of amusement visible beneath those lashes. "I fear you have very low standards, my lord, for I am a very long way from perfection."

A smile tugged a little at one corner of his mouth and he gave into the impulse, allowing himself to be teased. "There I must correct you, Miss Fernside. I have exacting standards, as anyone who knows me will attest to. I must also point out one very important fact to you, and I feel it is best you learn the lesson now. You see, I am *never* wrong."

"Never?" she said, her eyes widening a little. "My word. I did not understand I was in the company of such a paragon."

"Oh, no. I cannot pretend to perfection myself, Miss Fernside. I only mean to point out that you cannot criticise my opinion, for it is always exactly right."

"I see," she said, giving a forlorn sigh, though her eyes now danced with laughter that made his poor heart jitter about like a

March hare. "Then I must resign myself to the fact that I am perfect. How disturbing, when for so many years I believed I was merely adequate."

The temptation to reach out was too much and he dared to touch her cheek again, too aware of the rush of blood in his veins, of the pulse thundering in his ears as he felt the satin of her cheek beneath his fingertips.

"Adequate?" he repeated, dizzy with her proximity. He leaned a little closer as a delicate scent teased at him, luring him closer still. "*Adequate?*"

He laughed this time, thoroughly dazed as his eyes fell to the softness of her mouth, the sweet tantalising pink that beckoned him. His hand slid to the back of her neck, pulling her closer, and she came to him without the least resistance.

Solo had considered himself quite the ladies' man once upon a time. He'd had any number of pretty light skirts vying for his attention, and he'd even gained something of a reputation. Oh, he'd been no rake, no seducer of innocents, and once he'd proposed to Hyacinth he'd been faithful to her, but before that he'd had his fair share of amours, and never been short of a willing woman to warm his bed. Yet suddenly none of that counted a damn. It was as though he'd never been kissed at all, for this kiss and those kisses seemed to bear no relation to each other. It was not a passionate kiss, there was nothing practised or erotic about the soft press of her lips against his, and yet the sensation rocked him to the core.

Shaken, he drew back to see Miss Fernside flushed and wide-eyed. She pressed trembling fingers to her lips, to that lush, perfect mouth, now shaped into a little 'o' of surprise. Solo braced himself, wondering how she would react. Yes, she was his mistress and she was no fool, she must know what that would entail, and realise he'd been very patient not to just order her to his bed as many men would have. He was no brute, though—not that manner of brute, at least—and he knew she'd been raised a lady, knew how shocking this change in her circumstances must be to her. He had no wish to frighten or alarm her. There was no trace of alarm in her eyes, however, nothing that spoke of shock or fear. The stormy skies he saw in her gaze had only darkened, and the sight made his blood run hot.

"Miss Fernside," he said, somehow speaking her name, which was a wonder as his mind had turned to treacle the moment their lips had touched.

"Jemima," she whispered, still gazing at him, a look of wonder on her face. She looked very much as if she wanted him to kiss her again. "You ought to call me Jemima."

"Beautiful," he murmured, thinking that was more appropriately what he ought to call her. "Beautiful, sweet, Jemima."

He leaned towards her, and she moved too, closing the distance between them when suddenly there were voices beyond the door, which opened a moment later.

"*Oh!*" A young woman Solo assumed to be Miss Butler, and whom he wished to the devil, gave a little shriek. "Oh, I do beg your pardon," she babbled and tried to back out the door again.

The ample charms of Mrs Attwood, who had not seen him and was still coming in, hampered her retreat, however. This resulted in a collision that saw the lace on Miss Butler's gown caught on the small buttons on Mrs Attwood's sleeve.

To his great relief, Miss Fernside—Jemima—rescued them all.

"Oh, dear, what a mess you have made! Do come and stand by the light so I may untangle you."

A moment later they were freed, and Solo heard them both whisper mortified apologies to Jemima.

"My lord, may I present my very dear friend to you. This is Miss Butler."

Remembering his manners, even if the circumstances were somewhat trying, Solo got to his feet and bowed. It occurred to him that Jemima must have confessed the situation she was in, as Miss Butler did not appear thoroughly scandalised by the fact he'd been kissing her friend. Though she had been having an affair with Inigo these past weeks, so she was in no position to throw stones.

"A pleasure, Miss Butler. I collect we have an acquaintance in common."

Although Solo had surmised that Inigo had made a hash of everything, he was unprepared for the way that Miss Butler's eyes filled, and her lower lip trembled.

"Oh," she said. "Oh, I'm so… so… Please forgive me, I—I don't feel terribly—"

With that, she rushed out of the door. Mrs Attwood dipped a hurried curtsey and rushed out after her. Good riddance, as far as Solo was concerned. He was more than content to help Inigo put things right, but for the moment he was selfish enough to want only to be alone with Jemima.

"Oh, the poor dear," Jemima said, one pretty hand pressed to her heart. Solo wanted to rest his head there, upon that soft place, and it took a considerable effort of will not to act on the desire. "I wish there were something I could do."

"Well, there's something I can do, and I shall. Once I've gone, you may comfort her that all is not lost. I know the damn fool is head over ears in love with her. He's just made a mull of things, the dolt."

Jemima stared at him and Solo grinned. It was a rather wonderful sensation to discover that he could at least put something right for her.

"Inigo is my closest friend," he said, daring to move closer and take her hand in his. "I promise you he won't let Miss Butler down. He's only a little befuddled, never having been in love before. It does odd things to a fellow, I'm afraid."

"You mean he *wants* to marry her?"

Solo experienced that same sensation of falling from a great height as she gazed up at him, all her hopes shining in her eyes. It made him feel like a knight of old, promising to fight dragons for his lady. God, how nauseating, but nonetheless true for all that.

"I cannot speak for my friend, but unless something has changed drastically since last I saw him, then yes, I believe he does. Perhaps you'd best not tell Miss Butler that, but I hope I may reassure you, at least, that I will do my best to help them to put all to rights."

It was as though she blossomed in front of him, the tender flush of colour at her cheeks, the sparkle in her eyes, the smile that made him feel like he'd been kicked in the head by a cantankerous donkey.

"How kind you are," she said with a sigh. "I just knew you were a good man, and there, you have proven yourself already."

Solo chuckled and shook his head, though he felt about ten feet tall all the same.

"Not good," he amended. "Just never wrong."

He lifted the hand he held to his lips and kissed her knuckles, one by one, experiencing every little hitch in her breath like an echo as his heart thudded behind his ribs.

"I wish we'd not been interrupted," he murmured, daring to put his free hand to her waist.

"S-So do I," she stammered, rather to his amazement.

Not being an idiot, some of the time at least, Solo did not need further encouragement. He bent his head and kissed her, careful not to overwhelm her and scare her off. This gradual unfurling was too delicious to rush, or spoil. He'd been alone long enough to savour the moment for what it was, the first lowering of her defences. She wanted his kisses, which was more than he could have hoped for. He was proud enough to admit he wanted her to want him in other ways too, ways which he would show her when she was ready. For now, he forced himself to draw back, which was no easy task.

"Do you think we might dine together tomorrow night?" he asked, and then cursed himself as he saw the troubled look flicker across her face. She had a guest, did she not? "And Miss Butler and Mrs Attwood too," he added, wishing them to the devil.

Mrs Attwood could be left at home easily enough, she knew the situation, but Miss Butler....

"I'm so sorry, my lord. I did not expect to have a guest staying with me and know I have made difficulties for you. It is your right to dine here whenever you wish, and... and yet...."

He smiled, wanting to chase away the forlorn look on her face, though her friend's presence was indeed a bother he had not counted on. "Yes, you should have refused her entry and turned her out into the cold and dark," he said with mock severity. "Whatever were you thinking?"

Her lips twitched, which only made him want to kiss her again, so he did, overcome with delight at not only being allowed to, but that she did not seem the least bit horrified or missish about returning his kisses.

"I had best leave you," he said, with real regret. "I think I have scandalised your friend enough for one day."

Jemima blushed a little. "I am fortunate in my friends, my lord. I believed I should lose them all when... when they discovered my situation, but it appears I may not be abandoned."

"I should think not," he said, frowning over the idea he had forced her to make such a choice, and that she had chosen him believing her friends would disown her.

"You know how society works as well as I do. I could not condemn them for avoiding me when the association would tarnish them, if the truth got out. Perhaps it is not so dreadfully grave for those who are married, though it would still cause disagreeable gossip, but for the single ladies it is a considerable risk to their reputations."

Solo grunted, knowing she was right but disgruntled all the same. Damn busybody gossips with nothing better to do than poke their noses into other people's affairs.

"Don't look so cross," she chided, and he felt the frown that had gathered at his brow ease away under the soft, caressing tone that teased him just a little. "Not when I have worked so hard to chase away that daunting scowl."

"Perhaps I should make you work a bit harder," he countered and stole another kiss. It was only a brief touch of lips, yet his heart was thundering all over again and he did not wish to leave her, especially when she looked so adorably flushed and flustered.

"Goodbye, Jemima," he said, knowing he would count the minutes until he could return to her company.

"Goodbye, my lord."

"My name is Solomon." He hesitated. "My friends call me Solo."

"Solo," she repeated, shy now though a smile played over her lips.

He stared at her for a long moment, fighting the urge to kiss her again, and then forced his unwilling limbs to take him to the door. He returned to The Priory in a daze, smiling like a fool the entire way.

Chapter 4

My dear old friend,

I regret the need to ask a favour of you, but I have returned from India for a time. There are things I can no longer ignore, things I have left undone and must rectify. I am not getting any younger and so it cannot be delayed any more than it has been by my cowardice to face the truth. As you know the situation between myself and my nephew is beyond saving, despite my best efforts. It breaks my heart to admit that there is no hope for reconciliation, but there it is. I am afraid of him and what he may do should he discover my return to England. He has become a powerful and ruthless man and I would be a fool to believe he holds any remaining fond feelings for his old uncle. The rift between us saddens me more than I can say, but I dare not make another attempt at rapprochement. I do not believe I overstate when I tell you our last encounter left me in fear for my life.

How I envy your close relationship with your nephew, the duke, but then Bedwin was always a good-hearted boy and was only led astray by a bad woman and circumstance. I fear my own nephew is beyond saving. His cruelty and contempt for all those he deems below him has grown past anything I could have foreseen. I believe he is utterly corrupted and there is not a drop of compassion left within his wicked heart.

This being the case, I am in need of a place to stay for the duration of my visit, a place where I may be safe from Montagu and among friends, and hope I may appeal to your kindness and the camaraderie between us that has endured these many years.

—Excerpt of a letter from Mr Theodore Barrington to Charles Adolphus, Baron Fitzwalter.

26th January 1815. Briar Cottage, Mitcham Village, Sussex.

After Solo's promises to intervene, Jemima was a little astonished when—later that same night—Inigo de Beauvoir presented himself on their doorstep to declare his love and intention to marry Minerva. Jemima had not expected such a speedy resolution. She was baffled by the sack of coal, which Minerva seemed beside herself over. Apparently, it was a romantic gesture, but the girl was so overcome with emotion she did not seem able to satisfactorily explain in what way it was romantic. Still, one could not be unmoved by the sight of the poor man, soaked to the bone and dripping a puddle onto Jemima's new carpet, and obviously out of his mind with loving Minerva.

Their betrothal settled between them, Jemima packed Mr de Beauvoir back to The Priory, sighing happily over the fact that Minerva would get her happy ever after. Coal notwithstanding, it was very romantic.

Now tucked into her own bed, she stared up at the ceiling, remembering her own brush with romance, or at least the closest she'd ever come to it. How very bold she'd been! Her hands had trembled so when she had touched his and pressed it to her cheek. Even now she could feel the soft press of his mouth against hers, as though he'd branded it, branded her. She had not expected the rush of... of warmth and excitement, of desire he had brought blazing to the surface with such a brief touch of his lips. Was she wicked to feel this way for a man she barely knew? The idea disturbed her even as she experienced a surge of relief. It would be a sorry fate that awaited her if she was forced to be mistress to a man for whom she felt nothing but revulsion. It was not revulsion she felt for Baron Rothborn, though. Oh, no. Did that make her lustful, to want his touch, to welcome his kisses? Should she be ashamed? Had she been destined to become a fallen woman from the start, her position as a man's mistress a foregone conclusion because of her salacious nature? Perhaps Mr Briggs had seen that in her? Perhaps others could tell what kind of woman she was, and that was why he had suggested such a scandalous arrangement.

Realising she was becoming overwrought, Jemima forced herself to take a deep breath. Whatever she was, or was not, it would not change her circumstances. Besides which, Lord Rothborn—Solo—had told her she was perfect, and he was never wrong.

Smiling to herself, she relaxed and allowed herself to fall asleep at last.

***

Much to Solo's relief, Inigo returned to town with his beloved Miss Butler the next morning. Not long after, a handwritten note had arrived, inviting him to dine with Jemima that evening. Though Solo was beside himself with impatience and could have made a dozen excuses to visit, he knew that the village was in a flurry of curiosity over the new arrival in their midst. That the newcomer was a beautiful, elegant and unattached female of marriageable age only heightened the intrigue and speculation.

"I heard from Mrs Tuttle that the vicar was visiting this morning, and the Misses Granger and that dreadful mother of theirs," Mrs Norrell informed him mid-morning, when he wandered into the kitchen in search of tea and biscuits. "And the schoolmaster wasn't shy in coming forwards yesterday. I hear he's had a haircut since, and no wonder. The whole village is abuzz with talk of how pretty she is, and such a lady besides. My, you've set the cat among the pigeons and no mistake."

Solo scowled. It was something he had not considered before now. Whilst he was all for saving Jemima's reputation—after all, he had no wish to cause her embarrassment or be at the centre of a scandal—how was he to keep the other single men at bay? He could not scare them off without showing his hand, and it would hurt Jemima when the gossip began.

Damnation, he should have foreseen such difficulties, but he'd been so overwhelmed by his own good fortune and anticipation at having her near, he'd not thought it through. Not that he could see any way of changing things. Either they knew she was his mistress, or they believed she was a respectable unmarried woman and was therefore free to be courted. A flare of jealousy and irritability chased away his previous good humour.

Mrs Norrell paused in her preparation of the tea to give him a considering look. Solo rearranged his face into something slightly less murderous, but the damage had been done.

"What's she like, then? Is she the kind to play you false?"

His scowl darkened once more as he turned a black glare upon Mrs Norrell, who looked thoroughly underwhelmed by such an expression.

"No," he said, with frigid civility.

"Well, then there's nowt to fret over, is there?" the lady said with an imperturbable shrug, as though the matter was settled. She arranged a teapot, milk and sugar, cup and saucer, and a plate of shortbread onto a tray and hefted it. "I'll set this in your study for you."

Solo stalked after her, his cane clattering against the flagstones with more force than usual as he considered Mr Stickles the schoolmaster and the vicar Mr Pemble. Both were unmarried men in their late twenties. Mr Stickles was tall and thin, with regrettable ears that stuck out like a carriage with both the doors open, but otherwise he was a pleasant enough looking man. Mr Pemble was smaller, pockmarked and rather rotund, and had an unfortunate habit of sucking on his teeth. Surely, such men would hold no appeal. Yet those men were likely honest and good and could offer her marriage, and respectability. Irritation simmered beneath his skin and he wished—could not help but wish—but no, that was his punishment, to never marry, never have a family. It was a punishment he deserved and had accepted as his due, but never had it had consequences for anyone else but him before. Why should Jemima suffer for his failings?

Though he'd been well aware of his good fortune on first meeting Jemima, he'd been wholly focused on saving her from poverty. In his mind he had been doing something good for her and had even congratulated himself on how lucky she was to have fallen into his hands rather than a man who would use and abuse her. Now, though, the reality of how good and sweet and innocent she was fell upon him like a weight. She ought to be a good man's wife, a woman he loved and honoured and was proud to call his own, not a mistress to be kept in secret and cloaked in shame.

It was in this gloomy and introspective frame of mind that he whiled away the interminable hours until he was due to dine with her. Troubled and impatient, he presented himself earlier than he ought to have done and was further irritated to discover the lady was not yet ready to receive him.

***

"Oh, drat!" Jemima fretted. "Do hurry. You know how he despises tardiness, you told me yourself."

"Then he had no business arriving fifteen minutes early," Bessie muttered through a mouthful of pins as she arranged Jemima's blonde hair into something artful and lovely.

"Oh, you ought to have been a lady's maid, Bessie," Jemima said, turning her head this way and that with approval. "You are quite wasted on me in this little village."

"Nonsense," Bessie said stoutly. "I know a good mistress when I sees one, me mum an' all. She's right pleased with being here, and is all a-flutter to be cooking for his lordship."

"I'm sure she'll do us all proud, Bessie, so do tell her not to fret, but now I must make haste before he is out of all patience with me."

Jemima flew down the stairs as fast as she dared, spared a moment to catch her breath, and hurried into the parlour.

"My lord," she said, curtseying to him and feeling her heart pound in her chest.

It would have been easy enough to ascribe the fierce beating to her speedy descent, but Jemima was nothing if not honest and could not fool herself. He looked terribly dashing. The dark blue coat fitted his broad shoulders to perfection, and he stood tall and straight, every inch the military man from the shiny gold buttons to the brilliant sheen on his boots. Jemima felt suddenly overwhelmed by him, and by the way his kisses had made her feel: both cherished and yet in quite desperate danger all at the same time.

"Solo," he said, a note of irritation in his voice that put her on guard.

So, the good humour she had teased from him last time had faded already. Still, he had warned her he was not even-tempered, so she must do her best to lift his spirits.

"Forgive me, *Solo*. I'm afraid I find it difficult to address you so intimately when you arrive looking so splendid. I feel quite the dowd in your presence. It's a good thing poor Bessie did not see you. I fear she may have swooned."

"Nonsense," he said, his dark brows drawing together in confusion. "You…." He stopped then and his gaze swept over her, something hot and dark flashing in his eyes that made heat pool low in her belly. "You look like a fairy queen."

The admission made her smile, as he was still scowling.

"Well, if I do, I shall endeavour not to do so again as it seems to make you most dreadfully cross. Was it because I kept you waiting?"

"No, it was not," he said, pacing away from the fire with impatient strides, his tense face telling her that his leg was paining him, and then he returned to scowl at the flames again. "You did not keep me waiting. I was early, as you well know, and why you must endure my… my wretched temper with such grace I cannot fathom. You ought to throw me out for being such a dreadful boor, and I like the way you look," he added, sounding as sulky as scolded boy.

Jemima bit her lip, wondering if she was foolish to find him quite adorable. She dared to move closer to him and take his arm, looking up to discover his eyes upon her, wary now.

"What has put you all out of temper, my dear friend? What dreadful creature has undone all my hard work and taken the smile from your eyes? But never mind, you do not have to tell me. Bessie's mother, Mrs Jarvis, whom I believe you know, has come to work for me and she is as marvellous as her daughter. We have a dinner ready fit for Prinny himself, and surely that will lift your spirits, if I am so dismal company as not to manage the feat myself?"

"Dismal?" he said on a huff of laughter. "You could no more be dismal than I could stop the sun from rising." He reached out and Jemima felt her breath catch in her throat as a finger traced the line of her jaw, raising shivers that chased over her skin in tiny ripples of pleasure. "And if you must know the extent of my folly, it is Mr Stickles and Mr Pemble who have put me in such a wretched temper, damn their eyes."

"Mr...?" she began, and then trailed off, staring at him with uncertainty. "They both called upon me to make me welcome to the village."

"I know, and that is why I damn their eyes and their blasted intentions," he said, and then muttered a curse. "Forgive me."

He sounded weary and Jemima realised with a start that he was jealous. She almost laughed. Mr Pemble had been a dreadful bore and, whilst Mr Stickles seemed a good sort, if he stood beside this magnificent specimen of masculinity, he'd not fare well by the comparison.

Jemima had no experience of men, beside the usual polite interactions at dinners and parties, yet she was no fool. There appeared to be no obvious explanation why such a man as the baron—with his title and his wealth and good looks—should fret over two fellows he must know he cast in the shade, unless you considered that he had been through a terrible ordeal. What form it had taken she did not know past the fact he'd been shot in the leg, and yet she guessed it had wounded more than his limb, and this was why he was so fractious, so uncertain and so ready to believe the worst.

"There is nothing in the world to forgive you for," she said, keeping her voice soothing. "But now you must come and eat, or we shall both have to beg forgiveness for ruining Mrs Jarvis' hard work."

Wondering how she dared, she lifted on her toes and kissed his cheek. Heat flared in his eyes and she looked away to hide her blush.

"Come," she urged, tugging at his arm.

He did not resist, and followed her through to the dining room.

Mrs Jarvis was not the only new member of staff. They seemed to have employed the entirety of Bessie's family between here and The Priory, for Bessie's younger sister had come to Jemima as laundry maid, and her younger brother was to keep the gardens in order. As Bessie's eldest sister and her aunt worked with Mrs Norrell, her older brother saw to his lordship's horses, and her uncle was The Priory's coachman, it was quite the family affair. There were also some cousins who worked for the head gardener at The Priory, too, it appeared. Still, Bessie assured Jemima that the family had worked for the Rothborns for generations and would never tattle about so good and generous a master. With this, Jemima had to be satisfied. She knew it was unlikely their arrangement would remain private for long, but it had been nice to receive calls from her neighbours, even if some of them had been deadly dull. It would be far duller and more inconvenient to be thought a pariah.

As Bessie had warned, her mother was a plain cook, but a marvellous one. The first course of pea soup was delicious, and the pork cutlets that followed were tender and sweet. Jemima refused the rump of beef, which Solo declared a marvel, but she was pleased to watch him take second helpings of everything, including the vegetables. They finished with a bowl of preserved cherries, some good sharp cheese, and stewed pippins with cream. As Solo had sent wine from his own cellar, it was obviously excellent, though Jemima drank little, fearing what might happen if she allowed it to go to her head.

Bessie had set the table with his lordship at the head and Jemima at his right elbow. It was intimate and cosy and, little by little, she sensed him relax. Once the dishes had been cleared and the port brought in for him, she went to get up.

"I shall leave you to your port, then," she began, only to halt as he laid a hand on her arm.

"No, don't go. This port is exceptional. Won't you try some?"

Jemima stared at him for a moment, then nodded. If she was to be ruined, she may as well enjoy all the things previously forbidden to her.

She took a sip, pleasantly surprised by the rich texture of the drink and the warm glow it set alight inside her. She watched him as he turned his own glass back and forth in his hand.

"There, now. Has the excellent Mrs Jarvis restored your sense of equanimity?" she enquired, teasing him just a little.

Solo harrumphed, but there was amusement in his eyes, so she was not perturbed.

"Indeed she has, though if I am honest, the company has had the most beguiling effect."

"Oh, what a plumper," Jemima said, laughing. "You looked positively rapturous when you saw Bessie carry the beef in."

"Do you accuse me of dissembling, madam?" he said with mock indignation. "That is a very grave matter."

"I do, and what is more I pronounce sentence. You are guilty as charged."

"Not true."

Jemima fell silent, aware of the change in his voice, of the darker tone that matched the light in his eyes. He put down his glass and reached out, taking her hand. All at once the warm glow the port had set flickering to life erupted into something hotter and more insistent.

"Come here," he said, tugging gently at her hand as he pushed his chair away from the table.

She got to her feet, colour rising to her cheeks in a rush as she moved towards him.

"Closer," he urged, a breathless note to the demand that sent the breath from her own lungs, leaving her giddy as she realised what he wanted. Telling herself she was being a ninny for hesitating, she did as he asked and tried not to tremble. She was to be this man's mistress, to share his bed. Sitting in his lap was hardly too much to ask.

"I've shocked you," he murmured.

Jemima shook her head, too conscious of the brush of her own soft curls tumbling around her face, and of the heat of the hard body beneath her, the warmth of his chest pressed against her arm as she tried to relax.

"Now who is dissembling?" he said, a gentle reproof in his voice.

She dared to look at him, aware her cheeks must be scarlet.

"I'm sorry," she said, mortified by her obvious inexperience when he was a sophisticated man of the world. "I… I must seem very gauche, and not at all what you would wish for in your m-mistress, but I shall learn, I promise. If you would just be… a little patient."

"You are more than I dreamed of, as I believe I have already told you," he said, touching a thick coil of hair with such obvious reverence she found she could not doubt the sincerity of his words. "I am a wicked, black-hearted villain for despoiling such a prize. My only saving grace is that I know it. I know I am unworthy, and I shall do all in my power to compensate in whatever way I can, to make you happy, to keep you safe."

Jemima stared into his dark eyes, and this close she found they were not merely brown but flecked with every shade from russet and amber through to bronze and gold.

"You are no villain," she whispered, still trembling, but no longer from fear of what was to come.

This man would not hurt her. She'd known it before, for he had told her so and she'd believed him, but now she felt it in her heart, in her bones. He was troubled and a little careworn around the edges, but he was not the wicked seducer he painted himself, not when he took such care and patience to reassure her, not when he said such pretty things to her with painful honesty.

"I want to kiss you."

"Yes," she replied, that one word sounding too dreadfully like a plea, not that she could help it.

She was aching and fretful, wanting things she knew he could give her, even if the specifics of her desires were hazy.

One large hand cupped her cheek, his thumb stroking as he gently pulled her closer.

"Beautiful girl," he murmured, angling her head so he could press his lips to the tender spot beneath her ear.

Jemima gasped, unprepared for the force of sensation that slight touch of his lips sent surging through her.

"Your scent is maddening," he said on a groan, nuzzling into her neck, kissing and painting delicate pictures with his tongue that made her shiver with longing. "I dreamt of it last night. I want to wake with it upon my skin."

"Oh," she gasped, shocked by his words, but not in the manner of a well-bred young lady.

It was the way her body reacted that stunned her, the liquid heat that bloomed inside her and made her limbs feel both heavy and pliant all at once. As she imagined a morning where she might wake with him, in his arms, she could no longer conjure the dismay she'd previously felt. Yes, she was afraid still, but more that he should find her lacking, that she might fail to please him, for she wanted to please him. She wanted to keep the troubled look from his eyes, to chase away whatever it was that made him growl like a lion with a thorn stuck deep in its paw.

His mouth moved across her skin until their lips brushed and Jemima could not deny the instinct to turn to him, to press closer and wrap her arms about his neck. He groaned, and the sound vibrated through her with a thrill of exhilaration. How marvellous to draw such a sound from him! She wished very much to hear it again.

"Jemima."

Her name was a whisper, spoken in a way that made it sound altogether different. It was the name of a man's lover, the woman he dreamed of and longed for, and she wanted to be that woman. She gasped as the wet warmth of his tongue traced the seam of her mouth, startled by the intimacy of the touch. It became more intimate still as his tongue swept in, taking advantage of her surprise. Tentatively, she returned the touch with her own, beguiled by the silky slide and retreat. As she understood the way of it she became bolder, pressing her body closer. Solo's arms pulled her in tighter still, so close he crushed her breasts against his hard chest as he deepened the kiss. She felt giddy and hot and out of control and when he finally released her, she could hardly breathe.

"Oh my," she said, putting one unsteady hand to the place her heart thundered in her chest, as though it had become so frantic she needed to stop it escaping.

"Oh my, indeed," Solo repeated, staring at her.

He looked a little stunned himself, which was reassuring. His gaze dropped to the hand upon her breast, and he reached to take it in his. Lifting it to his mouth, he pressed a kiss to her palm, and then laid his head in its place, placing her hand upon his hair.

Jemima felt herself melting inside as she realised what he wanted. So she held him to her breast, stroking his hair and feeling the tension ease out of him at last. They stayed that way for a long time, his breathing having become so deep and even, she wondered if he was sleeping.

"I should go," he said, his rumbling voice disconcerting her a little as the room had grown so quiet. "It's late and I am keeping you from your bed."

"I don't mind."

It was the truth. She didn't wish for him to go, though she was not bold enough to ask him to stay. His kisses made her body ache and burn, and she knew there must be far more to come, but she was not ready to invite him to her bed. Perhaps he would invite himself. It was his right, after all. He'd been more patient and understanding than she had expected. He was treating her gently, still as a lady, for all that he was paying for her company. She pushed that thought away, not wishing to dwell upon it.

He raised his head at last and looked at her.

"Thank you," he said, so gravely she could not help but smile at him.

"I don't feel I have done terribly much," she said, daring to touch her hand to his cheek. "But if I have lightened your heart, I am very glad of it."

"You have. You cannot know how... how much this means to me. You... make everything seem better."

He looked perplexed by the confession, but it was so obviously heartfelt that Jemima's chest ached.

"That is undoubtedly the nicest thing anyone has ever said to me."

"It is only the truth," he said, sounding apologetic. "I can steal pretty words from cleverer, more romantic men, but the truth is that you ease my soul, Jemima, and I am very glad to have found you."

Jemima blinked. The world had suddenly become a little hazy. Impulsively, she leaned in and kissed him. His arms pulled tight once more, and the kiss became far more than the press of lips she had intended. Not that she minded, wicked girl that she was.

He let her go at last, and she found his hat and coat. It was late, and she'd told Bessie not to wait up for her.

"Come to The Priory tomorrow," he said, buttoning his greatcoat. "Bring Mrs Attwood to keep any busybodies happy.

She'll have a fine time with Mrs Norrell, who will be glad of the company. I should like to show you a little of my home."

Jemima nodded and handed him his hat and cane. "I would like that very much."

At the back door he kissed her hand, polite and chivalrous, and she bade him a good night, standing in the cold and dark, and watching his figure retreat into the shadowy garden.

Chapter 5

Dear Harriet,

How is life at Holbrooke House? Ireland is damp and dreary, and I long for the spring. Luke, however, is wonderful, and we have made our new house into a home. I wish you could come and see it. In truth, I am perfectly blissful, though I do miss you and the other Peculiar Ladies most dreadfully. Please send me all the gossip and tell me what everyone is doing. I heard from Ruth yesterday and she is full of plans for all the things she wants to do at Wildsyde. It sounds very exciting, and such a romantic place. I would love to visit her one day. Perhaps we could go together?

Now take your nose out of whatever book it is currently stuck in and get writing, you dreadful creature. I want to hear it all, especially if it's scandalous. Much love to you and Jasper.

—Excerpt of a letter from Mrs Kitty Baxter to Harriet Cadogan, The Countess St Clair.

28th January 1815. Mitcham Priory, Sussex.

Jemima shifted the basket on her arm and stared in awe at the building before her.

"Good heavens."

"It's huge," Mrs Attwood murmured, as they gazed with astonishment at the ancient priory. "I mean it's a fraction of the size of Chatsworth or Dern, but still. I never expected such a fine place."

"You've been to Dern?" Jemima asked in surprise.

Mrs Attwood nodded. "The Marquess of Montagu allows visitors when he's not in residence. I was lucky enough to see it last summer."

"What's it like?"

"Old, grand, and vastly intimidating."

Jemima returned her attention to The Priory. "It's haunted," she said, worrying her lip with her teeth.

"Not in daylight, I'm sure," Mrs Attwood said briskly. "Come along."

They were greeted by Mrs Norrell, the housekeeper, who—as Solo had predicted—was delighted to see them. Jemima wondered at it, having assumed she would be disapproved of, but the woman seemed genuinely welcoming. Tiny, yet with a quite considerable girth, the housekeeper appeared to be a force of nature. She bustled them into a comfortable parlour with leaded light windows that looked out upon the fine gardens. Every wall was panelled in oak from floor to ceiling, and the wood glowed in the reflected light of the fire.

"This is the cosiest room at this time of year, save the kitchens," she said cheerfully. "A wretched draughty place it is in the winter, though don't tell his lordship I said so. Loves the bones of the place, he does, for all he complains about it. He'll be with you in just a moment, and, Mrs Attwood, I should be glad of your company in the kitchen once you've had your visit."

She bustled out again, leaving the impression of a woman who ruled her domain with vigour and enthusiasm. As she'd said, a moment later Lord Rothborn appeared, and Jemima could not hide the blush that rose on seeing him again. Each time she promised herself he would not overwhelm her, and each time she felt a little stunned by his presence. It was not simply that he was handsome, but there was something indefinable about him that commanded attention. He seemed a man who had been born to take control and give orders, a man others relied upon.

"Miss Fernside, Mrs Attwood, how lovely to see you. I wish the sun was shining for you, but hopefully The Priory did not disappoint at first sight."

"Disappoint?" Jemima said with a chuckle. "Good heavens, it's marvellous. Quite the most romantic building I have ever seen. One look at it and my head was filled with villains and desperate heroines, with mad monks inhabiting every corner."

"Have you cast me as the villain?" he asked, a warm light in his eyes that made Jemima look away as she remembered last night.

"Certainly not, nor a mad monk either, before you ask."

"Well, that is a relief! And Mrs Attwood, how are you settling in at Briar Cottage? I hope you have both found everything to your satisfaction."

"Indeed, my lord, I do not see how we could fail to be delighted. It is warm and comfortable, and I believe we shall both be most content."

"Excellent," Solo replied, and all at once it was a little awkward.

Mrs Attwood cleared her throat. "Well, if you would excuse me, my lord, I know Miss Fernside is eager for a tour of the building, but I have been invited to take tea with Mrs Norrell."

"Ah, then you are in luck. I have it on good authority she is baking lemon cake today, which is a personal favourite. Please remind her to send some up to me, as I am awaiting it with anticipation."

Jemima watched, amused and a little mortified, as Mrs Attwood curtseyed and hurried away. Solo sent a rather crooked and boyish grin in her direction.

"There, I do have manners. Aren't you relieved to discover it?"

"You are charm itself this morning, my lord," she said, unable to resist the desire to tease him. "I believe you must have slept well and eaten a hearty breakfast to put you in such good humour."

He shook his head and closed the distance between them, taking her hand and raising it to his lips. "Wrong on both counts," he murmured. "I did not sleep a wink, and I was too distracted to eat, because I knew you were coming and so I have been counting down the minutes."

"Such flattery," she said, flustered and happy. "Yet I am relieved to hear it, for I have been just the same you know. I can prove it, too, for I awoke so early I baked you some scones."

Jemima gestured to the basket, feeling a little silly and unsophisticated, but at the look of delight in his eyes her confidence returned.

"You baked for me?" he said, obviously pleased and surprised.

Jemima nodded. "I'm afraid it's a rather shameful secret for a lady who ought to prefer needlework or painting, but I enjoy baking. I had to learn when my aunt was ill, and we could not afford staff. Imagine my surprise at discovering I was rather good at it. Scones are my favourite, though, and Mrs Jarvis was so kind as to put in a jar of bramble jam, and now I am no longer a lady I realised I could do as I pleased," she added with a laugh.

Her brows drew together as she noticed the smile had left his eyes and he looked troubled once again.

"Don't say that." He lifted her chin and pressed a soft kiss to her lips. "You are and will always be a lady. I am sorry that life has been hard for you, yet I am selfish enough to be glad of it too, because it has brought you into my life, and I am too greedy for your company to wish it otherwise."

"I have no regrets," Jemima said, realising that—in this moment, at least—it was true. Perhaps that would change when she was shamed before her neighbours, but today, in this man's company, she was happy.

"Come," he said, offering his arm. "I shall show you a little of the place. It's too big to see all in one go, and besides, I need something to lure you to come back and visit me again."

Jemima took his arm, knowing that there was already lure enough, and she needed nothing else to make her want to spend time in this romantic setting with such a man.

***

Solo glanced down at Jemima, entranced by her delight in the old place that he loved so dearly. He realised it had been important to him that she liked it. The Priory was as cold, inconvenient, and troublesome as any ancient building, and he knew well enough that many people would far prefer a smart new house with every fashionable accoutrement. Yet her enthusiasm had been genuine, he was sure. She had peppered him with questions, not least about the ghosts, which seemed at once to fascinate and terrify her.

"Very well," he said, laughing as she insisted on hearing more. "But do not blame me when you have nightmares."

She grinned up at him and, for the first time in longer than he could remember, he felt happy. It was such a departure from his usual frame of mind that he just stood staring at her for a moment, basking in the emotion and in the light she had brought into his life. It was as though he had turned his face to the sun after living in the dark. He cleared his throat, trying to marshal his thoughts, which always seemed trickier to do when she was near.

"Along this corridor there is the ghost of a monk."

"Oh!" she said, clutching at his arm. "I knew it, a mad monk!"

Solo laughed, delighted by her. "Well, whether he was mad I cannot say. He is purported to walk here at night, though, and sometimes he is seen in the gardens beneath the yew tree."

The shiver that ran over her was noticeable and too good an excuse not to pull her into his arms. "Are you cold, Jemima, or have I chilled your blood speaking of such fiendish creatures?"

"A little of both," she said, stealing his breath as she snuggled against him and laid her head on his chest. "Such stories seem fanciful and not the least bit scary with you by me, but I know if I were here alone, I would be terrified."

"Then you had best always keep me by you," he said softly, before lifting her chin and kissing her.

She responded to him at once, sliding her arms about his neck, and Solo's heart soared. This… this was everything he had been missing, longing for. His hands slid to her tiny waist, so slender he could span the width with ease. She was too fragile from too many years of scrimping and saving and putting on a brave face. It made him ache to know how close she had come to disaster, to know that *he* was a form of disaster for her, albeit a less uncomfortable one. He wanted to protect her. He *was* her protector, he realised with disgust. That was what he would be named, the man profiting from her desperation. He pulled away from her, suddenly ashamed of himself.

"What is it?" Her soft voice penetrated his self-disgust, the uneasy note making him realise she was concerned. "Did I… did I do something wrong?"

"No!" he said at once, returning to her and gathering her in his arms. "No, no, how could you think it?" He kissed the top of her head and sighed. "It is I who is forever in the wrong, taking advantage of your desperation. I feel ashamed, but not so fiercely as to want to find another way to help you. I'm a wretched excuse for a man."

"Stop that at once."

The severity of the command was rather astonishing to him and he looked at her in surprise. There was a glimmer of something powerful and perhaps even dangerous betrayed by the glitter in her eyes, something that suggested this frail, gentle creature was not as helpless and delicate as he might think.

"I like you very much," she said, putting her chin up. "You tell me you still think me a lady, that I ought not feel ashamed, and I believe it... until you speak in this fashion. If not for you, I don't know where I would be. You have given me a home, security, and you have been so very, very kind and patient. I may be innocent in some ways, my lord, but I am not so naïve to not realise how rare that is. I am happy to be here with you. Indeed, I could not wait to be in your company again this morning. So, do you not think we can forget the morality of the situation? There are people enough who will pass judgement upon us when they discover the truth, I believe we can afford to be kind to each other in the meantime."

Solo let out a breath and nodded. "*You* are too kind, and you give me far too much credit, but I have no wish to spoil the day. I have no wish for you to ever leave."

"Kiss me then," she demanded, and Solo was only too happy to comply.

***

The invitation to the wedding of Miss Minerva Butler to Mr Inigo de Beauvoir arrived mid-morning, to both their delight. Although it was to be only the next day, for them at least it was not unexpected, and Solo had made plans to travel to town as soon as the date was announced. Jemima was touched to see how very pleased he was to be asked to stand as best man for the groom. It clearly meant a great deal to him and gave her further proof as to his character and the kind of friend he was to those for whom he cared. As they were neighbours and both friends of the happy couple, Solo insisted it would be quite unexceptional for them to travel together in his coach, with Mrs Attwood and Bessie playing chaperone. Jemima would spend the night with Matilda, assuming her friend did not mind the imposition, and Solo would return to collect her the next day for the return journey.

In truth, Jemima was rather jittery to be in the company of all her friends with Solo in attendance. Minerva already knew the truth, and whilst Jemima had been pleasantly surprised—not to mention relieved—at the way Minerva had reacted, she could not help but experience a qualm of misgiving. Despite meaning what she'd said to Solo, she realised she did not want her friends to know her circumstances, not yet at least, not while she was still getting used to those circumstances herself. The sensation of not knowing quite who she was had grown stronger over the past days, since Solo had taken her in his arms and kissed her. That she had kissed him first was still something she could not quite believe, and only added to her anxiety. Everything her aunt had brought her up to believe desirable in a young woman of quality, everything she had taught her, Jemima was casting aside. All those lessons seemed meaningless when Solo was beside her, and far less important than she'd always believed them to be. She was happy. Yet she felt she was living apart from reality, as though this was a sweet dream, and she very much feared waking up.

Mrs Attwood seemed conscious of her distraction and kept up a merry stream of inconsequential chatter. Jemima did her best to join in, more than grateful for her companion's efforts on her behalf, but she was aware of the way Solo watched her, and of his growing impatience with Mrs Attwood. Eventually, the lady desisted, and by mutual if silent agreement, they feigned sleep for the remaining hour of the journey.

Minerva's obvious joy in the day did much to revive Jemima's spirits, that and the tactful way in which Solo kept his distance. Now and then, she felt his gaze upon her and turned, but he was always looking elsewhere. The ceremony was brief, which was just as well for the poor befuddled bridegroom, who stumbled and stuttered over his words, much to the exasperation of the poor clergyman trying to marry them. Mr de Beauvoir was obviously so overwhelmed by his good fortune that no one could doubt the sincerity of his feelings, and there was much laughter and a deal of surreptitious eye wiping from the ladies. Matilda had a sodden hanky clenched in one hand when Jemima gave her a gentle nudge and offered her a fresh one.

"Thank you," Matilda murmured, and gave an audible sniff. "I always cry at weddings," she said, giving a little hiccoughing laugh and taking Jemima's arm in hers.

Though she was sorry to say goodbye to the others, it was a relief to leave with Matilda and enjoy a comfortable evening together. Jemima suspected her refusal to allow Matilda to come and stay had hurt her friend, and now that Minerva knew the truth, she felt she owed Matilda an explanation. Yet when it came to the point, it seemed a deal harder to do than when Minerva had appeared on her doorstep.

Jemima knew, as all the Peculiar Ladies knew, that Matilda and the Marquess of Montagu were drawn to each other. That Matilda desired him was clear to them all, though whether or not she actually *liked* him was another matter. He wanted her for his mistress, yet despite what must be a dreadful temptation, Matilda continued to resist him. She had held her head up and rebuffed every advance, and for Jemima to concede that she had capitulated when Matilda held firm, made her feel a little ashamed.

Shame turned to frustration, however, as she looked about the luxurious and elegant home on South Audley Street. Matilda had every advantage, for she did not want for money. Yes, her reputation meant that she suffered the indignity of men who believed they could purchase her for the right price, but she did not have to fight hunger, or worry if the next night would be her last with a roof over her head.

"Is everything all right, Jem, dear?"

Jemima looked up to find Matilda watching her with concern in her eyes.

"Yes, of course. Why ever not? It's been a lovely day, though a little fatiguing after the journey and all the excitement. I confess I slept ill for fear I should oversleep and keep Baron Rothborn waiting for me."

"Yes, he seems a rather prickly fellow," Matilda said, lifting her cup of tea to her lips. "St Clair tried to speak to him, but he was terribly curt."

Jemima bristled on Solo's account, and then reminded herself that the observation was likely fair enough, even though the man himself was far different when you got to know him a little.

"He doesn't do well in company, that's all," she said, still feeling the need to defend him. "He was very kind to us on our journey here."

Matilda set her cup down, thoughtful now. "A military man, I recollect. So many suffered during that dreadful conflict and I can imagine returning to the civilised world must be a difficult adjustment after everything he's seen and done. Thank heavens that monster, Napoleon, is dealt with at last."

Jemima nodded, trying to commence a conversation that would end with, *and I am his mistress*. Before she could contrive a way in which to do so, Matilda stifled a yawn and begged her pardon.

"I must go to bed or I shall do something unforgiveable and fall asleep before you. I promise you it is not your company, however. I confess I have missed you dreadfully and it is good to have you here again, if only for a night."

Jemima smiled, knowing this was the moment she ought to explain why she could not invite Matilda to stay, but the words caught in her throat.

"I have missed you too," she said instead, feeling like a dreadful friend. "But bed sounds like a wonderful idea, or I risk snoring in the carriage tomorrow and making poor Lord Rothborn most uncomfortable."

Taking up her candle, Jemima gave Matilda a brief hug, and took herself up the stairs.

Chapter 6

Dearest Aashini,

I have just had the most dreadful and shocking news about Mr Burton. It will be in all the scandal sheets tomorrow and I can only thank heaven that I have had such a narrow escape. Except it is not heaven I must thank for my liberty.

I feel the world has been turned on its head. I ought to believe that Montagu was motivated by his desire to have me for himself. It would be what any sane person believed. Yet I think he truly acted out of concern for my happiness and then could not ignore what he discovered when the horror was revealed to him. I do not know if that makes me the biggest fool that ever lived.

Oh, my friend, when you read of the conditions found in Mr Burton's mills, of the treatment of those poor children… and he <u>must</u> have known. How can I ever trust my own judgement again when I believed him a good man, when <u>everyone</u> knows Montagu is cold and cruel, and yet he is the saviour here. I do not know what to think. Montagu has taken it upon himself to bring the awfulness of these people's lives to the public notice. Perhaps even a bad man can act for the good, or perhaps he is playing a deeper game than I can comprehend? Is it possible that the *world has misjudged him? Or is it simply that I am still a fool with no reason when it comes to men, and I am seeing what I wish to see?*

—Excerpt of a letter from Miss Matilda Hunt to Aashini Anson, Viscountess Cavendish.

4th February 1815. Briar Cottage, Mitcham Village, Sussex.

Jemima was kept busy for the next few days with a constant stream of visitors from the village. Though she knew this irritated Solo no end, for he felt compelled to keep his distance until the furore died down, it was certainly entertaining. The Grangers returned, which comprised Mrs Granger and her two daughters. Jemima and Mrs Attwood had immediately recognised the mama as a spiteful cat who would sooner speak ill of someone than give them the benefit of the doubt. She had two pretty daughters who seemed to have escaped their mother's bitter tongue, but who were rarely given the opportunity to speak. Noting the envious glances Mrs Granger cast around the elegant parlour, and that her gown—though of quality—was last year's style, Jemima treated her with unflagging courtesy and noted her down as someone to treat with extreme caution. Mrs Tuttle was next, a good-natured busybody who knew everyone and everything. A pretty, softly rounded lady of middling years, she was all ruffles, ribbons, and frills that rustled and fluttered when she moved. Her visit coincided with yet another by the schoolmaster Mr Stickles, with whom her dialogue alternated between motherly teasing and outrageous flirting until the poor man was the colour of a beetroot. His embarrassment aside, Mr Stickles was an amiable fellow with good manners and interesting conversation. The day after, Mr Pemble the vicar returned, and Jemima was put quite out of countenance by the way the clergyman had of addressing her bosom rather than looking in her eyes. Mrs Attwood nearly choked on her tea with the effort of not laughing. Young mothers Mrs Finton and Mrs Pellet followed him, bearing gifts of sugar biscuits and homemade elderflower cordial. Next came the widowed Major Hawkins, a rather dapper old soldier with a twinkle in his eyes for Mrs Attwood. He gifted two bottles of his own peapod wine with a jovial warning to underestimate it at their peril.

So the villagers of Mitcham came and went, making themselves known to their new neighbour with various degrees of warmth and welcome, until Jemima felt quite giddy with the effort to remember all their names.

"Well, you've certainly made an impression." Mrs Attwood chuckled once the last of the guests had left.

"Yes, but what manner of impression?" Jemima retorted, only half joking.

She wondered how many of those amiable people would cut her dead if they knew the truth. Ah, well, that was the risk inherent in her new life and she ought not dwell upon it.

They had no sooner sat down and picked up their abandoned needlework when the front door knocker sounded again. Jemima looked up in surprise as Bessie escorted Mr Stickles in for his third visit in little over a week. At this rate, it would not be Lord Rothborn everyone was gossiping about and linking to her name. The fellow carried a delicate posy of snowdrops and was blushing profusely.

"Forgive me for the interruption, ladies," he said, giving a very formal bow. "Only I was out walking, and I came upon the most glorious expanse of snowdrops I've ever encountered by the woods behind the vicarage. They were so pure and lovely, I... I felt compelled to pick some to bring to you, Miss Fernside."

He offered the little posy to her, flushing hotly as Jemima took them from his hand.

"That was most thoughtful of you, Mr Stickles. Thank you."

Mr Stickles beamed with pleasure as the front door knocker sounded again and Bessie hurried to answer it. A moment later, Lord Rothborn strode in.

Jemima felt her breath catch and was at once certain that the room shrank by half and the temperature plummeted to arctic climes as his lordship's hawk-like gaze descended on Mr Stickles and his posy.

"My Lord Rothborn," Mr Stickles said, bowing deeply and looking more awkward than ever under Solo's brittle greeting.

Jemima felt dreadfully sorry for the poor man and watched with a combination of embarrassment and irritation as he stammered and stuttered through a stilted conversation whilst *Baron* Rothborn seemed determined to play up to his role of high and mighty lord of the manor. It was one she'd never seen him use before. Suitably crushed, Mr Stickles fled, and Mrs Attwood muttered something about being needed in the kitchen before doing likewise.

The room seemed to shrink an inch or two more as Mrs Attwood closed the door, leaving them alone. Solo's scowl indicated his mood. He thumped his cane on the floor a few times. She wondered if he knew he'd done it.

"It is good to see you," Jemima said, testing the water with care to see just what she was dealing with. He grunted and rested the cane against a chair before limping to the window. She studied him with curiosity as he stared outside, hands behind his back.

"I'm surprised you even noticed my arrival, judging from the swarms of visitors that have scurried to and from your door these past days."

Jemima could not see his expression, but the words were terse enough to clarify his mood was one of deep annoyance. Whether with her or her guests, she wasn't certain.

"They have been very kind, and most welcoming."

There was an impatient harrumph, and Solo folded his arms over his chest. "Yes, Mr Stickles has been *most* welcoming. Three visits in as many days and a posy to boot. Everyone in the village believes he means to court you, and I see no evidence to contradict them."

Jemima's eyebrows shot up, and she was so surprised she spoke without thinking, which was most out of character. "Frankly, I suspect I am unlikely to see him ever again, now you've frightened the poor man out of his wits. Why do you not just paint a sign and pin it up over my front door, *The Property of Baron Rothborn?*"

Solo stiffened, clearly shocked by her impatient words, but no more than Jemima herself, who couldn't believe she'd said such a thing. Something about this man made her forget she was a lady, but then she'd agreed not to be a lady for him, so perhaps it made sense. She was on the verge of begging his pardon when he turned, and the uncertainty in his eyes halted her words.

"Did... Did you wish for him to return?"

Jemima let out a breath of surprise, and then reminded herself of what she'd learned of the man before her, that he seemed to have forgotten just how handsome he was, how magnetic his presence, and how lucky any woman would be to have his attention. She liked having his attention.

He stared at her as she studied him in return, noting the stiff way he held himself, the arrogant tilt of his chin, and the doubt in his eyes.

"He is my neighbour, and I should like to be on friendly terms with all those in the village, for as long as I may hold their good opinion. I assure you I am quite capable of rebuffing Mr Stickles, should the need arise. However, to answer the question I believe you meant to ask me... No. I have no interest in Mr Stickles. There is no reason on earth for you to be jealous, nor to act as though the poor man was something unpleasant you had rather not look upon."

Solo's dark eyebrows drew together, his gaze troubled. "You do not mince your words, Miss Fernside."

Jemima felt a jolt of unease at being addressed so formally and wondered just how deeply she'd offended him.

"I beg your pardon, Lord Rothborn," she said, staring at the floor, her fingers twisted in a knot. Had she'd ruined everything by allowing her foolish tongue free rein.

There was a taut silence and then Solo moved stiffly towards her, sitting down at her side on the love seat. Jemima let out an unsteady breath as he untangled her anxious hands, taking hold of one and lifting it to his lips.

"Forgive me," he said, bringing her hand to his chest and holding it there. "It's been damn frustrating having to keep away, and then to see that… that blasted twit of a schoolteacher mooning about over you." He sighed, shaking his head and scowling. "I'm sorry. I behaved very badly, and you were quite right to scold me."

Jemima stared at him, astonished by his apology.

"No, indeed, I had no right at all," she said, too stunned to just accept his words and be pleased by them. "Only you looked so terrifying and poor Mr Stickles has no defence against a man like you. He was quite outmatched and, you frightened him half to death."

"A man like me?" he repeated, a glimmer of interest in his dark eyes.

"Now you are just fishing for compliments," she said tartly, though she smiled at him to let him know she did not mean it.

"I am. Shall I get any?"

"No," she said, though her lips twitched. "I do not believe in rewarding bad behaviour."

Solo snorted.

"Then I have nothing to lose in admitting it was my intention to frighten him," he said, sounding just a little belligerent. "Though you are correct that such behaviour could easily be construed as possessive and I was a fool to act so. The problem is... I *am* possessive."

Jemima swallowed as his thumb traced a circle around and around her palm, and shivers went racing up and down over her skin in a delicious if horribly distracting manner. His next words made matters far worse.

"I want you all to myself."

She could see that possessive light in his eyes clearly enough, and though she disliked the way he had behaved, she could not deny a little thrill at his jealousy. It was a new and wondrous thing to be wanted, and by such a handsome man. With chagrin, she acknowledged that her head had not only been turned, it was still spinning.

"You came to the front door," she observed, wishing she didn't sound so breathless.

"It would have been as remarked upon if I had not visited as if I had come too often, and I was a fool not to realise how badly it would chafe to see all the young blades cast their lures at you. Damnation, I cannot abide gossip and I hate having to be so circumspect when I want to see you all the time."

Jemima smiled at the idea of Mr Pemble and Mr Stickles resembling young blades of any variety, but said nothing. His hand still held hers, warm and strong, his thumb tracing that same path which was making her feel fractious and odd. Jemima stared at it, bewildered by too many emotions. Unease stirred in her belly and momentarily pushed the other, intriguing sensations to one side as she wondered if their agreement didn't please him as much as he'd hoped it would. He'd been annoyed this morning, and he still sounded irritated.

"Do... do you regret our arrangement and wish I had not come?"

"*Regret?*"

Jemima looked up, struck by the incredulity in his voice.

"Little fool," he whispered, his gaze hot and dark. "Come here, and I will show you how much I regret it."

Though it was terrible to admit, Jemima wanted nothing more than to go to him and did not need a second invitation. He kissed her, his mouth a slow, sensual assault as he pressed closer and closer, and still closer. It was a moment before she realised she was being pushed back against the cushions and he was following her down. How strange, that all the world should go away, so far away, when he was close. It was as though time had been suspended, and nothing mattered, nothing even existed beyond the press of his lips, the caress of his wicked tongue against hers, and his warm hands mapping her like an undiscovered world. It was all new to her, though no doubt she held no surprises for a man like him. Perhaps the war and circumstances had changed him, but before there would have been no shortage of lovers for such a dashing, handsome officer.

Perhaps she ought to be alarmed or ashamed, despite the agreement between them, but in that moment Jemima could not muster either response to his touch. She was at once languid and taut with anticipation, her limbs heavy whilst excitement coiled within her, a slow burn that grew hotter as his questing hands explored. Perhaps she should have protested a little at least when his hand closed over her breast and gently squeezed, and perhaps she might have done if the sensation that jolted through her hadn't been so glorious. So, instead of protesting, she moaned and arched into his hand, somewhat appalled by her own abandon, but falling too fast to make it stop.

"So beautiful," he murmured, kissing a path down her neck.

He expertly tugged aside the fine lace fichu that demurely covered the décolletage exposed by the dress, and kissed all along the border of the gown, over the swells of her bosom. Jemima's breath hitched as his tongue dipped into the valley between her breasts, her hands sinking into the thick silk of his hair. She was increasingly frantic, an insistent burning ache having begun between her thighs. It was maddening and she longed to be closer to him, responding by pressing her body against his and thrilling in the low moan that rumbled through him.

"Jem, my beautiful girl, oh God, you're so sweet."

"Solo," she gasped, wanting to ask—no, to *demand*—something, but not knowing how to articulate what exactly it was she wanted. "Please," she said, struck by the desperation in that one word, but unable to take it back.

He seemed to know, though, to understand, and he tugged her bodice down, undoing the ribbon on her chemise and easing her breasts free of her stays. Jemima cried out in shock as the heat of his mouth closed over her, but the sensation was too delicious, and she wanted more. Oh, this was sin. The road to the devil's door must be paved with kisses so sweet. This was wickedness and debauchery. She was immoral and depraved, and how very good it felt. This was what her aunt and every maiden's mama had warned them about. This was why innocent young girls were closely chaperoned, because how could anyone possibly resist... *this*.

Any relief was short-lived, however, as the maddening desire for more only grew. The fire that had been smouldering inside her only burned hotter and hotter beneath his mouth and hands. She needed more of him, needed to be closer, wanted his skin on hers.

"Let me touch you," he murmured, and she wanted to shout *yes* at the top of her lungs.

Yes, please ruin me now. All at once, she was riveted to the slide of his palm as it moved beneath her gown and up the inside of her calf. Her breath caught and held as his touch moved inexorably higher, until his fingers traced the delicate skin above her garter.

"So soft," he marvelled, taking her mouth again, making her giddy with kisses that seemed to act like an opiate, easing away her cares and making everything so easy and perfect and pleasurable.

"Solo?" His name was a combination of pleading and uncertainty on her lips, and he hushed her with soothing noises of reassurance.

"It's all right. It will feel good, so good."

She was relieved to discover he was breathing as hard as she was as he eased her thighs apart, and then his fingers brushed the hidden curls, the touch so intimate she jolted even as her body ached for more.

"I won't hurt you," he promised, kissing her mouth, her face, the warm, damp trail of his lips and tongue moving over her skin. "This is for you, to please you, my lovely Jemima. Let me make you feel good."

She gasped as his touch became more insistent, his fingers gently insinuating their way inside, and then she was lost. Any pretence that she might still be the nice girl her aunt had brought her up to be had been abandoned and cast aside beneath his clever hands. The sensations were delicious and maddening, at once too much and not enough, and she squirmed restlessly, wanting both to scream with frustration and purr like a cat. Shamelessly, she moved under his caresses, arching into his touch, desperate for more, her vocabulary reduced to little sounds of pleasure, gasps and moans and broken cries that he swallowed with kisses until her body betrayed her entirely. At last it gave itself up to him without regret, shuddering and swept away on a tide of sin and joy, sparks glittering behind her eyes as she fell into the flames.

Jemima was floating on a dark sea, her limbs heavy as lead, too weighty to move an inch. Even her eyelids refused to cooperate, though perhaps that was the knowledge that shame must surely await her if she dared to lift them. She was dimly aware of Solo's hands upon her, setting her to rights. With those clever fingers that had undone her so comprehensively, he put her back together again, her skirts rearranged, her chemise tied, and stays and gown eased carefully in place.

She couldn't look at him. She'd never be able to look at him again. What must he think of her?

"I've shocked you."

There was something she recognised in his words, a touch of masculine pride that made her dare to peek at him. His expression matched his tone. He looked smug, undeniably pleased with himself. Well, he wasn't disgusted by her then, that was a relief.

"A little," she said, thinking that must be the biggest understatement of anyone, anywhere, *ever*. "H-have *I* shocked *you*?"

His eyebrows shot up and then he grinned, looking as pleased as a schoolboy promised sweets.

"You were total perfection. Just as I predicted. I told you, I am never wrong. You may as well accept that now."

Despite this unequivocal statement, Jemima regarded him doubtfully.

He leaned down and pressed a soft kiss to her mouth. "I know morality would have it otherwise, but I do not believe you've done anything wrong. I wanted to please your body and I did. Why should you not enjoy my touch? I know I will enjoy yours when I am allowed the privilege. It is not right that men alone enjoy such pleasure, and it is foolish to believe a woman wrong to enjoy it too. Why would God have given you the means to experience such a thing only to deny it to you?"

That sounded reasonable, she supposed, but she must have still looked uncertain as he frowned a little.

"Do you regret—?"

"No!" she said at once. "I mean... I don't know what I mean," she said, laughing a little. "I don't regret it, though a part of me insists I ought to be ashamed of myself. I am changing, and I don't feel like those changes are for the worst, yet everything I have been brought up to believe... I don't know what to think. I don't even think I know who I am anymore."

"I'm sorry. I wish—"

She pressed a finger to his lips, suddenly certain she did not want to hear what he wished. For if he expressed regret, she might feel she really had done something shameful, and she was still floating in some happy place she had no desire to abandon just yet.

Yes, she was confused, but she was not ashamed, and she did not wish to be. Solo took her hand and kissed each finger in turn with such tenderness that she ached for him. Why hadn't this lovely man married? Why hadn't someone seen how good and kind he was and snatched him up and given him a family? Why had he been left by himself to become brittle and lonely?

"Will you dine with me tonight?" he asked, his eyes warm and hopeful, and she could not think of a single thing she would rather do than spend time in his company.

"Yes. I would like that very much."

He smiled with pleasure and, her heart seemed to give an odd little lurch in her chest.

Oh, Jemima, she thought with a sigh. *You are in very deep trouble.*

Chapter 7

My Lord Marquess,

The sale of the mills is confirmed, and I shall be pleased not to have to deal with Mr Burton again. Though he did not dare say it clearly, he implied that he had been slandered and ill-used, the mills swindled from him for a paltry sum. Since the news broke, no one will receive him. He is cut in the street and treated as an outcast. I believe he intends to go to abroad, and heaven help the poor devils who fall into his path.

I have made the arrangements you requested and set up an anonymous charitable fund for those who were injured and the families of those who have died. The new procedures we discussed are being implemented as we speak, and the mills will not reopen until we have completed a safety inspection. No children will work in these places ever again. The increase in wages will cover any loss of income for families whose children will no longer bring in a wage.

I look forward to your visit and to showing you everything we have accomplished in such a short time. We have done a good thing, and I am proud to have been a part of it.

—Excerpt of a letter from Mr Richard Glover to The Most Honourable Lucian Barrington, Marquess of Montagu.

4th February 1815. Mitcham Priory, Sussex.

Jemima smiled at Mrs Norrell, whilst butterfly wings swept about in her stomach. Mrs Norrell had been struck down with a megrim, much to that lady's distress, and could not accompany her. So, Bessie had chaperoned her to The Priory for propriety—in case some disaster struck and they were seen—but also as Bessie wanted to visit her brother and his wife who was expecting their second child. She'd hurried off as soon as Jemima was safely inside and in Mrs Norrell's care.

"What a lovely gown," Mrs Norrell said with a gasp as she helped remove Jemima's cloak. "If you don't mind me remarking it, miss," she added, a tinge of colour in her cheeks as she realised she ought not have commented. "I beg your pardon, but it's so long since we had anything resembling company at The Priory. I've forgotten my manners."

Jemima smiled. "Thank you, Mrs Norrell, and please do not apologise. I have no idea how we are supposed to treat each other in such circumstances, but... but I do thank you for your kindness. I did not expect it."

There was an impatient huff, and Mrs Norrell gathered up her cloak and put it away.

"That man needs a bit of love and gentleness. I don't see what business it is of anybody else's what goes on. It certainly isn't mine, and I've seen enough of life not to judge you for it neither. If not for that wicked fiancée of his...." She broke off, her lips thinning into a hard line.

"His... *fiancée*?" Jemima echoed. "He was engaged?"

Mrs Norrell nodded, her expression still hard and angry. "She broke it off when he came home."

"Oh," Jemima said, her heart sinking as she realised. "Surely not because he was lame?"

She watched as Mrs Norrell studied her, judging what and how much to tell her, perhaps.

"Mrs Norrell, do you plan to keep my guest to yourself for the entire evening?"

Jemima jumped a little as Solo's terse voice echoed across the entrance hall and Mrs Norrell turned to tut at him. He was standing some distance from them, too far to have overheard their conversation, thank heavens.

"I was just about to bring Miss Fernside to you, my lord," she retorted.

"Ha, when you'd finished gossiping, no doubt," he muttered. "Hurry and bring the dinner in, and stop chattering with my guest. I'm famished, and the lady looks likely to swoon from hunger. Oh, and don't forget that Rhenish wine for the dessert course. Keep it chilled until the last moment."

"Right you are, my lord," said Mrs Norrell, muttering as she went. "*And I'll stick a broom up me arse and sweep the floor as I go.*"

Happily, Solo hadn't moved and still could not hear her, but it took a great deal of effort on Jemima's part not to splutter with mingled shock and amusement. With regret, she watched Mrs Norrell go, wishing they'd had time to finish their conversation.

"You look astonishingly beautiful."

Jemima felt a little shy suddenly as she moved towards Solo, aware of the quality of his gaze as he watched her approach.

"Thank you," she said, smiling and doing a twirl for him despite her nerves. "It's my favourite of the gowns I bought before

I left London, and really quite shocking. I thought you would like it, though."

It was a dusky pink crepe robe with a demi-train. The dress dipped low at the back and off the shoulders with a soft satin border the same shade as the gown. Her hair was curled in thick waves, with a few thick coils falling to one shoulder. Truly, it was the most daring thing she'd ever worn, and she'd never have done so in public, but then she was dining alone with her lover, so… why not?

"I do like it," he said, as he led her into the dining room and closed the door. "I like you," he added, and bent to steal a kiss.

Jemima closed her eyes, her body thrumming to life with even that brief touch of his lips. Memories of how he'd touched her earlier that day came back with a rush, stirring her blood with anticipation. Would he touch her like that again? Tonight? A blush rose to her cheeks, and he let out a shaky breath as he watched her.

"Don't look at me that way, or we will never make it through dinner."

Jemima bit her lip and hurriedly averted her gaze. She moved forward as Solo drew out a chair for her.

"I don't have many staff, as you see," he said, sitting down at the head of the table, with Jemima seated at his right elbow. "I prize my solitude, and cannot abide people poking about and disturbing me, so I only keep on the bare minimum. On the plus side, they are loyal and not the kind to gossip."

Jemima nodded. "Bessie told me as much. Between the cottage and The Priory, you employ most of her family."

Solo nodded. "I discovered by accident that my grandfather was, er… rather a profligate and wild character. I have reason to believe we may well be related, though I did not know that until a few years ago. Still, the least I could do was keep them in employment. They're good people, too. Loyal to a fault, as Bessie has shown you."

"She thinks the world of you," Jemima said with a smile. "They all do."

Solo coloured a little and harrumphed, reaching for the wine. "Try some of this. It's very good."

After a glass of wine and the first course of beef broth, which was rich and tasty, Jemima relaxed. Solo was excellent company, and she soon discovered they shared a love of books. In fact, he seemed to have read everything she had, and a great deal more besides. Most surprising, however, was his unabashed love of novels: a thing most men would deny vehemently, even if it were true.

"Well, no wonder you were so impatient with me when we first met in the bookshop," she said, laughing now as she realised. "You were no doubt disgusted that, with so much choice, I failed to choose a single title."

"I was not impatient," he said, sounding impatient.

Jemima bit back a smile. "Indeed you were. You looked so formidable. Such a handsome, precise military man, and I was so terribly nervous that I nearly knocked that poor old gentleman flying and succeeded in wresting his book from his hands. If not for you, it would likely have given the salesman a shocking blow to the head, as he was the only other person in the shop that day and I was therefore bound to strike him with it. You were utterly horrified, which I compounded by admitting I didn't wish to buy anything. I was certain you'd taken me in immediate dislike. I was only surprised you didn't run in the other direction."

Solo stared at her in wonder. "How odd that two people can remember the same event so differently."

"We do?"

He let out a little huff of laughter. "I was convinced there had been some mistake and spent the entire time waiting to get my face slapped. I couldn't believe that someone as beautiful, as perfect as the vision before me could ever... that you would even consider....

If by some miracle you were the woman Mr Briggs had sent me to meet, I knew you'd take one look at me and change your mind. I was certain of it."

"Why on earth would you think such a thing?" Jemima asked gently. "You are a very handsome man."

He frowned and looked away, and the conversation dwindled as they served themselves the next course. Little by little, Jemima coaxed him back by speaking of books. She was reading *Undine*, a romantic and tragic tale of a woman who was really a water nymph and married a knight. Naturally, he had read it too, and she found herself charmed by Solo's enthusiasm for the tale. Truly, it was a romantic fairy story, but he seemed just as beguiled as she was, both by the story and the glorious illustrations that followed lovely Undine to her fate. The urge to reach out and touch him made her ache, the desire to hold his head against her breast and stroke his hair as she had once before so strong it was a pain in her heart. How this brave, careworn soul fascinated her. His willingness to open his heart to such a story, and his obvious sadness for the way the tale turned out when the knight betrayed poor Undine with unthinking words, only made her long to see him happy.

Perhaps this was why she spoke without thinking, but once the table was cleared after dinner and they were alone, the question slipped out.

"Did you never think of marrying?"

Jemima did not know why she asked. He obviously had thought of it, if he'd been engaged. She was simply prying, wanting to satisfy her curiosity about him. His tension was immediately apparent, and she regretted her inquisitiveness at once.

There was a sharp silence, and Jemima was about to change the subject when he answered her.

"I was engaged once. She declined to go through with it on account that I killed her brother."

Jemima stared at him. Though it had been a shocking thing to say, worse was the bitterness and self-loathing in his eyes. It was painful to see.

"You did not kill her brother."

Her words were full of certainty, and she didn't know where that assurance had come from, but the sense that he was punishing himself was too strong to deny.

He made a disparaging sound and drained his wine glass, reaching to fill it again. "And you know this how, Miss Fernside?"

The question was full of mockery and Jemima found herself a little shocked by his tone, and by the fact that they were back to Miss Fernside again.

"Did you fight a duel?" she asked.

"No."

Jemima nodded. "Then it was while you were at war. Perhaps there were events you feel responsible for that led to his death. I could understand a sense of guilt in such circumstances, but I doubt you put a gun to his head. Did you?"

"I may as well have done."

Solo drained his glass and then got up, snatching up his cane and going to stand by the fire. He poked irritably at the uppermost log with the tip of his cane and it collapsed the stack below, sending a shower of sparks up the chimney as the flames leapt higher.

Jemima watched him for a moment and then followed, standing behind him, uncertain of what to do or say. His head was bent, and he stared at the flames while the flickering light made his dark hair gleam like bronze. He looked terribly alone, and she could not bear for him to feel so. Gathering her courage, she moved closer and put her arms around his waist, laying her head against his back.

"Forgive me. I ought not to have pried. It's not my business."

For a moment he didn't react, and then he cast the cane to one side and turned, pulling her into his arms and kissing her hard. Jemima felt she had fallen into a shower of sparks too as the fire leapt inside her and seared her skin, dissolving her into molten heat. His tongue was urgent, devouring, and she gave what he asked with no hesitation, leading where he followed until he drew back, breathing fast.

"Forgive me," he said.

His voice was still harsh, the tension singing through him not lessened a whit, but he evidently meant it.

"There's nothing to forgive."

He let out a breath and leaned his head atop hers, still holding her close.

"Stay."

Oh.

"S-Stay?"

"Yes. Stay here tonight."

Jemima's heart skittered madly in her chest as she fought not to react. She'd known this time would come, of course she had, but... but she hadn't expected....

"I... I don't have any of my things...."

"Yes, you do. I asked Bessie to let me know what items you might require before you moved into the cottage and I ordered all she suggested, including clothes for the morning. There ought to be everything you should want but, if there is anything missing, you need only name it."

Oh.

Too late, she realised she had gone rigid in his arms. He stepped back a little, regarding her.

"Jemima?"

"Yes," she said, too brightly. "Yes, of course."

He let out a breath. Relieved, she supposed. At least she'd managed not to have a fit of the vapours, though something panicked and trembled at the corners of her mind.

"I'll ask Mrs Norrell to show you to your rooms, and Bessie will attend you."

Jemima nodded. The motion was too jerky, but he seemed not to notice. She stood by the fire as he went off in search of Mrs Norrell, wondering what to expect. It had been her hope that Mrs Attwood would instruct her and give an explanation of what she was letting herself in for before this night, but now it was too late. The woman had tried a couple of times to raise the subject and enlighten her, but each time Jemima had shied away, not quite ready for such a frank discussion as Mrs Attwood would grant her. How stupid not to have taken the woman's instruction and counsel while she could. Foolish of her to think Solo would continue to wait. She had made no such stipulation and she was his property, or her body was, all the while she abided by their agreement. The idea made her hot and cold and a little sick, but there was no backing out now. Besides, she was being silly. She had not disliked his touch earlier, far from it. The thought of repeating the experience had excited her, so there was no point in getting all missish about it. So, she put up her chin and forced herself to appear calm when Mrs Norrell came to fetch her.

"If you would come with me, Miss Fernside?"

"Jemima, please," she said, hardly able to look the woman in the eyes but grateful that she had still been addressed with respect and kindness.

They climbed the stairs, and Mrs Norrell led her along a long, gloomy corridor that seemed to go on forever. The candle guttered, the floor creaked, and a succession of long-dead Rothborn ancestors glared balefully down at Jemima, making her feel as if she'd been plunged into a Gothic novel. It was most unsettling.

"The old house makes a lot of odd noises, moaning and groaning," Mrs Norrell said, sounding unreasonably cheerful. "But there's nothing to worry about."

"There isn't?" Jemima said doubtfully, shivering in the chill as a draught whistled down the passageway, stirring her hair and making her look over her shoulder.

Her heart banged against her ribs as she contemplated being in this place alone at night. Except she wouldn't be alone, she assured herself. She wasn't certain whether that was entirely comforting.

After what seemed to be an eternity, Mrs Norrell opened the door and led her into a bedroom. It was a large, impressive room, and clearly part of the Tudor addition to the building. As with downstairs, the walls were panelled and the ceiling heavy with beams. Rich brocade curtains covered the windows, and there were luxurious rugs over the polished wood floorboards. A huge, ancient bed dominated the room, the covers just as lavish as everything else. The only sound was the snap and pop of a hearty fire in the beautiful carved stone fireplace. Much to Jemima's relief, Bessie was waiting for her, arranging things on an elegant mahogany dressing table with a marble top and an adjustable octagonal mirror.

Mrs Norrell bade her a good evening and left them alone.

"Oh, miss, just wait till you see!"

Bessie giggled, then rushed to a large armoire and flung open the doors. With something approaching awe, she withdrew a folded scrap of material that fluttered open as she held it up with careful fingers. Jemima gaped as she realised she was looking at a chemise, though it was unlike any chemise she owned. Made of cambric so fine it was almost sheer, it was edged at the hem with a wide band of the most delicate lace she'd ever seen in her life. The neckline was wide and deep and trimmed with a tiny frill. With a gasp, she noticed how short the item was. It would barely cover her to mid-thigh.

"Good heavens."

"Isn't it beautiful?" Bessie stared at the chemise with wide brown eyes. "I never saw nothing so lovely in all my days."

"Lovely," Jemima said faintly, discovering it was hard to breathe.

"You'll hardly know you've got it on."

Jemima blushed, a furious rush of colour that only made Bessie giggle harder.

"Oh, if you could see your face…! But surely you're not frightened, are you? I mean, you like him and he's devilish handsome. I'd take your place if he'd only take a fancy to me."

"Bessie!" Jemima said, shocked, but she couldn't help but laugh at Bessie's enthusiasm.

"You ain't frightened, are you, miss?" Bessie asked again, her tone more serious now.

Jemima bit her lip. "N-Not frightened, exactly."

"And you do know… what goes on…."

Jemima's gaze snapped to Bessie.

"Why, do *you*?" she asked, a little astonished, as Bessie was younger than she was.

There was a snort of amusement. "I grew up in the country, miss. Ma told me years ago and even if she hadn't, my brother works with horses and I seen the stallion servicing the mares. Aye. I reckon I know well enough."

"Oh."

Bessie grinned at her. "Wait there."

Not having a great deal of choice in the matter, as there was no way on earth she was leaving this room alone, Jemima sat before the dressing table and waited. She allowed herself a moment to look about, and almost at once noticed the door… the one that must connect to the master's chambers. Good heavens.

She turned away, as if not looking at the door would change anything. Not too much later, Bessie returned with a decanter and a crystal glass.

"Reckon you need a nip of brandy, settle your nerves, like," Bessie said, pouring out a generous measure and handing it over.

Jemima practically snatched the glass from her hand and took a large swallow, coughing a little as the liquor lit a fire down her throat.

Bessie took the glass back and set it down on the dressing table. "Right then, miss. Let's get you ready, and I'll tell you everything I know."

Chapter 8

Dear Minerva,

Oh, how dull it is without you here to entertain me. Prue and Robert are dreadful company now. Prue is forever falling asleep and Robert fusses about her, doing a fine impression of Matilda at her most maternal. It is terribly sweet and I'm happy for them, but from my point of view it is terminally dreary. I shall run mad if something exciting doesn't happen soon.

Speaking of excitement, the shining light on the horizon comes from my Uncle Charles (Baron Fitzwalter), who is hosting a small house party. He's very good company and always invites the most amusing people. For instance, Harriet's brother, Henry Stanhope with be there – he is sweet on me, you know – and guess what…

He's bringing Mr Gabriel Knight.

Perhaps all is not lost.

—Excerpt of a letter from Lady Helena Adolphus to Mrs Minerva de Beauvoir.

4th February 1815. Mitcham Priory, Sussex.

Solo paced his dressing room and did his best to reassure himself that he was not being unreasonable. He hadn't *thought* he was being unreasonable, until Jemima had gone as stiff as a board in his arms, her eyes doing an alarming impression of a frightened doe caught in a hunter's sights. Yet, earlier in the day, she'd been willing enough, enthusiastic even, so he'd simply assumed.... He was an idiot, naturally. To think that he'd once been considered quite the ladies' man. Of course she was terrified. She was an innocent, forced into this situation through no fault of her own. The poor creature must think him an absolute beast. The least he could do was take things slowly and not frighten her any more than needs be.

He remembered how she'd felt then, soft and pliant in his arms, the delicate scent of her skin still fogged his brain like opium smoke. It was a scent he still hadn't identified to his satisfaction, only that it was enticingly feminine and made him think of the garden in spring after a shower of rain, lush and fertile. Oh, bloody hell. His body ached with desire, a longing to lose himself in her, and he took a deep breath, willing himself to be patient. He wasn't some fool boy, and she'd not been displeased earlier. There were plenty of ways to bring them both pleasure without frightening the wits out of her and, if she was too nervous to allow him that much, he would simply wait until she was ready. She hardly knew him, after all. He hadn't employed a doxy to service his needs, but a companion, a mistress, and he did not believe any woman deserving of impatience or ill treatment for being afraid.

Resolved to behave like a gentleman—even if it killed him—he knocked on the adjoining door and waited until he heard a soft reply bid him enter.

Solo walked in, and froze, his heart leaping to somewhere in the vicinity of his throat and his body tightening with anticipation. Letting out a slow breath, he reminded himself sternly that the brain in his head was in charge, not the smaller, badly behaved one that resided somewhat lower.

She was standing by the fire, something she'd likely have decided against if she'd realised what the firelight did to the sheer fabric of her night-rail. Solo had imagined her wearing it almost every night since the day he'd ordered it. His imagination had fallen a long way short of reality. Her blonde hair was loose and cascaded down her back, shimmering gold in the light of the flames. The arms were bare and crossed protectively about her middle, pulling the fabric over her breasts, making the peaks of her nipples visible, pressed tight against the night-rail. The hem of the gown was short and a good proportion comprised fine lace which covered little, allowing him a generous view of slender legs, all the way to her bare toes.

Solo tried to find words, to find some pretty quote from any number of the poems he'd read over his lifetime, but as he reached to find something it slid from his mind like a fish darting into deep water. It was sometime before he realised he'd just been staring at her in silence.

He cleared his throat, deciding actions would have to speak for him, and moved towards her. She was breathing hard, but so obviously trying her best to look calm and unruffled that tenderness welled inside him. Solo held his hands out to her and, with rather stiff movements, she unwound her arms from about her body and put her hands in his. He lifted first one and then the other to his lips, kissing each knuckle in turn.

"Exquisite," he managed, the word sounding like a growl.

She gave a little half smile, still trying so hard to please him.

Solo tugged at her hand and led her to the chair by the fire. He sat down and then gestured for her to sit in his lap. She did, stiff and awkward.

"Come here," he said, gently easing her back against him. "There's nothing to be afraid of. We don't have to do anything you don't like. My word upon it."

She put up her chin and turned towards him, though she didn't meet his eyes. "I… I know what is expected of me. It's q-quite all right. You have been very patient already and—"

Solo hushed her by pressing his lips to hers and kissing her. Gently he coaxed her, teasing her mouth with his, with touches of his tongue that tempted her to respond, to seek more of him. Little by little, he felt some of the tension ease away and her body relaxed against him. He pulled back and drew her head onto his shoulder, stroking her hair.

"There. Is this all right?"

She sighed and nodded and Solo smiled, pleased.

"I told you, there is no need to fear me. I would never hurt you. I know this is all new and no doubt you are afraid, but I would never force you. I want you to want me, Jemima. I want nothing that is not freely given."

"I do want you."

She spoke so quietly he almost missed what she said, but the admission had desire simmering beneath his skin.

"I'm just… I wasn't expecting…."

"I know," he said, smoothing his hand up and down her back, lightheaded with the sensation of her nearly naked body in his lap, the heat of her skin burning his palm and making him breathless with the need to slide his hand beneath the cambric and find the silk of her flesh under his fingers. "I'm a thoughtless brute. The truth is, I'd not intended to ask you to stay, not yet, but… but I did not want you to go. I'm sorry if I frightened you."

She looked up then, her storm cloud eyes troubled. "I don't want to be silly and missish. I knew what I was agreeing to, and had no illusions. You have been so generous, so patient, and I feel so foolish to… to fret over what is inevitable."

"Hush," he said, sliding his hand about her neck. "There is no rush, and you're not being silly. Tonight we will talk, and you will get used to having me close. Perhaps you will stay again, like this, just to talk, and then we shall see how you feel. If you are still unsure, we will wait a bit longer."

"How kind you are."

Solo felt uncomfortable when faced with the soft look in her eyes. *Kind?* He was the wicked seducer, the man who would ruin her, take her innocence and make her a whore in the eyes of respectable society. Oh, yes, how kind he was. He reminded himself that she had a warm, comfortable home, plenty of food and firewood, pretty gowns and the company of women who would not judge her. He had done all of that to please her… yet the knowledge did not ease his guilt. His guilt was not enough to halt what would happen, though. He needed this woman and now, having met her, he knew no one else would do. It had to be her.

"What shall we talk about?"

Solo smiled. "I'll tell you a little about The Priory, shall I? That will send you to sleep in no time."

"Oh, I'm sure it couldn't do any such thing," she said, and he found himself pleased by the enthusiasm in her voice. "It's such a beautiful place, and it must have such an extraordinary history. Do please tell me."

So he did. Solo told her about the moat—one of the longest in the country—that enclosed The Priory and eight acres of gardens, making it an island all its own, where you could shut out the world if you wished to. He'd been doing it for some time. He told her about the ancient parts of the building, the original Augustinian priory and about the later Tudor additions. He told her some of the bloody history of his ancestors and found himself delighted when he made her laugh with some of the naughtier tales most people never heard. She asked questions and soon seemed quite at ease in his arms, welcoming his kisses when he became distracted by her nearness and his desire to have just a taste of her. After a while, she relaxed against him, one hand resting on his chest, over his heart, her head on his shoulder, and it was some time before he realised she was asleep.

"There," he said ruefully. "I told you I'd send you to sleep."

To Bed the Baron

He gazed down at her, mesmerised by the sight of her in repose, the soft sweep of dark gold lashes and the luminescence of her skin. Her mouth was a dusky pink, the top a perfect cupid's bow, the bottom wider and fuller. The longing to taste her again was almost too strong to resist, but he didn't wish to disturb her. Then he wondered how the devil he was to get her into her bed without waking her. Well, he'd just have to carry her. Once that would have been an easy matter. Now, with his blasted leg, it presented more of a challenge.

Somehow, he got to his feet, trying not to jolt her and biting back a yelp as pain lanced down his thigh to his knee. Jemima stirred, nuzzling against him and sighing before settling back to sleep. He was unsurprised to discover she weighed next to nothing. She was still far too fragile, her limbs too slender, though there was more colour in her cheeks than when he'd first met her, and he looked forward to watching her blossom as regular meals and an end to financial worries worked their magic. Still, light as she was, the unfamiliar burden taxed his injured limb as he tried not to jostle her. The pain made him nauseous, a fine sweat breaking out on his forehead and down his back with the effort of keeping quiet as he made his way towards the bed. Good God, how had he never noticed how bloody big these rooms were.

Finally, he made it, and set her down with care, taking a moment to steady himself by clutching at a bedpost and forcing himself to take a few deep, steadying breaths. Once the dizzying pain had subsided, he reached for the covers and tucked her in, lingering for a long time. With a wry smile, he reflected that it had been the most enjoyable evening he'd ever spent, and he'd barely touched her.

"Goodnight," he said softly, and made his way back to his own chamber.

7th February 1815. South Audley Street, London.

"Oh, I know I'm horribly selfish, but I wish you didn't have to go," Matilda lamented, reaching for a slice of plum cake.

Aashini laughed and set down her teacup. "It has been a lovely visit, but I offered for you to come with me. Why don't you?"

Matilda smiled and shook her head. "You are already missing Silas most dreadfully, that much is obvious, and I'd just as soon miss the romantic reunion," she said, laughing and hoping she didn't sound like a bitter old crone. "Besides, I'm to stay with Nate and Alice. They've been pestering me for ages, and I want to be there for the birth of the baby, though I think there are five or six weeks to go yet. Still, it will be lovely to see them both again, as long as they don't start matchmaking."

"I thought you wanted to make a match, though?" Aashini said, frowning a little as she took a fresh baked roll and tore it into pieces. "Why would you object?"

Matilda shrugged and broke off a corner of her cake, staring at it with a frown before setting it down again.

"I... I don't know, it's just...."

It was just that there was only one man she wanted. There was no point in trying to deny it any longer. How could she try to find herself a husband when her mind was full of thoughts of him? It would be unfair to any man, and to herself. So what did that mean? Montagu was still an enigma to her. Why had he stepped in to expose Mr Burton? Because he was a good man at heart, one who cared that people were being ill-treated?

"It's just because a certain marquess is the only thing on your mind," Aashini finished for her. There was no condemnation in her eyes, no judgement, but there was concern, and sadness too.

Matilda let out a little breath of laughter. "I'm the biggest fool alive."

"Never that." Aashini reached out and took her hand, squeezing. "Do you love him?"

"Love him?" she repeated, a desperate ache settling in her heart. "How can I love him? I don't know him. It is merely desire, I suppose, though *merely* seems a pitiful description of what he makes me feel."

The words sounded rather caustic and defiant, but a little voice in her head screamed *liar, liar, liar*, and her heart was full of an emotion to which she refused to put a name. She didn't know him, not really, though she wanted to very badly, but her heart didn't seem to care. It had made up its mind.

"I had a letter from Mr Burton," she said, changing the subject before Aashini could question her further.

"No!" Aashini said in astonishment.

The scandal sheets were glorying in his downfall, never having liked to see a self-made man succeed. That made his disgrace all the worse in Matilda's eyes. How hard people had to work when they were not born to privilege, and for such a man to be exposed as a villain, how much harder it would become. His wickedness in treating his workers worse than beasts had shown him to be vile and heartless, and she could not believe she had been so mistaken. She had thought him a good man! How flawed her judgement must be.

Strangely, Montagu's part in his downfall was never mentioned, nor was the identity of the mysterious benefactor who had bought the mills, set about making them safe places to be, and promised to create a school for the workers' children... though Matilda had a strong suspicion she knew. This anonymous benefactor had also set up a charitable fund for those injured and the families of the dead.

Had the cold-hearted, wicked marquess been as ill-judged as Mr Burton?

"He tells me it is all lies," she said, her scorn apparent. "Apparently, Montagu set out to ruin him because he wants me for himself. He blames me for having played with his affections whilst angling for a carte blanche from the marquess. I shall spare you the names I was called, but he was very disagreeable."

Matilda's voice shook a little as she tried not to remember. She had flung the letter into the fire and spoken of it to no one until now.

"Oh, Matilda," Aashini said, leaping to her feet and moving around the table to throw her arms about her and hug her tight. "Oh, love. I'm so sorry. What a beastly, disgusting excuse for a man he is, but even Silas was taken in and that's no easy feat. They had some business interests in common—not in the mills, thank heavens—but we both believed him good and honest. So, you see, it was not just you that was taken in. Now, you must put him out of your mind, do you hear me? I can't quite believe I am saying this, but… thank goodness for Montagu. I shall thank him myself the next time I see him, if he deigns to notice my existence, that is," she added with a smile.

Despite everything, Matilda chuckled and hugged Aashini in return. "I fear I must as well. I tried when he was here, but I was so shocked and distressed I suspect he misunderstood my words. I think he believed I was angry with him, which is so… *so…* ridiculous."

Her voice broke as regret at having not properly shown her gratitude to him for what he'd done made her feel stupid and emotional.

"I'm sure he'll understand," Aashini said soothingly. "It was a horrid shock and he is an intelligent man. That is the last thing you need to fret over."

Matilda nodded, but found in her heart, the marquess' opinion was the only thing that mattered at all.

***

Three days later, Matilda had settled in at her brother's home, with a heavily pregnant Alice fussing about her as if *she* was the one who need looking after. Matilda had been welcomed with open arms and genuine pleasure, and realised how much she had missed them both. It seemed foolish now to have stayed away, afraid she might feel resentful for their happiness and joy at the imminent arrival of their baby. Yes, she wanted that for herself, with all her heart, but never could she begrudge their obvious contentment in their new lives together, especially as they so clearly wanted her to be a part of it.

To her surprise, an invitation arrived on the same day from Helena, who was staying just a few miles away with her uncle, Baron Fitzwalter. The baron was giving a dinner and had allowed Helena to invite some guests of her own. Nate, Alice, and Matilda were duly invited.

"Oh, but you must go," Alice insisted that morning at breakfast. "You'll have little enough society here now that I am confined, but I insist you take what opportunities are presented to you."

"But I've only just arrived," Matilda protested. "How awful of me to go gallivanting about when you can't come too."

Alice gave an impatient eye roll. "What nonsense. I'm quite content, indeed I feel like a cow put out to pasture," she said, giving her belly an affectionate rub before reaching for her third bread roll and liberally piling it with butter and jam. "Besides, Nate won't leave me, so I'll have company. It's you who must go alone, I'm afraid, but it sounds as if you must keep an eye on Helena, if Minerva's worries about her interest in Mr Knight are sound. I've heard the most shocking stories about him. Affairs with married ladies and all sorts of wickedness. He's a member of *Hunter's*, you see, and Nate knows him. He says the man is a dreadful libertine. He also says he intends to marry a lady of quality, to help him get a foothold in society."

Matilda narrowed her eyes at Alice, who returned a beatifically innocent smile, knowing full well that Matilda hadn't known Mr Knight would be there, nor that he was such a dangerous prospect, and she'd now have to chaperone Helena who had a reckless streak a mile wide.

"You… are sneaky and underhand, Alice Hunt. No wonder my brother loves you so much."

Alice snickered and batted her eyelashes at Matilda.

"I don't know what you can mean," she said with a straight face, and bit into her roll with relish.

Chapter 9

My Lord Marquess

~~*I will never know how to repay you for what you have done…*~~

~~*Have I misjudged you so badly…*~~

~~*I cannot stop thinking of you…*~~

—*Excerpt of a letter from Miss Matilda Hunt to The Most Honourable, Lucian Barrington, Marquess of Montagu—never completed.*

7th February 1815. Mitcham Priory, Sussex.

"Good morning, Mrs Norrell."

"Miss Fernside," the woman said, smiling broadly. "We didn't expect you until this evening."

"I know," Jemima replied, pleased to be made to feel welcome. "I came to see you. If that's all right?"

"Oh!" Mrs Norrell looked rather taken aback and then beamed at her. "Well, of course it's all right. I'm flattered."

"Don't be," Jemima said, laughing at her. "I've come to wrest the recipe for lemon pond pudding from you by any means necessary and I don't mean to leave without it. I even brought a bribe." She lifted the basket she carried and Mrs Norrell gave a delighted bark of laughter.

"As if you need to bribe me. It's yours and gladly. I'm only pleased you enjoyed it so much."

"It was heaven in a bowl."

Jemima gave a genuine sigh of pleasure as she remembered and followed Mrs Norrell to the kitchen. Although fitted with all modern conveniences, the kitchen showed clearly how things had been centuries past, with thick stone walls and a lintel over the fireplace so large she wondered how it had ever been hoisted into place. The air was warm and scented with delicious things that made her stomach rumble in anticipation.

"So, what's in the basket?" Mrs Norrell asked with obvious amusement.

Jemima reached in and brought out two bottles. "My very own blackberry wine," she said with a touch of pride. "And if I do say so myself, it's very good."

"Oooh," Mrs Norrell said, her eyes lighting up. "That sounds just the thing for these cold nights. Keep the chill out, it will."

"Oh, it will," Jemima promised, grinning.

"Have you tasted the Major's peapod wine yet?" she asked, taking the bottles and putting them away. She then bustled about the kitchen making tea.

"How did you know I had any?"

Mrs Norrell snorted and put a plate of queen cakes down on the table. "He gives it to everyone. Lethal, it is. There's more than one marriage in these parts that's been put down to the Major's wicked brew. Help yourself to cakes."

"Heavens!" Jemima laughed and did as she was told. "Lethal indeed. I shall have to try it...."

She blushed as the implications of her words sank in. Mrs Norrell gave her a kindly smile.

"It would do him the world of good to marry you, and I hope such a thing may come to pass. You'll get no complaints from this quarter if you manage it, however it happens."

"Oh, but I wasn't... I'm not...." Jemima protested, mortified now.

"Hush!" Mrs Norrell rolled her eyes as she hefted a large brown teapot over to the table. "I know you're not. I'm only saying good luck to you if you do. He needs a good woman, someone to bring him back into the world. I think that woman could be you, but I know well enough what a stubborn fellow he is. Honourable and loyal to a fault, but to all the wrong people for all the wrong reasons. Not that he can see it."

She sighed and shook her head before concentrating on pouring the tea.

"What do you mean, he's loyal to the wrong people?"

Mrs Norrell's face set in a frown. "Not my place to say, miss. I've said too much as it is. You must winkle the story out of him yourself. Milk?"

Jemima nodded and accepted the cup handed her, pondering this. She liked Mrs Norrell very much, and was glad for her kindness, but she could not deny she'd also come to find out more about Solo. He was so reluctant to share anything of himself. Oh, he'd speak for hours about his family history, or that of The Priory, and he was very entertaining too, but any mention of his own past and he changed the subject with such speed it made your head spin. She'd spent another night here since that first one, cuddled in his lap as he told her the exploits of long-dead relatives. Although anticipation and desire simmered between them, he'd made no move to touch her. In all honesty, she wasn't certain if that pleased her or not, as she burned for him too. She felt far more at ease with him now, though, which had obviously been his objective, and one she was more than grateful for.

"You said before that he'd been engaged. You didn't like her?" Jemima asked, well aware that she was fishing but unable to stop herself.

There was a derisive sound of contempt from Mrs Norrell, who folded her arms across her ample bosom and scowled.

"I did not."

Jemima bit her lip, desperate to find out more. "Why?" she asked, wondering if she was about to get her head bitten off. One thing was clear about the staff at The Priory, they were just as loyal as their master appeared to be, and fiercely protective of both his privacy and him.

She could almost see the struggle behind the woman's eyes as she debated what to say. Jemima recognised her dilemma. She was clearly hoping for a romantic conclusion to their arrangement—one which Jemima was dangerously close to hoping for herself, even though it was beyond foolish—but she did not want to betray a confidence.

"I won't tell a soul, Mrs Norrell," she said, eager to sway the woman in her favour. "I… I only wish to understand him better. He said she refused to marry him because he'd killed her brother."

To Jemima's dismay, Mrs Norrell's face darkened like an approaching storm and she surged to her feet, stalking away to the kitchen shelves. There was a deal of crashing and slamming of cupboard doors as the woman muttered furiously and Jemima didn't move an inch, wondering what on earth would happen next. Would she be thrown out?

After what seemed to be an eternity of holding her breath, she dared relax a little as Mrs Norrell came back to the table and sat down again. She put a plate of ginger biscuits down too, and placed them rather than throwing them at Jemima, so she thought perhaps she'd been forgiven.

"I beg your pardon, Mrs Norrell. I ought not pry."

"Oh, bugger that," she said, rolling up her sleeves. Jemima's eyebrows rose as Mrs Norrell leaned in, a confiding tone lowering her voice. "He never killed no one, and that miserable bitch knows it. I know I ought not say so, especially as she lost her brother, who was a dear, sweet soul. That much is true, but to make the poor man suffer so when she knows full well it was none of his doing… well, it's wicked, pure and simple."

"What happened?" Jemima asked, finding herself whispering and leaning across the table too.

"His lordship was injured at Sahagun in Spain in eighteen oh eight, and not for the first time, but it was certainly the worst. A dreadful battle, it was, miss. His lordship's Dragoons defeated two regiments of French cavalry in the dead of winter, a night attack in heavy snow, it was, too. So many medals that man was awarded for that encounter, it would make your head spin, not that he'd ever mention them."

"The villagers speak of him with something close to awe," Jemima agreed, feeling a swell of pride herself. "They say it was his strategy that won that encounter but he refuses to speak of it."

"Aye, that's him, right enough." Mrs Norrell gave an exasperated sigh and reached for a ginger biscuit, turning it around and around in her fingers. "Did they tell you he was shot in the leg at the beginning of the battle, but carried on? Never faltered, they say. No one even knew he'd been injured until the conflict was long done and all his men accounted for. Then he falls off his horse, dead to the world from loss of blood. He was taken to a field hospital and, at first, he seemed all right, demanding he be allowed to go back to his post, but then the wound got infected and he was out of his head with fever."

"Oh." Jemima felt her breath catch, her heart aching and something close to terror making her skin prickle. Strange, when it had all happened long ago, and yet he had been in such danger, she had been so close to losing him before they'd even met. She forced her attention back to Mrs Norrell who was speaking again.

"They'd got word by then that Napoleon was on his way and that they were dreadfully outnumbered. The lot of them had to retreat to Corunna. The journey was so bad and weakened him so much, they didn't think he'd survive amputating his leg. Reckon they thought he'd die either way, so best to save him the pain." Mrs Norrell's expression darkened, but Jemima recognised the concern behind it, the worry she'd felt for him. "If he'd got it seen to right away, it likely wouldn't have been so bad, but he'd never shirk his responsibilities that one, never let anyone down. The men under his command were his responsibility, every last one of them, and he'd have died for them. He's always too quick to sacrifice himself, to do the right thing. He'd let no one else suffer for him, not while there was breath in his body."

Jemima shuddered and put her hand over her mouth as she tried to comprehend the horror of what he must have gone through.

"Well, anyway. Miss Hoity Toity Hyacinth Jackson had extracted a promise from him to look after her brother, though a sillier fellow you never did see. A good-hearted lad to be sure, but a silly fribble who never ought to have been in the army at all. Lord Rothborn tried his best to keep him from signing up, worried himself sick too, but when the fellow wouldn't be swayed, he vowed to Miss Jackson he would keep her brother safe. From all accounts, the young man was a good horseman but barely knew one end of a sword from t'other. How his lordship kept him alive as long as he did, I shall never know. Though I do know he kept the lad close to him at all times, protecting him. Once Lord Rothborn was laid up, though, his guardian angel was gone. Poor fool didn't last the week."

"Oh." Jemima sat back in her chair, trying to take it all in.

"He'd been badly injured before that, though, more than once. All while keeping young Jackson alive, too. Another time, he nearly got himself killed with a bayonet. Got in the way of some fellow trying to finish off a fallen soldier," Mrs Norrell said, her voice low and reverent. "Not an officer, mind, just an ordinary serving man. How many other titled gents do you think would have done such a thing? Well, he's a hero round these parts, not that you'd know it the way he hides himself away, like he's ashamed to face the world."

"Ashamed?"

The word hung between them, spoken with incredulity and mirrored in Mrs Norrell's eyes.

"It kills him that he was sent home. Fought it tooth and nail, he did. Think it sent him a bit mad for a while, and he lost himself in a dark place. He read the papers, drinking himself into a stupor when he found names of friends and men once under his command who'd died while he was back home, far away from the war. Then, as if his guilt wasn't heavy enough, that fiancée of his told him she'd not marry him because she couldn't bear to look at the face of the man that condemned her brother to die. She blamed him, in no uncertain terms. He was in love with her, and that awful woman looked at his lordship, still bearing the scars of his own pain, and she sentenced him to a lifetime of guilt. She broke his heart, she broke *him*... and that... that foolish man swore he'd never marry to atone for his sins."

Jemima felt her eyes burn as Mrs Norrell's voice wavered. *Oh, Solo.* She'd sensed the pain in him and had assumed the war had damaged more than his leg, but to know a woman was responsible for his pain... Her heart ached, but it was more than that. Anger burned inside her. Perhaps it was understandable that a woman would lash out in the heat of the moment if her beloved brother had died. It was not right, but grief made people do and say things they did not mean. Yet to never recall her words, to never tell him she'd not meant it, that she knew it had not been his fault... that was sheer wickedness.

Hyacinth Jackson. Jemima burned the name into her mind. She would not forget it. There was likely nothing she could do, for she was a woman with nothing of her own, her reputation balancing on a knife's edge, but she would not forget.

"Do you see, miss?" Mrs Norrell reached out a hand to cover Jemima's. "Do you see why we are so happy to have you here? You've made him smile, made him take a moment to drag his head out of the books he loses himself in and look about him. You're bringing him and The Priory back to life, and we're grateful to you. So, don't you go fretting about propriety. His lordship explained you was a lady, that things had been hard for you and we're not about to judge you harshly. We're too pleased to see the change in him, it's so obvious a fool could see it, and I'm no fool, Miss Fernside."

Jemima swallowed past the lump in her throat and squeezed Mrs Norrell's hand.

"Thank you," she said, meaning it. When she had agreed to this scandalous proposal, she had assumed she would lose all her friends, but not only did it appear that would not be the case, she was finding new ones. It was more than she could ever have hoped for. "He makes me happy too, but I asked you to call me Jemima. I wish you would."

Mrs Norrell huffed and blustered. "Well, it don't seem right, a fine lady like you, but… well, there's no harm when we are alone I suppose, if it would please you, Jemima."

"It does please me." Jemima smiled and Mrs Norrell gave a nod.

"Well, in that case, I'm Martha, and I'm very happy to know you."

That settled, Mrs Norrell slid the plate of biscuits across the table to her. "Now, tuck in. You're all skin and bone, and these biscuits won't eat themselves."

Chapter 10

My Lord Marquess

I felt I must write and thank you for everything you have done in exposing the appalling conditions in Mr Burton's mills. I fear that when you came to bring me the dreadful news that day, I did not sufficiently show my appreciation. My only defence is that I was so terribly shaken that I hardly knew what to make of it and had no words to give you.

Please, my lord, would you inform me of what exactly is happening to those mills and all those who relied upon the work they gave? I understand some kind soul has set up a charitable fund giving provision for those injured, and for the families of those killed in such dreadful circumstances. I would be grateful if you could give me any further information, as I should like to contribute to any fund at the very least. I feel somehow responsible, for what I'm not exactly certain. For not seeing Mr Burton for what he was perhaps, or for not knowing the conditions those people were forced to work in? I cannot answer, but the guilt lays heavy and I should be glad to make amends.

I feel I ought to inform you that I received a letter from Mr Burton. I confess his vile language was upsetting and most disagreeable. He blames me in no uncertain terms for what has happened to him. He believes — well, I shall not, cannot write down his words verbatim. Suffice to say he holds me responsible for your 'campaign to ruin him.' For my part, I am glad for it. I am glad for all those you have rescued from such hellish conditions and I thank you from the bottom of my heart.

—Excerpt of a letter from Miss Matilda Hunt to The Most Honourable, Lucian Barrington, Marquess of Montagu.

The evening of the 7th February 1815. Hillcrest House, Otford, Kent.

Matilda beamed and held out her hands to Helena, who hurried to meet her.

"How lovely to see you," Helena exclaimed, looking beautiful in a gold silk gown with long white gloves. A gold and diamond necklace circled her elegant neck, with matching bracelet, earrings, and hair clips that sparkled among her thick tresses.

"Good heavens, Helena, you look stunning," Matilda said, realising that Minerva had been right to worry.

Helena was always beautiful, but she'd gone to some lengths this evening and, if Mr Knight had a pulse, he'd have no choice but to notice her. If he was the rake that Alice believed him to be, there could be trouble in store.

Helena appeared pleased by this before looking Matilda up and down. "Well, I might say the same thing, darling. That blue is simply ravishing on you. A man could drown in the colour of your eyes."

Matilda snorted and took Helena's arm. "So long as I don't tempt Mr Knight to come for a swim, I suppose," she said, casting a sideways glance at her friend.

Helena flushed just a touch, narrowing her eyes and then sighed. "The little birds have been chattering merrily, I take it."

"Of course," Matilda said, giving Helena's arm a gentle squeeze. "We worry for you. The man has a wicked reputation."

Helena rolled her eyes. "There's nothing to worry about."

Matilda must have looked sceptical, for Helena laughed. "No, I mean there really isn't. The provoking fellow won't even look in my direction."

Somehow, that didn't soothe Matilda's anxiety. No one could ignore Helena, which meant Mr Knight must be concerting a remarkable effort of will to do so. Why?

"Come," Helena said. "Let me introduce you to our guests."

Helena moved easily among the guests, and Matilda followed. She knew some of the people here, including Helena's uncle, Baron Fitzwalter, who was charming and greeted her warmly.

"How lovely to see you again, Miss Hunt, and looking as lovely as ever. Theo, do let me introduce you," he said, turning towards the man standing beside him.

He was of an age with the Baron, perhaps five and sixty with a merry twinkle in his eyes—eyes that seemed strangely familiar—and a kindly face. He turned to Matilda with obvious enthusiasm.

"Oh, I wish you would," he said, beaming at Fitzwalter.

"Mr Theodore Brown, this lovely creature is Miss Matilda Hunt."

Mr Brown bowed deeply, a courtly gesture that made Matilda smile.

"We will leave you two to talk," the baron said, giving Mr Brown a significant look which Matilda did not understand, and drawing Helena away with him.

"I'm afraid that was a lie," Mr Brown said, his gaze on Matilda steady. "My name is Barrington, not Brown.

Matilda's heart raced as she realised who he must be. She stared into eyes which were a darker grey than the ones she dreamed about—and his hair was pure white, rather than white blond—but Mr Barrington could be nothing but a relation of Lucian Barrington, Marquess of Montagu. So why the subterfuge?

She'd believed all the male Barringtons dead, that only Montagu and his niece survived, so who was this man, why had he given a false name and then revealed it, and how would he treat her, considering how high in the instep the family had always been?

"Ah," he said, a touch ruefully. "I see from the look in your eyes, you have made the connection."

"I do not know if I have, or why you were introduced to me as Mr Brown, but... but you *are* related to Montagu?"

"His uncle, for my sins," the man said, and an air of sadness swept over him like a wave, almost palpable.

Matilda frowned, wanting to ask a dozen questions at once, but knowing she could not voice a single one of them, for it would be vulgar to press for information. Oh, but how she burned to know more. His name, though... surely he could not expect her not to ask?

"Forgive me, Mr Barrington, but why would you hide the connection? Does everyone here believe you to be Mr Brown?"

"Come and take a turn about the room with me," Mr Barrington said, holding out his arm to her. "I believe we have much to talk about."

Though she couldn't imagine what this man wanted to speak with her about, or what kind of game he was playing, Matilda took his arm, too curious to refuse.

"I know my nephew has treated you very ill, Miss Hunt," he said, once they were out of earshot of anyone who might overhear.

She stared at him in shock, astonished that he should refer to the incident in which Montagu had ruined her in the first place, and speechless that he should openly criticise his nephew, the marquess.

He gave a rather bitter laugh. "Oh, I know, how disloyal of me to censure the head of our ancient line." The genial face darkened suddenly. "You know, it is not surprising you were unaware of my existence, Miss Hunt. Polite society believes me dead. Indeed, I know Lucian would infinitely prefer it if I were. He did try his best."

Overwhelmed by this revelation, Matilda didn't know how to respond, so she said nothing, waiting for what came next, for surely there was more. She was not disappointed.

Mr Barrington turned to her, holding her gaze, his expression serious and full of regret. "I am sorry for the wrong my nephew did you, Miss Hunt. Sorry, but not surprised. The truth is, he is spoiled beyond measure, spoiled and cold-hearted and cruel, and it is all my fault. Much as I would like to deny that, to say he was born wicked and I had no hand in his corruption, I cannot pretend that is true. He saw so much tragedy in his young life that I indulged him far more than was prudent. His younger brother too, to some extent, but I confess Lucian was always my favourite." He gave a wistful smile and shook his head. "My word, you should have seen him as a boy, the face of an angel. It was impossible to believe him capable of the slightest wrongdoing, or to refuse him anything, and so I didn't, and now you suffer the results of my foolishness."

Still Matilda said nothing. She had no idea *what* to say. Despite his words, his expression was open and kindly, and she could not mistake the hurt and regret in his eyes, or the sincerity. If she had heard such things about Montagu just a few short weeks ago, she would have not struggled to believe them, she *had* believed them.

Now, though….

"I have shocked you," he said, and Matilda did not contradict him. He sighed. "From what I have heard of you, I know you to be a generous and kind young woman, and I know what you must think, how faithless you must believe me. But the truth is, I am afraid of my nephew, of what he is capable of." He paused and glanced about them, as if checking no one was paying them any mind. His voice lowered to a whisper and it was impossible not to hear the urgency and fear behind his words. "I beg you, do not mention to him that you have seen me here. I am only in the country for a short while, before I return to my exile in India. That is where he sent me—forcibly, I might add. I tremble to think what he would do if he discovered I had returned."

"Why would you believe I should have any contact with him?" Matilda said, disturbed by this whole conversation as her opinion of Montagu was tested once more.

His face softened. His eyes were filled with compassion and understanding, and it was impossible not to feel sympathy for him. Matilda started as his hand covered hers, such an intimate gesture from a near stranger that she stiffened in surprise.

"My nephew was a beautiful boy, and he has become a very handsome man. Handsome, powerful, and wealthy. A heady combination for any young woman, is it not, Miss Hunt? He is the kind of man who can do something quite unforgivable and then beguile you into forgiving him. Believe me, I know, but it is just a game to him, a sick and twisted game. You mean nothing to him, no more than I did in the end, for if he can do his best to put an end to a beloved uncle, what chance does a young woman with an uncertain reputation stand?"

Matilda withdrew her hand from his, unsettled and shaken by this whole encounter.

"I'm sorry, Miss Hunt," he said, distress making his grey eyes glitter a little too brightly. "I had no wish to upset you and I can see that I have, but I could not allow Lucian to destroy another life. Though he has already tried, I think. You are nothing but his latest plaything. You are not the first, and you will not be the last. Why do you suppose he went to such lengths to crush your Mr Burton, your only chance at a respectable life?"

Matilda felt the words as a physical blow, and it took every vestige of will to keep her face impassive as a wave of ice water seemed to cascade over her.

Mr Barrington nodded with satisfaction all the same, having seen his words hit home despite her efforts. "I can do nothing for poor little Phoebe. That poor child, kept like a prisoner in that vast mausoleum of a house, though she is too young to understand or chafe against her restrictions yet. She will, though, and it breaks my heart to be so helpless, but I *can* help you, warn you, and I swore I would do so, no matter the cost to my own safety."

Matilda took a deep breath, striving for calm.

"You may consider me warned, Mr Barrington," she said, her voice cool if a little unsteady. "And I shall say nothing of having met you."

Barrington smiled, a sad smile that only highlighted the weariness in his grey eyes.

"Then I have done all that I can."

He bowed to her and left her alone.

***

Gabe downed his drink and cursed inwardly. Hell and the devil, but he hated these bloody affairs. He had so much to do, and making polite small talk made him irritable at the best of times, but Montagu had advised him that if he wanted Bedwin on side, his best chance was to get his uncle, the baron, interested. Although Bedwin had asked for more information about the project, Gabe had heard no more about it and knew he must explain the matter to the man himself. On paper it just seemed too much of a risk, a dangerous and ill-advised venture, perhaps. If only Gabe could have a few moments to explain that this was the future. He could feel it in his bones, feel the gathering excitement in his gut, and his instincts rarely led him wrong.

The duke held a high opinion of Lord Fitzwalter's business acumen and sought his advice as a matter of course. If Gabe could win him over, he had a good chance of meeting with Bedwin in person and bringing him on board. Gabe did not doubt the veracity of the advice. His dealings with the marquess were a delicate balance, a little like standing on a knife's edge, but he had never had cause to doubt anything he'd been told. He'd even come to trust the man, up to a point. That Montagu stubbornly refused to even contemplate dirtying his hands with his railway venture rankled more than Gabe wanted to admit, but the snooty bastard wouldn't even hear out his proposal. Bloody aristocrats made him furious. It would be easy to assume they were all stupid and vacuous, and Gabe had certainly had a bellyful of those that met the description perfectly. Montagu was not one of them. He was cold and ruthless, with a mind like a rapier, and God help you if you got on the wrong side of him. Gabe would not want to be on the wrong side of him, but their unlikely alliance had worked well enough these past few years. Not that anyone else knew about it, but Gabe could do things and go places the marquess could not, and vice versa. It was a mutually beneficial arrangement, but one that they both approached with extreme caution, aware of the danger. Like two lone wolves forming a pack to hunt down their prey, but ready to tear out each other's throat the moment one of them put a foot wrong.

Yet this business with the mills had surprised Gabe, and confirmed something he had suspected for a long time, for the man had stepped in and got his hands dirty when he'd seen the conditions. Of course, there was another, less charitable, explanation. He might have done it to get his hands on Miss Hunt. Any fool could see the marquess had his sights set on having her, and a man like that might go to considerable lengths to get what he wanted. Ruining Mr Burton was one way to leave the field clear for him. Either way, it was none of Gabe's affair, though he'd always despised Burton and was only too glad to see the man fall. He didn't give a damn what the marquess' motivation was, only that knowing it gave him insight into a man who held everyone at a distance. Knowing how his mind worked would help Gabe do business with him in the future.

So, here he was, doing the pretty to get Bedwin's uncle on the hook, but the old fellow was too busy playing nursemaid to some old friend of his. The only time Gabe had managed to speak a word to him was when he left his Mr Brown in the company of Matilda Hunt. Seeing Mr Brown with Matilda jarred in his mind, but he couldn't for the life of him grasp why, which did not help his temper. His instincts had driven his success, and rarely guided him wrong, and every sense told him that there was significance in those two speaking together. He was damned if he could figure out what it was, but something about Mr Brown nagged at him, and he didn't like it a bit.

"All alone, Mr Knight? How tragic."

Gabe sighed. Just to top off his evening, here was Lady Helena, temptation incarnate, come to plague him.

He turned an unfriendly gaze upon the young woman, the kind that made most grown men tremble, but she was made of sterner stuff and didn't so much as flutter an eyelash. That's what being the daughter of a duke gave you, he supposed: an unshakeable belief in your right to do or say exactly as you wished.

"Not in the least," he replied, not bothering to bow or even pretend civility. "I enjoy my own company more than most people's."

He gave her a significant look which she either did not understand or chose to ignore. In other circumstances, he would have vastly enjoyed seducing her just for the fun of it. It never occurred to him to doubt that he could, but he had other fish to fry and she would only hinder his plans. A pity, as a duke's daughter would have been the ideal candidate for the wife he'd been considering, but there you had it. There would be other opportunities to get himself leg shackled, but for the moment this railway line was of more importance. He knew when to get in fast, before anyone else had grasped how important an idea or invention would become, and this was it. This was his biggest venture yet, and he was damned if he'd get distracted by a pretty face.

"How fortunate for you," she said, studying him.

Her gaze was unsettling. There was something about this woman, the epitome of the perfect aristocrat, that made his skin prickle. It was as if she peeled away the carefully wrought layers of the façade he'd constructed with one dainty fingernail. Not that anyone was fooled, or even that he wanted to fool anyone. He'd been born in the gutter and he'd made himself one of the richest men in the country. He didn't care who knew it, he was proud of it. His factories had likely provided many of the buttons and buckles these people wore tonight. The bricks he made were rebuilding the face of the city. His efforts had already cleared vast areas of slum buildings, which were being redeveloped with shops and houses and yet another hotel to add to those lavish properties he already owned. No one could ignore him, whether they liked it or not—and that they did not was abundantly clear. Yet although he'd taught himself which fork to use, learned to dress properly, where to buy his shirts, and even had lessons to rid himself of his accent, he was not ashamed of what he was and where he'd come from. Not even a little. He'd done those things to pass among these people without making *them* uncomfortable, and he'd succeeded, up to a point. When this woman stared at him with those astonishing green eyes, though, she reminded him he didn't belong. She was so beautiful, so pristine and unspoiled... spoiling her would be a great deal of fun.

It was sorely tempting, he'd admit that. No doubt she was just like the rest of her kind, an overindulged, spiteful creature he'd enjoy teaching a thing or two, and then leaving, preferably once her family realised what she'd done and scurried to hush it all up. Forcing the duke to allow them to wed once he'd ruined her also appealed, yet that was no better option for now. He needed Bedwin, if Montagu would insist on being a stubborn bastard, and he didn't think seducing the man's sister would help his cause. Perhaps when everything was signed and sealed, and the man could not back out, though....

"Your glass is empty," she observed and, without the least effort, caught the attention of a servant.

A fresh glass of champagne was put in his hand a moment later. Ah, how lovely it must be, to grow up with everything handed to you with the slightest crook of one finger. Gabe glowered at the glass with distaste. He wanted a proper drink, not this sparkly nonsense. Still, he downed it in a couple of large swallows and had to try hard to resist the urge to belch. She made him want to act badly, to shock her and shake that cool, perfect exterior.

"My, you are thirsty."

Once more she gestured, and another full glass was exchanged for the empty one. Gabe sighed. Well, if she would insist on pestering him, he may as well get some use out of her.

"I want to speak to your uncle," he said, with no preamble. Either she'd arrange it, or she wouldn't.

Her eyes narrowed, considering, and he suspected she was a deal shrewder than most people gave her credit for.

"Why?"

Well, at least she was direct. He appreciated that.

"I have a business proposition I wish to interest him in."

Those emerald eyes scrutinised him and he stared back at her, unblinking. For once he kept any hint of flirtation from his gaze, just studied her as frankly as she did him. To her credit, she did not look away, nor falter in her perusal.

"It's not my uncle you want to speak with, it's my brother, but you think if Uncle Charles has an interest, he'll get Bedwin to take you seriously."

Gabe shrugged, a little surprised, both by her figuring out his motivation, and admitting to it. "I need someone with influence, a title, to open doors I cannot."

Lady Helena considered this for a moment. "Perhaps I could arrange for you to meet with him. Tomorrow, though. It is vulgar to discuss business at an affair like this."

He resisted the urge to say something that really *was* vulgar, just to see the look on her face and simply nodded. "I would appreciate that."

"Would you?" she asked, tilting her head to one side. "How much would you appreciate it? What's in it for me?"

Gabe narrowed his eyes. She'd surprised him. For all he'd been aware of her interest in him, he'd not believed her a tart.

She moved a little closer, looking up at him from under a sweep of thick, sable lashes.

"Why do you insist on ignoring me, Mr Knight? It's almost as though you are afraid of me, but I cannot fathom why. I find it frustrating, though, when you are the most interesting man here. I would like to know you better."

Her words were low, and certainly seductive.

Despite his assessment of Helena's interest in him, Gabe admitted himself shocked. She was so very young, and looked as fresh and innocent as a daisy, despite the uncompromising, bold quality of her gaze. Yet surely that had been an invitation? Women had suggested *getting to know him better* before now, and their meaning was never ambivalent. A wave of revulsion washed over him at what she was suggesting. He'd sold himself plenty of times in his youth, but had believed those days behind him. Never again would he need to bed a woman he didn't want to put food in his belly or pay his rent, yet here was the bloody duke's daughter demanding he debase himself for her.

Gabe gritted his teeth as he considered it. He could do it, if he must. It was possible to be discreet. He could use her as she used him and, when he'd gotten what he wanted, he could watch her fall. These people, they lived in their gilded cages, letting no one who didn't meet their requirements past the pretty bars. Well, he would find a way in, like a fox in a hencoop, and then they'd all have their feathers ruffled as he took control.

"Do you have a place we can meet, then?" he demanded, seeing little point in beating around the bush. If she wanted him to bed her, she could damn well acknowledge it. He kept his voice low all the same, not wanting to draw attention to them. "Private rooms? Or should I arrange it?"

For a moment there was nothing but confusion in her eyes, and then they widened so far that he felt a twinge of unease. His unease grew to discomfort as a searing blush scalded her cheeks and her mouth fell open. Her elegant hand rose to circle her neck as though she feared a physical attack, and Gabe took an instinctive step back, assuming she would slap his face and throw him out for his insult. Damn. He had misjudged her. How had he misread this situation so badly? Only, the way she looked at him, the hunger in her gaze... surely he'd not imagined it?

To his surprise, she let out a startled laugh, never taking her eyes from his.

"Good heavens, you... you thought I was suggesting... you *service* me? L-Like a st-stallion?" She gave a most unladylike bark of laughter and slapped her hand over her mouth. "Excuse me...." she said, as all eyes turned in their direction.

She fled, leaving Gabe standing alone and utterly perplexed. Not quite understanding why he did it, he followed her. He found her in the next room, alone before a window which she'd opened a crack to let in some cold night air. Her shoulders were shaking and an unfamiliar sensation of guilt hit him as he realised the shock had worn off and she was crying.

Bloody fool. Why the devil should he feel guilty? If she went around looking at men like she looked at him, she would get a deal more than she'd bargained for. The sooner she learned that lesson, the better off she'd be. He'd done her a favour and he was damned if he'd regret it. Gabe turned, deciding he'd be best served leaving her alone and pursuing his own path to get to speak with Fitzwalter. Henry Stanhope was here, and he'd use the fellow to gain the introduction he needed, as he'd first intended. Then he heard her laughter.

His head swivelled of its own accord as the surprisingly deep, throaty sound rose around him. She hadn't been crying, she was laughing herself stupid.

Gabe folded his arms and scowled as she turned and saw him—and went off in another peal of laughter.

"Oh," she said, clutching her arms about her waist. "Oh... I... I do b-beg your pardon. Only, no one has ever... *ever*...."

Off she went again, and Gabe rolled his eyes. It took some time for her to calm herself enough to speak, and even then, her eyes still glittered with mirth.

"I'll not apologise for the insult, if you are expecting such a thing," he said, deciding she'd better understand the kind of man he was right now. "If you look at a man in the way you look at me, speak such flirtatious words, you can expect him to form a conclusion of what you want."

"*Really?*" Helena said, looking fascinated. "Oh, dear. Well, it seems my brother was right. I am a danger to myself, though it is partly his fault for protecting me so hard. I confess I have been very little in society, as I was in mourning—oh, forever it seemed—and I never did do very well at being ladylike. We lived quietly, and no one could ever stop me putting my foot in my mouth. You see, I only came out a few months ago, and no one else has ever caught my attention."

Gabe hid his surprise at her honesty, too interested to hear what she'd say next.

"Men are usually falling over themselves to speak to me, so I've never had to exert myself before. I suppose I over-egged the pudding." She gave such an impish smile and spoke so candidly that Gabe found himself unwillingly charmed. "Though I rather think the gentlemen I know would not offer their services quite so… so *frankly*," she added, giving him a gently reproving look.

"I'm no gentleman."

She smiled at that. "I know. That's why you're so interesting. You say exactly what you think, and you don't flatter."

The chuckle that came from her seemed at odds with the elegant exterior. It had a naughty, irreverent edge to it that suggested she was not as buttoned up and haughty as she appeared on the surface. He was irritated to discover how much it intrigued him.

"I don't think you have the slightest idea how to flatter and cajole, do you, Mr Knight? A quality I find quite irresistible. You cannot imagine how wearying it is to always be told your opinions are right, to have your every joke laughed at, and odes to your beauty delivered daily. If I hear my eyes compared to emeralds once more, I shall scream. You, on the other hand, have the subtlety of a hammer, and I suspect pound your point across until your opponent is squashed flat."

Despite himself, Gabe felt his lips twitch upwards at this apt description. He wanted to tell her that that he knew her eyes were not at all like emeralds, not now he'd seen them up close. They were not as cold and hard as that. They were mysterious, with the shifting shades of a forest's canopy, where the sun filtered through the green and turned it every conceivable shade as the leaves stirred in a breeze. He bit the compliment back, irked that such a nauseating thought had even occurred to him.

"What did you want, then?" he asked instead, curious now.

Helena shrugged, and when she looked at him her expression was guileless and rather shy, her youth and innocence all too obvious. "What I said. To know you better—not in the biblical sense," she added in a rush. "Just to talk to you and hear about your life, how you made such a success of yourself. I find your achievements fascinating. How proud you must be to have accomplished so much in your life. I know I should be."

There was a wistful note to her words that struck him, but he shook it off. Lady Helena Adolphus was beautiful and interesting and bedding her would not be any hardship, but it would ruin his chances with her brother, so he'd best keep such temptations at a distance.

"Well, my stories are my own, and I don't share them with strangers for their entertainment. Find another man to practise your wiles on, my lady. This one has no interest in being your pet."

He ensured the words were hard, sneering at her to make certain she understood his contempt. Gabe did not bother seeing how she received them. He simply turned and strode away.

Chapter 11

My Lord Marquess

I regret to inform you that the 'item' you wished us to locate was found by my men yesterday evening but slipped through their hands. You may rely upon the fact they have been severely reprimanded. I give you my word I will do everything in my power to ensure said item is on a boat to New South Wales as soon as is possible. It is, as you requested, a priority. Although I know you will not thank me for observing it, I have discovered you were behind the exposure of the conditions in those mills and I congratulate you on all you have done. In the circumstances I am only too happy to oblige you in seeing the vile thing gone from these shores.

At the risk of incurring your wrath, may I ask if you have thought any more about the railway project I mentioned? Vulgar it may be, but I promise you it will be the most profitable venture you ever take part in if you change your mind.

—Excerpt of a letter from Mr Gabriel Knight to The Most Honourable Lucian Barrington, Marquess of Montagu.

7th February 1815. Mitcham Priory, Sussex.

Solo did his very best not to stare across the dinner table at Jemima, but it was nigh on impossible. She was growing lovelier by the day and his desire to spend every moment in her presence something he was struggling to contain. He had discovered that she had visited that morning, to see Mrs Norrell, and experienced a sharp and childish wave of jealousy. How ridiculous that a man of his years should behave like a spoilt boy. Nonetheless, he wanted to stamp his foot and yell that she was *his* friend, and demand all her attention for himself. Except she was only his because he paid her to be. It was like owning a wild, unbroken horse. He could claim ownership, feed and care for it, but he could not compel it to love him. His mood darkened as he wondered how she would view him if she had not been forced into the position in which he'd found her. Likely she'd have not given him a backwards glance. Why would she, when there were plenty of other men, lively, jovial, whole men who would want her as their wife, not to ruin her and use her for their own amusement? His appetite fled and he pushed away his dessert, barely touched.

"My, how serious you look. Is the apple tart not to your liking? I warn you I may be forced to eat yours too. I cannot risk having Mrs Norrell offended, or she might revoke her recipe for lemon pond pudding."

Jemima's soft voice was amused and coaxing, but with an underlying note of concern, and Solo only hated himself all the more. How it must disgust her to pander to his moods, to always try to please him because it was her job. Her *job*! He ought to remember that.

"It is not for me to tiptoe around Mrs Norrell's pride," he snapped, struggling to get to his feet and almost overturning the chair as his temper rose.

Damn him for being so blasted clumsy and ungainly. He was a bloody buffoon, always clomping about. He stalked awkwardly to the fire and stood staring down at it. It had rained all day and the cold and damp seemed to sink into his bones, making his leg throb like the devil. He wanted to sit down, but he was too aggravated.

"I don't suppose it is," Jemima said, her voice cool. "But she puts a great deal of effort into pleasing you. I do not believe it is too much to ask you to spare a thought for her hard work. She thinks the world of you."

Solo frowned, a little taken aback at being scolded, albeit it gently.

"Mrs Norrell knows well I appreciate her efforts." He was uncomfortably aware that he sounded increasingly like a sulky boy, but the knowledge only made him ever more belligerent.

"Does she?" Jemima enquired politely. "How?"

"What?" he barked, irritated that she hadn't given up on the conversation now she realised he was in a bad mood.

She ought to change the subject for something soothing, surely she knew that much.

"How does she know?"

Solo considered this, frowning with annoyance as he turned around to regard Jemima. She was not looking at him, but eating her dessert, so still and placid and poised he felt the overwhelming desire to ruffle her.

"She knows! She knows because I have never given her cause to believe otherwise."

Jemima nodded. "So, she knows you are pleased because you have never complained. You have, in fact, said nothing at all."

"Quite." Solo thumped his cane on the floor to punctuate his answer, glaring back down at the flames.

"Well, my lord. This may surprise you, but not complaining does not equate to a show of appreciation. We all need a kind word now and then, a compliment. Everyone likes to know their efforts have been noticed and that they are valued. You ought to tell Mrs Norrell how much you appreciate her."

"Perhaps you should tell her for me," Solo muttered. "As the two of you have become so close. Thick as thieves, it seems."

Solo regretted the words at once, for they showed him up for the resentful child he was acting like, though he was damned if he knew how to stop. He'd noted too that she had addressed him formally, illustrating her annoyance. Though he wished he'd kept his mouth shut, he could not find a way of backing down from the foolish argument now. Jemima's eyes were fixed on him, and he struggled to meet it, but found he couldn't ignore the weight of her gaze.

There was curiosity there, a thoughtful appraisal that made the back of his neck hot.

"Would you have liked me to visit you, my lord?" she asked, her tone softening. "I would have, if I'd thought you wished it. Only I did not like to intrude, and you had invited me only to dine this evening. I promise you I meant no slight by it. Indeed, I should have liked to have seen you."

Solo frowned, his jaw rigid even as his heart felt buoyant and soared in his chest at her words, but surely, she was just being polite still, trying to please him. *She desired him*, a desperate little voice whispered. She did, he knew she did, yet desire did not equate to love or even liking. *Love?* Where the devil had that thought come from? He did not need or want love.

The words were so obvious a lie that he felt a pain of longing stab deep in his chest. Well... he did not deserve it, at any rate.

He watched, wary now, as Jemima got to her feet and moved towards him. He didn't move an inch, curious what she would do next. Her job was to tame the beast, to flatter and coax him to a better humour. It was what any good mistress would do.

"You're being very silly," she observed, tilting her head and regarding him with interest.

Despite himself, Solo's temper rose another notch. Well, that was not what a mistress should say to him, more like a nagging wife, and he'd not asked for one of those.

"Silly?" he repeated, outraged. He was never silly. Bad tempered and irascible maybe, but never *silly*. It made him sound like a little girl with ringlets.

Jemima folded her arms and nodded. "You are jealous because I spent the morning here but did not seek you out."

"Don't be foolish. You are free to spend our time apart as you see fit, it is no concern of mine." He sounded so stiff and pompous he almost cringed.

"Yes," she said. "I am. It is in the terms of our agreement, is it not? Yet I would have enjoyed spending time with you, if you had indicated the idea pleased you. You see, this is what I mean. You must tell people how you feel, or they mistake you. Like Mrs Norrell thinking you do not appreciate her. Or me, believing I would be an unwelcome bother if I called on you unexpectedly."

Suddenly, he couldn't remember what the devil they were arguing about. She was so close, but still too far away to reach for, and he wanted to reach for her very badly. He didn't want her to be cross with him.

"You could never be a bother, and you will never be unwelcome. I long to see you, Jemima, all day... every day."

He hadn't meant to say it, not that last bit at least, but the words had tumbled out of him, too honest, too desperate, and he could not take them back. His heart was pounding so hard he felt giddy, the sensation only intensifying at the pleasure he saw in her eyes at his words.

"I long to see you too," she whispered, such a rush of colour to her cheeks that he could not help but believe she meant it.

Likely he was being a fool but... but damn it, he didn't care. He wanted to believe she meant it so badly.

"Jemima."

It was only her name, spoken with all the reverence he felt, but somehow it meant far more. Did she hear everything he could not say aloud? For her name spoken thus said, *come to me, stay with me, let me be your love*, and she did. With a soft rustle of skirts, she closed the gap and threw herself into his arms, almost knocking him off balance. Not that he cared. He cast his cane to one side and pulled her to him, as close as possible, holding her tight as he took the kiss he'd been aching for.

"Jemima, Jemima," he murmured, kissing her mouth, her cheeks, her jawline, the beautiful length of her neck. "Oh, how I want you."

Her arms around his neck, the way she pressed herself closer to him, the urgency with which she returned his kisses all made him hope that this time, she would not shy away from him.

"Stay," he said, aware it sounded like begging and not giving a damn. "Stay with me, *please*."

She nodded and he wanted to shout with triumph, to laugh and spin her around, and promise he'd never let her regret it, regret him, even though such a thing was beyond his power. It was the hardest thing to pull away from her, to break the kiss and take his arms from around her slender waist, but he wanted more, so much more. He might be the villain of this piece but the least he could do was treat her right, and debauching her on the dining table did not seem to equate with that idea.

So, although he was nigh on trembling with desire and anticipation, he saw her up to her room and left her there to give her time to ready herself, knowing the next half-hour would be the longest of his entire life.

***

Once Jemima had dismissed Bessie, she sat at the dressing table and brushed out her long hair until it shone like silk. She noticed her hand was not entirely steady but realised it was not fear that disturbed her equilibrium. Though nerves fluttered under her skin as if her every limb was full of tiny butterflies, she was not afraid. Not this time. This time, she wanted him, wanted what was to come, and if there was regret for her situation, it was not enough for her to find no pleasure in what was to come. It was pointless to regret what was already lost. Perhaps it made her wicked not to wish to dwell on her loss of innocence. The situation she had found herself in was not of her own making and she did not see why she must punish herself for it. There would be plenty of others to do that job for her, to make her ashamed, if ever the truth was discovered. So she would enjoy the pleasures offered her, even if it was a pretty path to the devil, though she could never see Solo in such a light. The more she knew him, the more her heart yearned to know, to smooth away the rough edges that made him brittle and irrational. She wanted to please this man, wanted to touch him and hold him and make him smile, to take away whatever those dark thoughts were that would steal into his mind and shatter his peace.

She had seen it happen tonight, before her eyes. He'd seemed perfectly content, at peace, and they'd enjoyed a splendid dinner and animated conversation, and then he had fallen quiet. Little by little, she'd noticed the tension in him, seeing it roll over him like an incoming tide as his mood darkened. At first, she could not fathom what had started it, but she'd been rather astonished to discover he was jealous of Mrs Norrell, of all people. She felt certain he was aware he was being foolish, and she was not about to pretend otherwise. Perhaps, if she really wanted to please him, she ought to flatter his ego and coax him out of his sulks, but she thought he was too intelligent a man to want to be treated in such a way. There had been a shaky moment when she'd doubted she'd done the right thing—he really did not enjoy being told he was silly—but, in the end, he'd come around.

I long to see you, Jemima, all day, every day.

She smiled, holding the words close to her heart. Perhaps it was only lust he spoke of. Indeed, she should expect nothing more from him, but her heart was foolish and wilfully hopeful no matter how often she warned it of the danger it was in. Now she saw the connecting door open behind her in the looking glass and he came in, wearing a dark green silk banyan. The fine fabric moulded to his body, lovingly clinging to powerful shoulders and a broad chest. Jemima's breath caught. His legs and feet were bare, and something hot and urgent tightened low in her belly as she realised he was naked beneath the gown.

Oh goodness. Oh, good heavens above.

He paused, staring at her, and her smile widened, even as her colour rose. He returned her expression, such sweetness to his smile that her chest ached. She watched as he moved to the bed and sat on the edge, setting his cane against the bedside table before getting on and making himself comfortable. He looked quite at ease as he adjusted the pillows and folded his arms behind his head.

Uncertain of what to do next, Jemima hesitated, brushing her already smooth hair a little more to give herself time to consider.

"I love watching you do that. You put me in mind of Rapunzel."

Jemima laughed. "Only if I was a prisoner on the ground floor, I'm not sure it's long enough to reach any further."

"It's beautiful, like spun gold."

Jemima set the brush down. "Thank you," she said, staring at his reflection in the mirror.

"Will you come to me?" He held out his hand to her and Jemima got to her feet, discovering her knees felt wobbly as she moved towards the bed. When she reached him she placed her hand in his and he lifted it to his mouth, kissing each knuckle in turn. "Nothing you don't like, Jemima, nothing you don't want. You have my word."

She nodded, the movement a little stiff, the smile at her lips hesitant, but reassured all the same. It was a relief to discover she believed him still, she trusted him. He would be kind and careful and there was nothing to fear.

"Would you take this off for me… please?" He gave a gentle tug on the scandalously indecent night rail and, if not for the breathless, desperate edge to his voice, she might have balked at his demand, but she heard his desire, saw the warmth in his eyes, and could not refuse him.

With trembling hands, she undid the tie at the neckline and allowed the garment to fall to the floor with barely a whisper of sound as it pooled at her feet. Far louder was Solo's sharp intake of breath, and the way his eyes grew dark and hot made her skin heat too, as though she could feel the quality of his gaze upon her naked flesh.

"I'm dreaming," he said with a shaky laugh. "You cannot be real."

"Real enough, my lord," she said, wondering at her own boldness as she moved closer to the bed. Jemima held her breath as he reached out and touched her with the back of one finger, sliding over the gentle curve of her belly as shivers rippled over her.

"So you are," he said, sounding as though he truly was astonished by that fact. "Warm and soft and lovely, and so very real." He looked up at her then. "My name is Solomon, have you forgotten? I don't like hearing you say 'my lord.' I do not desire such formality, and it makes me believe you are angry with me."

"I could never be angry with you."

His lips quirked, a remarkably boyish expression which made her smile.

"That's a Banbury story if ever I heard one. You were cross barely five minutes ago."

Jemima laughed, feeling astonished that she could feel so at ease standing in nothing but her skin before this man. "I was not angry, just…somewhat irritated."

"I like it when you scold me," he said, drawing her closer to the bed. "It makes me believe that you care, at least a little."

"I do care," she said, wondering too late if she ought to have revealed such a thing, but what was the point in hiding it?

The way pleasure lit his eyes at her words made any regrets dissolve into thin air, and when he patted the place at his side she moved around the bed, obedient and willing. Her chest felt tight, her breath coming fast as she lay down beside him, arms and legs straight, rigid with tension as her nerves flooded back.

"Jemima," he said.

He had turned on his side, his head cradled on his hand, and his expression was gentle and just a little amused.

"Turn towards me."

Awkwardly she did, mirroring his position.

"You are very beautiful. I am honoured that you are here with me."

She smiled and allowed her gaze to travel over him. The silk robe had fallen open to reveal the strong line of his throat, and a tantalising glimpse of his chest. The coarse hair that curled there was dark, and her fingers twitched with the urge to reach out and see how it felt to touch.

"Were you ever in love?"

The question startled her, and she looked back at him in surprise.

"I know you had your come out at least, and were in society for a while. You must have had hordes of beaus desperately in love with you."

Jemima felt her eyes widen and a burst of laughter escaped before she could stifle it.

"No!" she exclaimed. "I certainly did not. Who on earth would want the penniless girl whose dress has clearly been made over, no matter how cleverly my aunt contrived it? I had no connections to speak of, either. My family only ever clung to the fringes of the *ton*. In truth, I never expected to meet anyone, though I hoped, but I did it to please my aunt. It made her so happy to see me attend such affairs, and I believe she enjoyed them more than I did."

"Those men were fools not to notice you."

She was so touched by the real scorn in his voice that it took her a moment to reply.

"I think you judge them too harshly. I doubt very much you would have given me a second glance, either, had you been there. There would have been too many beautiful ladies vying for the attention of such a handsome war hero. You'd never have noticed a faded wallflower."

"No," he said, the word fierce as he reached out and cupped her cheek. "I cannot believe that. I *will* not believe it. You stole my breath the first time I saw you, and I don't believe it has ever been fully returned to me."

Jemima's heart felt as though it would burst at his words, and no matter that he did not speak of love, of his feelings for her, she knew her own were throwing themselves headlong into danger. She was falling hard and fast and there was nothing she could do to stop it, despite knowing how foolish she was, despite knowing her heart would likely be broken when he tired of her. She turned her face into his palm and closed her eyes, luxuriating in the warmth of his hand, the gentle caress of his thumb over her lips.

Her breath caught as his hand moved, fingers tracing a path down her neck as shivers followed in their wake. She sighed as his hand found her breast, caressing and teasing her nipple.

"Look at me."

Her eyes fluttered open and she blushed as she found his heated gaze upon her.

"Don't hide from me."

It was difficult to give him what he wanted as his lazy hand slid down her body, but she watched him watch her, and found herself glad of the effort she'd made as she saw the change in him. His eyes darkened, almost black in the shadowy candlelight, his lips parting as his breathing quickened. As her gaze travelled over him, she saw the fine silk could not hide his awakening body, the thick, hard length a blatant show of masculine arousal that made liquid heat pool between her thighs.

"I won't hide if you don't."

How she dared say it she couldn't fathom, but the longing to see him was too fierce to deny.

He hesitated, and it occurred to her that he was nervous. For a moment she couldn't understand why, and then she realised that his injury must have left scars and that he might be sensitive to their appearance. Whatever his qualms, when he moved he was quick and decisive, tugging at the robe's fastening and shrugging it from his shoulders. He still lay atop the heavy silk, but it no longer covered him and Jemima drank him in. There were a lot of scars, more than she had anticipated. She could only see the ragged edge of the injury to his leg as he lay flat now, the scar hidden from her.

"What's this?" she asked, bold enough to reach out and trace a long white line that ran across his shoulder, down his arm, almost to his elbow.

"From a sword at the Battle of Alkmaar," he said, his voice husky.

She thought perhaps he shivered under her touch.

"It must have hurt dreadfully," she said, a pinching sensation assaulting her heart at the thought of anyone causing him pain. She had no scars, no visible marks upon her skin, and it frightened her to think of the violence he must have witnessed, and been subjected to. "Does it still?"

He smiled and shook his head.

"And this?"

His muscles twitched and leapt under her touch as she traced a puckered divot in his side.

"Bayonet, Battle of Alexandria."

She gasped, frowning over that, remembering the story Mrs Norrell had told her and trying not to imagine the cold metal piercing his flesh. He had saved one of his men and had this scar to show for it.

"This one?"

She touched a fingertip to his left arm, and he turned it to reveal two scars, one a short precise line, the other a faded but uneven scar some three inches long. She touched the straight one.

"Sabre wound from a French dragoon."

"And this?" She traced the one further along his forearm and his mouth twitched.

"Fell out of a tree when I was six."

She laughed, and held his wrist, pulling his arm closer to her and pressing her lips to each scar in turn, lingering over the childish injury and kissing him once, twice, three times, until she'd covered every part of it.

"Poor boy," she crooned.

"Grazed by a musket ball here," he said, motioning to a mark on his neck she'd not noticed. "Sword and bayonet cuts here." He raised his hand to show fine white lines across his fingers. "And this." He indicated a starburst of tiny scars that bloomed over his right side and back. "Shattered glass from a bombardment that hit our army camp." His eyes glittered as he looked at her. "Aren't you going to kiss them all?"

There was no challenge behind the words, only a breathless curiosity, and though her cheeks flamed she nodded.

"Of course. Such bravery should be rewarded."

"Idiocy for the most part," he said with a short laugh, though his voice was raspy and uneven.

"You are too modest," she scolded him. "You have been hurt, suffered for your country, and you should wear these scars with pride. I am proud of you."

She lowered her head to his shoulder and made words deeds, touching each scar in turn with her lips, starting with the sword scar there, then the mark on his neck, each and every tiny scar that peppered his side and back, and finally by kissing each fine line that crisscrossed his fingers. His breathing had grown increasingly erratic and, as she pressed her lips tenderly to the last mark on his hand, his breath hitched and a sound close to pain left him. She looked up to see his eyes filled with tears, and she wondered if anyone else had ever given him such words, or treated him with the tenderness he deserved.

Reverently, she kissed the scar on his side, and felt his large hand in her hair, stroking as her palm smoothed over his hip. As she moved lower, her gaze snagged on the part of him she'd not dared focus on before. A combination of nerves, excitement, and desperate curiosity lanced through her. The desire to touch him there was overwhelming, though it seemed a shocking thing to want, but then her hands slid over an uneven, bumpy patch of skin, and he flinched. Her gaze moved to his thigh.

"Oh," she said, staring at the mess of ropy, raised scars and the large indent that made it look as though some ferocious animal had torn a large chunk from his thigh. "Did I hurt you?" she asked, appalled as she removed her hand.

He shook his head, but the motion was taut, his lips compressed, his face rigid. Only his eyes showed any emotion, wary and mistrustful as he watched her. He expected her to be revolted, she realised, when all she could feel was pain for the suffering he must have endured.

"Does it hurt if I touch the scars?"

He shook his head again, a sharp movement. "You don't need to…" he began, but Jemima ignored him.

"A bullet did this?"

He shrugged. "The bullet wound was ugly enough, especially once it got infected and they had to cut away the dead flesh, but the scarring is mostly from where they cauterised the wound."

Her eyes filled with tears.

"Don't pity me, damn it!"

The words were hard and angry, making her jump with shock. The intimacy of the moment fled in the wake of his fury, leaving Jemima raw and exposed, until she looked back at him and saw the anguish in his expression.

"I don't pity you, you damned fool," she said, surprising herself with the harshness of her own words. She'd never sworn in her life before. "I admire you, you silly man, beyond anything I can express. All you have suffered and endured, the violence you must have experienced, and yet you are still so kind, so gentle. You can growl and snarl all you like, my lord, but I see you and you'll not scare me away no matter how you bare your teeth."

He stared at her in confusion, obviously wondering why she hadn't fled the room weeping, and Jemima took advantage of his momentary bafflement. She leaned down and kissed his thigh, where the scars were thick and white and shiny. She moved her lips tenderly over every inch of the ugly wound, and it *was* ugly, and yet there was a beauty to it as well. He had survived this, he had endured, and he was still here. These marks upon him showed his strength and his fortitude, and that made the twisted results before her a thing she could only find pride in and tenderness for.

She looked up at him and her heart leapt at what she saw in his eyes, at the adoration and wonder she saw there. She smiled and he held his arms out to her. It was an invitation she could not accept quickly enough, and she sighed with pleasure as he gathered her close, holding her to him. His body was hot against hers, sending such delicious jolts of sensation bursting through her and awakening such fierce desires she could never remember feeling so alive. She shivered as her body blazed to life, sighing as he reached down and tugged the covers up over her.

"I'm not cold," she murmured, snuggling against his chest. He stroked her hair, his hand carrying down the length of her back and resting at her waist. She almost pouted as his hand came to a halt, willing him to keep touching her.

"You will get chilled in the night. You should sleep now." There was an odd note to his voice, and she glanced up in dismay.

"*Sleep?*" she repeated, quite unable to keep the consternation from her voice.

He nodded, his expression strangely fierce.

"But... but aren't you... aren't we...?"

"There's no rush, is there?"

"N-No," she said, hesitant as she wondered if she'd done something wrong and killed his desire for her. Yet the body so intimately pressed to hers was as hard and virile as ever, blatantly so. Nonetheless, she had to ask. "Don't you want to...?"

There was a harsh bark of laughter. "I don't think there is much room for doubt on that score, is there?"

The words were vaguely mocking, but she knew they were not directed at her. Somehow, he'd gotten all tangled up in his head again and she must find a way to unknot him and set him free.

Gathering her courage, she moved her hand down over his chest, enjoying the sensation of the warm, hard muscle sliding under her palm, but he grasped hold of her wrist before she'd even made it to his waist.

"No," he said. "Not... not tonight. I cannot pretend it won't happen, my... my desire for you is too strong to deny, but...." He shifted down the bed until their faces were level and reached out, tracing the line of her jaw. "You deserve so much more than I can give you."

Jemima opened her mouth to object, but he pressed a finger against it.

"The things you said, the way you made me feel this evening." His eyes glittered and he shook his head, his voice shaky and full of emotion "I have no words. But I... my heart...." His mouth clamped shut, and he swallowed hard. "Just let me hold you tonight. Please."

How could she deny such a request? Indeed, her own heart swelled with hope at the idea there might be more between them than simply friendship and physical desire. She settled against him, enjoying the warmth and the nearness, and trying to ignore her body's insistent clamouring for more, until the candles guttered and left them in the dark and she slept.

Chapter 12

My dear Miss Hunt,

You will not credit how relieved I was to receive your letter. I feared I had ruined any chance I had at gaining your good opinion with my actions. I know well how easy it would be to perceive what I have done in the light Mr Burton has presented it and I am humbled by your belief in me, if you can imagine such an unlikely thing. I confess no one has ever achieved it before. Only you.

I enclose the address of the charitable foundation you enquired about. It is admirably run by Mr Bernard Wheatcroft. I am certain he would be pleased to hear from you.

I will not deny that I am happy to have ruined Mr Burton's chances with you. I am wholeheartedly glad to have done so. I promise you that if he ever has the misfortune to cross my path, I shall make him pay for having abused you so, the vile wretch. I don't believe it can come as a surprise to you that I have disliked him from the outset. Whilst I cannot pretend that my personal feelings have not played a part in my animosity, it was by far the only reason. My only regret is that I have caused you a moment's pain. For that I do have regrets, and yet I would not change what I have done. I hope you can forgive me that. I have seen men do wicked and horrifying things during my life, but what I discovered in those mills will haunt me the rest of my days.

I think of you more than I ought, Miss Hunt. I would see you again. If you would allow it.

—Excerpt of a letter from The Most Honourable Lucian Barrington, Marquess of Montagu to Miss Matilda Hunt.

7th February 1815. Mitcham Priory, Sussex.

Solo stared up into the darkness of the room. Never had he felt such a barrage of emotions battering him from all sides. He'd been turned inside out, his heart laying unprotected on the wrong side of his ribs. The scars he bore prickled with awareness, as though her touch had brought the dead skin back to life, as though she'd brought *him* back to life. He'd been damn close to weeping at her tenderness, at the pride in her eyes... pride for him. The longing to make love to her, to make her his own, had been matched only by the regret and confusion he felt. This woman, this extraordinary, beautiful woman cared for him, for surely there was no actress born who could play the part with such sincerity? The idea of taking her virtue and not offering her marriage in return had been a physical pain in his heart, as though the bayonet that had struck his flesh had returned to skewer him for his wickedness. It wasn't only that he wanted to make things right for her; he wanted her beside him, always. He wanted to walk through the village with her on his arm, to have everyone know that she was his, and that he loved and admired her beyond... beyond anything. The thought of her being shamed before everyone if they discovered their affair made his skin hot, his stomach roil. It was him who ought to feel ashamed. Not her. Never her.

So, although he'd been painfully aroused, although he knew she would welcome his body into hers, he'd not made love to her. Even now his body ached with desire, with her proximity, and he did not know what to do for the best. He was only flesh and blood, and he doubted his ability to deny himself the pleasure of the warm body curled about his for long. He was not that noble, and yet he must do it. For the first time in his life, he regretted the promise he'd made Hyacinth. Not because he deserved her forgiveness, not because the ghost of her brother would ever leave his heart, but because the vow he made hurt one who ought never suffer a moment's pain. Jemima deserved a man to honour and love her, and he could only love her, and how could that ever be enough?

It seemed ridiculously foolish to have lost his heart with such speed, but he realised it had been happening since the first time he'd seen her, blushing with nerves in the bookshop. Had that only been a month ago? It did not seem possible.

Jemima stirred in his arms, murmuring his name, the syllables softened and hazy with sleep as she snuggled in closer to him. His cock twitched, desire lancing through him as her hip nudged it, her silky skin the devil's own torment to his tortured flesh.

"Hush," he murmured, stroking her hair and battling the longing to allow his fingers to wander elsewhere, to explore the undiscovered places he longed to seek out with his hands and mouth. "I'm here. Sleep now."

His vision blurred, the dim outline of her face clouding as he blinked hard. *Oh, God.* What was he to do?

***

10th February 1815. Briar Cottage, Mitcham Village, Sussex.

"Matilda!"

Jemima exclaimed as Bessie showed Matilda into her parlour. Her friend looked as exquisite as always, in a fine Jaconet muslin morning gown with a deep rose pink spencer and matching kid boots, gloves, and bonnet. She was the height of fashion and utterly stunning. When Jemima considered how very kind and generous she was too, she could not understand how the idiot men of the *ton* did not see her true worth. They were fools.

"My word, what a surprise this is," she said, flinging her embroidery to one side without a backwards glance and rushing to greet her.

"A good one, I hope," Matilda said, and her hesitant enquiry made Jemima realise she really wasn't sure.

With regret, she remembered how she had refused Matilda's offer to accompany her to her new home and stay until she settled in. Jemima had hurt her, when Matilda had been so very kind, and she regretted that profoundly.

"The very best," she said firmly.

Matilda smiled, the doubt Jemima had noticed fleeing. Impulsively, she hugged Matilda tight.

"I'm so sorry," she whispered, having by now seen the scandal sheets and all the news of Mr Burton's perfidy.

Matilda took a deep breath as Jemima released her.

"I am not," she said, lifting her chin, a flash of fury in her blue eyes. "I only regret being so taken in by that… that wicked man. Thank heavens I never married him, but I have no wish to discuss him further. Not now, at least."

Jemima nodded, knowing Matilda would speak of it in her own time if she changed her mind.

"Now, come and tell me everything," Jemima said, once Bessie had taken Matilda's spencer, bonnet, and gloves and hurried off to prepare a tea tray. Jemima tugged at Matilda's hand, pulling her to sit down at her side. "What have I missed? What news from the Peculiar Ladies?"

Matilda laughed and Jemima felt a rush of happiness at seeing her here, in her new home. A sliver of apprehension struck at her heart as she wondered if Matilda would be so happy for her once she knew the truth, but she pushed it aside. Her friends would not forsake her. She was certain of it.

They discussed everyone's news and devoured a goodly quantity of cake as they sipped their tea and Matilda caught her up on everything she'd missed. There was not so very much as letters flew back and forth between all the women with astonishing regularity and Jemima felt privileged to be included among their number. They had never forgotten her, despite her fading into the background. Once their gossiping and laughter abated, Jemima decided she ought to tell Matilda the truth. Her heart picked up speed as she set her teacup down, afraid her hands would tremble too badly once she spoke.

"There is something I must tell you."

There must have been a note to her voice that alerted Matilda to the seriousness of what she wished to say, for she too set her cup and saucer aside, and reached for Jemima's hands.

"What is it, Jem? Is something wrong?"

"No," Jemima said, smiling. "At least, I don't believe there is anything wrong, and I hope that you will not judge me too harshly."

She hesitated, wondering how to put into words what had passed between her and Solo. She didn't want it to sound cheap and tawdry, not when... Jemima remembered the night they had spent together and felt her heart ache. She did not know how things stood between them now though. He had treated her so tenderly, not taking what she would have willingly given, yet in the morning she had woken alone. When she'd gone down for breakfast, he had been waiting for her, smiling and kind and so very attentive, and he'd avoided her ever since.

"Jemima, I could never judge you."

Matilda's words were firm, her eyes filled with concern, and Jemima forced herself back to the moment.

She nodded and took a deep breath. "My aunt died penniless. In fact, there were bills I could not pay."

"Oh, Jem." Matilda squeezed her hands tight. "Why ever didn't you tell me? You must know I would have helped you. I would have done so gladly."

"I know." Jemima blinked back tears as she regarded her friend. "I know you would have, but where would it have ended, Matilda? Would you have kept me until I was an old lady? How could I burden you so, and how could you stop supporting me once you'd begun? I would have become a millstone about your neck. I have no skills with which to find employment, I could not gain a situation as a governess, and my stitching is adequate at best. You know the only options open to me."

She saw the moment Matilda understood, saw the acceptance of how she had gained this lovely home, the pretty new gown, all of it. There was no judgement in her eyes, only anxiety.

"What kind of man is he?" she asked, her voice faint, gripping Jemima's hands tightly. "Is he kind to you? Does… Does he…?"

"Yes, and I love him."

The words startled Jemima far more than Matilda, who let out a breath of relief. It was true, though. She loved him. She loved Solo.

"Oh, Jem." Matilda threw her arms about Jemima and burst into tears.

"Oh, Tilda, dearest, don't cry for me. I'm happy. Happier than I could ever have believed. I know perhaps I ought to be ashamed of what I have done, of what I have become, and perhaps I will be when it becomes known. I suppose it must become known one day, these things always do, but I cannot regret it. I will not."

Matilda fumbled for a handkerchief, wiping her eyes and blowing her nose noisily. Once she had calmed herself, she looked back at Jemima, her gaze direct and unblinking.

"You're truly happy?"

Jemima nodded. "Strange, isn't it? I cannot help but think fate has put us together. He is such a good man, Matilda. So kind, and he has suffered. He does not believe he deserves happiness and has shut himself away from the world, but the opposite is true. If anyone deserves to be happy, it is Solo."

Matilda started. "Solo? Not Solomon Weston? Lord Rothborn?"

Jemima nodded.

"Good heavens." She stared at Jemima for a long moment and then smiled. "Well, I did not expect that. I always thought he'd been ill used, though. That such a man, a war hero, should be treated so by that awful woman." Matilda tutted and shook her head. "I never did like her."

"You know her?" Jemima said eagerly, realising she was hoping that Matilda would tell her how dreadful the woman was. She found she was unwilling to chastise herself for such unchristian behaviour.

To her disappointment, Matilda only shrugged. "Barely. Nate knew her better, I believe. I know that she jilted Lord Rothborn, though. Broke his heart, by all accounts."

A burst of jealousy surged through Jemima, so fierce it left her breathless and a little shaken.

"She did more than that," she said, quite unable to keep the anger from her voice. "She's burdened him with the death of her brother, blamed him for something he had no hand in."

At Matilda's enquiring look, Jemima explained the story, and was gratified by the disgust in her friend's eyes.

"What a heartless creature she must be. It is gratifying to know I am not always such a terrible judge of people, for I thought she had a cruel streak."

There was such bitterness in Matilda's tone that Jemima was taken aback.

"We were all taken in by Mr Burton, Tilda. How many of us encouraged you to marry him?"

Matilda stared down, plucking fretfully at the lace edge of the clean handkerchief Jemima had given her. "It's not just him."

Jemima sighed. "Montagu."

"It was Montagu who exposed the scandal in the mills, Jemima. He's taken them over and is making them safe, giving the workers fair wages and providing schools for the children. He's established a charity to provide for those injured, and for the families of those who died."

"My goodness." Jemima had to admit that was a shock. She would never have believed the proud marquess to even be aware of the lower classes, let alone imagine he would bestir himself to help them. "He has done all this?"

A flicker of doubt clouded Matilda's eyes. "I know he exposed the scandal. I know those things *have* been done, though anonymously. I… I *believe* he is responsible." Yet there was a tremor of uncertainty in her voice.

"Matilda?"

Little by little, Jemima coaxed the rest of it out of her, the letter from Mr Burton and his accusations, the meeting with Montagu's uncle, and the letter from the marquess. Jemima could well understand her confusion. It was easy to believe Montagu the devil of the piece, and she was on the verge of telling Matilda that she should run from him when she thought of Solo. He had punished himself for years for something that was not his fault. What if Matilda's instincts had been correct, and Montagu was a good man beneath the ice cold exterior? It was hard to believe, nigh on impossible if Jemima was honest, but perhaps he deserved a chance to explain himself.

"What will you do?"

Matilda made a choked sound. "I have no idea."

"Will you tell him about his uncle?"

"I promised I would not, though it troubles me to keep such a thing secret. Jem, you must not breathe a word of it either. Promise me."

Jemima tutted at her. "As if I would! Of course I promise. What else is known about his family, though? I know his parents and his older brother, the Earl of Lyndon, died in a carriage accident."

"What?" Matilda paled, staring at her, and Jemima looked back in surprise.

"You didn't know?"

She shook her head.

"Well, it was years ago," Jemima said. "My aunt lived for the scandal sheets, though. I always knew far more about what was happening in the *ton* than about our own neighbours," she said with a laugh and then grew serious when Matilda said nothing. "Montagu could only have been a boy at the time. I think his brother, the earl, was only seventeen and Montagu is a fair bit younger. The only reason I know is that my aunt would indulge in stories of all the highborn fashionable people and tell me their histories. I think secretly she longed for me to marry a duke."

"I must have been too small to hear anything of it then," Matilda said quietly. "I knew he had a brother who'd died, and that he's his niece's guardian, but little more than that. I assumed he had always been the heir to the marquessate."

"You were perhaps thinking of the death of his younger brother, then. Miss Barrington is Lord Thomas Barrington's daughter. That's much more recent."

Matilda's hand went to her throat. "Oh, my. He lost two brothers *and* his parents?"

"Yes." Jemima wondered for the first time what that might do to a man. "I don't know the circumstances of the younger brother's death. I seem to recall my aunt was curious about it. She said there were murmurs about the circumstances in which he died, but if there was a scandal it was hushed up. It must have been five years ago, at least." She watched as Matilda absorbed this. "Have you met the niece?"

She nodded. "Twice. Once when he took her for ices at Gunter's, the other time at an art gallery."

Jemima considered this. "That hardly seems like she's being kept a prisoner."

"No," Matilda agreed, her face softening. "And she clearly adores him. I would say the feeling is mutual. He worries for her."

"But you still doubt him?"

Matilda threw up her hands. "Not in my heart, no. When I'm with him, I believe the things he tells me, but it appears my judgement is not to be relied upon… and you didn't see his uncle. How can one judge a man on such a brief meeting? But he seemed so… so genuine, so sincere. He was also a good friend of Lord Fitzwalter, who is such a dear man."

Jemima studied her, wishing she could help. "Will you see Montagu again, as he has asked you to?"

There was a short laugh, full of frustration and sadness.

"Yes," Matilda said hopelessly, before turning a direct gaze on Jemima. "What is it like, Jem? To be a man's mistress?"

Jemima blushed and looked down, taking a moment to arrange her skirts. "Surprisingly liberating," she said with a wry smile, and then realised what Matilda was asking for a reason. "But he is a good, kind man, and he makes me very happy. With another man I might have a very different answer for you. I am content, though. I have made peace with my sin, if sin it is. We have a little idyll for ourselves here and I shall live every moment without regret. I am blessed, Matilda, so do not pity me. I have a comfortable home, friends who do not judge me, and a good man who I am falling more in love with as the days pass. I shall not repine for more."

Matilda nodded, understanding in her eyes.

"Then I am happy for you, too. I may even envy you," she added, so quietly Jemima only just caught the words. "And now I must away. Alice asked me to give you her best love and demand you write to her at once and come and visit soon. You realise the journey took me little more than an hour and a half from their home?"

Jemima smiled as she remembered Nate and Alice had settled in Kent, and then realised Dern, the Kentish seat of the Marquess of Montagu was likely close by too. Did Matilda know that, she wondered?

"I did not realise they were so close, and I shall be delighted to indulge both requests," Jemima said, following Matilda as she got to her feet. "How is our mother-to-be?"

"Blooming and ready to be put out to grass—her words, not mine."

Jemima laughed, quite able to imagine Alice saying such a thing. "A boy or a girl, do you think?"

"I don't know, and it won't matter a whit to either of them. That child will be the most beloved to have ever been born."

They were silent as Bessie helped Matilda on with her spencer and handed her back her gloves and bonnet.

"Goodbye, Jem, dear."

Matilda embraced her so warmly that Jemima's eyes prickled. How she could ever have believed she would lose her friends she couldn't understand now. They would stand by her, even though they ought not.

"Matilda, if people start to talk… about me…."

Matilda's face grew stern in an instant. "Whatever you are about to say, swallow the words down now, and never consider them again. I keep my friends, no matter what. I've faced scandal before now, and I doubt it will be the last time. You did not shun me for my reputation, and I will hardly be the one to do so. I shall visit you when I wish. I trust that is clear?"

Jemima gave a choked laugh and nodded. "Bless you, Matilda, and thank you."

"Thank you, Jem," Matilda said, before walking away to her waiting coach.

What she was being thanked for Jemima wasn't certain, but she was very glad Matilda had come.

Chapter 13

Dear Minerva,

I feel my dare is hanging over my head like the sword of Damocles. The longer I wait the more nervous I become. Thank heavens Prue and Robert are finally going away at the end of this month now Prue is feeling so much better. I must strike in their absence – once Robert is far enough away to give me a head start at least. He will be furious with me! May I hide in your husband's laboratory if things get too heated? Perhaps he can turn me into a frog?

I spoke with the intriguing Mr Knight the other evening. For a wicked rake and seducer, he's rather blunt. I always supposed such men to have silver tongues and charm in abundance. Well, there's been none of that on display on any of the occasions we've met, but I suppose he dislikes me for being a peer's daughter, though it seems a little unfair. I can no more help my birth than he can. You were right, by the way; I am far too direct and need to watch my tongue more carefully. Do you know he thought I wanted to arrange a tryst with him! I confess I was shocked. Though it was thrilling, too.

Is it true, do you think, that he wishes to marry a lady of the ton in order to enter polite society?

—Excerpt of a letter from Lady Helena Adolphus to Mrs Minerva de Beauvoir.

17th February 1815. Mitcham Priory, Sussex.

Jemima regarded her reflection in the mirror and studied the new hairstyle Bessie had been practising for the past few days. The morning sunshine bathed her bedroom in its golden light and made her feel hopeful that she would see Solo today. She had missed him dreadfully.

"It's lovely, Bessie, thank you."

"You look like the goddess of spring, Miss," Bessie said. "That silly man won't know what hit him."

Jemima sent Bessie a reproving look, but prayed she was right. The pale green gown was trimmed with yellow and put her in mind of spring and primroses, and everything fresh and new. She hoped Solo liked it.

"Well," Bessie said, shaking her head and making a final adjustment to the coiffure she'd spent the best part of the past hour perfecting. "He *is* silly. Running away to London like that. I don't believe there's any business he needs seeing to up there, not for one moment. He's never stayed away for more than a day or two, Mrs Norrell says. I reckon he's in love with you, miss, and he's scared half to death."

"Bessie!" Jemima scolded. "You must not gossip about Lord Rothborn, especially not such foolishness as that."

Despite herself, her heart fluttered as hopes that Bessie had the right of it made her chest ache with longing. Bessie mimed buttoning her lip and flounced out of the room.

Why had Solo deserted her so abruptly, though? Where had he gone? Well, today she would get an answer. He had called on her before he'd left. He'd kissed her, too, but there had been a reserve in his manner which had not been there before, and it had been a chaste kiss with none of their previous passion. All the intimacy and warmth that she'd felt between them the night she'd spent in his bed had faded and gone. During his absence, she had resolved not to be a fool for him. Better to know the truth, to know where she stood. Mrs Attwood had agreed.

As if she had conjured the woman, she appeared at the bedroom door, which Bessie had left ajar. With a soft knock on the doorframe, she peered into the room.

"Can I come in?"

The woman was elegantly dressed as always, in a deep blue morning gown today, and at Jemima's invitation she came and sat on the bed.

"You look as pretty as a picture," she said, looking Jemima over with approval. "Now, you remember what we spoke about?"

Jemima sighed. Mrs Attwood, or Violet, as they were now on more familiar terms, had been a great comfort and confidant to Jemima, but it had baffled her to discover the woman was as wilfully romantic and silly as Bessie.

"He is not going to propose to me, Violet."

"A man does not get the woman he desires into bed and then stop short of ruining her for no reason."

Jemima groaned and rolled her eyes. This same argument had been raging between them for days now. "I expect there was a reason. Likely he… he was tired or didn't want me after all. Perhaps he didn't find me to his taste."

Violet made a sound of disgust. "Piffle. He told you plain he wanted you, and a man like that don't go in for fits of the vapours. He didn't ruin you because his conscience wouldn't stand for it. 'Tis why he's playing least in sight and all, you little goose." She shook her head, curls bouncing with impatience. "That man's fallen for you, Jemima, you mark my words, so don't you go messing it all up."

"It's you and Bessie messing it all up!" Jemima protested, surging to her feet with a swish of fine material, fighting the urge to cry. "You are raising my hopes of something I never dreamed of, have no right to expect, and how foolish I will look when he offers me nothing more than he promised. I shall blame you for my weeping and wailing in that event, and you'll just have to stand it, for it was your own fault."

"Away with you," Violet commanded, getting up and making shooing motions until she'd ushered Jemima out of the room to where Bessie was waiting for them downstairs.

"Really, you are both impossible."

Jemima's complaints fell on deaf ears, and she submitted to their fussing and primping as they hustled her into pelisse and gown and rearranged the flowers on her bonnet until they proclaimed she was quite perfect.

"Now, go and get yourself a husband." Violet ordered whilst Bessie smothered giggles behind her hand.

Jemima groaned but didn't bother to argue as they thrust her outside the back door and watched her walk out of sight.

***

Solo knew he was in trouble the moment he saw her walking through the gardens towards the house. Not that he hadn't already accepted that fact, but it was brought home to him with such force as he watched her come to him that he wanted to weep with frustration. Even seeing her from afar made his heart leap, and she looked so very lovely in the sunshine, every bit as fresh and perfect as a spring day. It seemed to him she'd dressed with the sole purpose of breaking his heart.

What a fool he had been. He'd thought an educated lady would make a fine companion, someone to talk to, and to ease his loneliness when he could not bear another night alone in his bed. He'd never considered someone as young and lovely as Jemima would accept the position. Damn Mr Briggs for bringing them together, and yet what might have happened to her if he hadn't? Might she had gone to some other man, someone who did not appreciate what he had, who would have ill-used her? Solo felt his stomach clench, nausea rising in his throat. Not that he could claim to have done so very well by her, but he would do better. He could not marry her, but he could put things back on a proper footing. They could still be friends. He was not strong enough to remove her from his life altogether, but he believed he was not so weak as to give into his baser instincts. Not after spending the past week away from her. If the alternative was all or nothing, he would take what he could get. He would not ruin her, and he could not marry her. So, she would be what all her neighbours believed her to be— a respectable spinster—and he would be her friend, nothing more.

He steeled himself as he heard Mrs Norrell greeting her, the sound of the two women's voices making it clear they were pleased to see each other. How quickly she made friends and gained the good opinion of everyone she met. What a perfect wife she would have made him. His heart ached with longing, imagining her living here, with him, waking beside her every morning and sharing his life with her.

Stop it. Stop it, you damn fool.

He forced himself to smile warmly as Mrs Norrell showed her into his study, and he asked the housekeeper to bring them tea.

"This is a pleasant surprise, Miss Fernside," he said, hating himself for the formality, more so when he saw the confusion in her eyes.

"A surprise?" she repeated, standing in the middle of the room. She looked uncertain, and he hated it. "But you have been gone for days. I came the moment I heard you had returned. Did you not expect me to, when I missed you so very much?"

The desire to close the space between them was a sharp pain in his chest. He wanted to take her in his arms and hold her to him, swear he would never leave her again, not for a moment. Instead he acted as though he'd not heard her words and pretended to busy himself tidying the papers on his desk. He ought to look like a man with things to do, one who did not have time to spare on social calls.

"I had business to attend to. Nothing very exciting, but one cannot put such work off." He hated the brisk tone of his voice. Good God, but he sounded like a pompous ass. For both their sakes he did not mention that he'd spent the entire time in the room he'd taken at his club, drinking too much and trying desperately not to give into the urge to return to her.

Silence filled the room, and he did not dare look up.

"I think you have been working too hard," she said, her voice soft with concern. "You look tired, Solo."

"I think you had best address me as Lord Rothborn."

Though he still didn't look at her, too afraid to see the hurt in her eyes, he felt the impact, felt the sting of his words.

Before she could form a reply, Mrs Norrell returned with the tea tray. She had evidently been expecting Jemima's visit, even if he had not. No doubt Mrs Norrell had sent word to the cottage the moment Solo had come home. The woman gave him a quizzical glance, clearly aware of the tension in the room. Solo dismissed her, curtly enough to earn himself a glare of displeasure.

Neither of them made a move towards the tea things. Solo turned his back on the room, staring out of the window and willing himself to be strong. He was doing this for her, because he loved her too well to ruin her. He heard her moving, the soft rustle of skirts as she came closer, and still nearly leapt out of his skin as she slid her arms around his waist.

"No!" he said the word like it was a curse, panic surging through him at having her touch him. There was only so much he could endure.

She jerked back as he moved away from her, putting distance between them before her touch could snap the fragile threads of his will.

The shock and hurt in her eyes made him want to howl with misery.

"I'm s-sorry," she said, blinking back tears. "What have I done, my lord? I know I have given you a disgust of me, but I-I don't know... I don't understand...."

Solo shook his head, horrified she should think such a thing but unable to get the words out. His throat was too tight, his grief too encompassing.

"Nothing," he managed, forcing the word out. "You've done *nothing* wrong."

"Then why?"

Solo turned away again, staring outside at the garden. He'd lived here alone, for years now, with only the ghosts for company. As much as he told himself he did not believe in such things, he knew they were there. Not that he'd ever seen or heard one, but they haunted him all the same. Not only those that came with The Priory, but those he'd brought back from war with him and those that had followed after him too, because he'd not been there to do his job. He ought to have been with his men, ought to have died with them, alongside them, rather than sitting at home, safe and warm and far from danger. He drew on every reserve of courage and honour he had, knowing she deserved the truth, or she would blame herself, find fault when there was only perfection.

"I cannot marry you."

He turned and hated himself all the more for her quizzical expression. She'd never expected him to offer. He'd made his intentions clear to her.

"I know that," she said, staring at him in confusion. "I never—"

"You ought to have expected," he snapped. "God damn it, Jemima. You're a lady. Any man would be proud, beyond proud, to have you as his wife. I know I would, but I cannot marry you, even… even if it is what I would wish to do, more than anything."

Her eyes widened, glistening with tears. She took a step closer, but he halted her with a terse word.

"No. I cannot offer marriage, but I can refrain from bringing you dishonour."

"You… You would send me away?"

"No!" he protested, knowing he ought to. If he truly wanted her happiness, he should find her another home, far from him, but he was not as strong as that. "I cannot send you away. I am selfish enough to want…to want your friendship still. I cannot deny myself that much."

She stared at him for the longest time and he could not read her expression, could not decipher the myriad of emotions that flickered in her eyes. Then she took a breath, and he recognised the one she settled on: resolve. Her jaw set, a flicker of anger in her eyes as she undid her bonnet and flung it aside, quickly followed by the gloves.

"What are you doing?" he demanded, unsettled by the sharp, furious movements, and more by the way her slender hands reached for the buttons on her pelisse.

She ignored him and made quick work of them, stripping off the coat and letting it fall to the floor in a heap. The moment she reached for the fastening on her dress, he knew he was in deep trouble.

"Stop that. Stop that at once!"

She stared at him, expressionless, struggling to twist about and untie the fastenings at the back of her dress. With relief, he realised she'd never manage it without a maid to help, and he thought he was safe until she gave up and tried another tack. When she lifted her skirts, showing him her slender legs clad in silk stocking, and began to untie the garter, his mind snapped.

"No! Jemima, for the love of God, what are you doing?" He crossed the floor, snatching at her wrists, forcing her to stop.

"Giving you back the things you bought me, my lord," she said, the anger in her voice unmistakable. "As I've not earned them."

"Jemima, stop. Stop this, I'm trying to do the right thing by you, damn it."

She stared up at him, such an expression in her eyes he felt his own burn.

"I don't want the right thing," she cried, tears threatening to overspill and cascade down her cheeks. "I want *you*. I love you, Solo, and I don't care a damn for my reputation. I want to be with you, if you'll have me. Say you want me."

She reached up and pressed her mouth to his, and he could not fight this battle. She didn't play fair, bringing such powers to bear against him as the softness of her lips, and the words he'd seemed to have spent his entire life longing to hear. He let go of her wrists and pulled her to him, kissing her ferociously, with anger and frustration, and with tenderness too. She clung to him, returning everything he gave, sinking her hands into his hair, putting every part of herself into the kiss, holding nothing back. She would never hold anything back; she would give and give to him until she destroyed herself.

He broke the kiss, still holding her tight, and discovered he was trembling.

"I won't ruin you. I won't have you as my mistress. I love you too much to dishonour you, to cause you any harm."

She pushed away from him with a cry of frustration. "But this hurts me, Solo. You brought me here. We had an agreement, and I was content with that. I never expected love, affection, but to discover it has been a joy, a blessing I had never dreamed of, and now... now you wish to take it from me, from us? You would condemn yourself to loneliness once again, or will you bring another woman here, to serve you as you will not allow me to do?"

"Hell and the devil! What do you take me for?" he raged, her words tearing at his heart. "You think I could touch another woman, *look* at another woman, now? With what I have in my heart for you? I would rather die."

"Then you punish us both for no good reason."

To his horror, he heard the tremor in her voice and watched as she dropped into a chair, as if her legs could no longer hold her. She put her head in her hands and began to cry.

"Jemima, please," he begged, falling to his knees before her but not daring to touch her. If he took her in his arms again, he wasn't sure he'd have the strength to let her go. "Please, please, don't cry. Damn me to hell, I ought to be horsewhipped."

She stopped crying abruptly and looked up, her cheeks still wet, tears spangling her eyelashes.

"No, Solo. You ought not to be punished a moment longer, but it is you who punishes yourself, for things you are not responsible for."

That brought him up short.

"You're wrong," he said in disgust.

"I know." He heard the anger in her voice, shocked by the force of her word. "I *know* what that awful, heartless woman told you and you ought never to have listened to her. She was wicked and cruel to say such things to you."

Solo stiffened. Damn Mrs Norrell and her bloody interfering. No doubt he had her to thank for his. He got to his feet, dragging himself up by clutching at the chair beside him, the movements clumsy and awkward as his leg protested.

"You know nothing of the situation," he said, hating how cold his words sounded, but she had to know. "You do a blameless lady a disservice by speaking of her so."

There was a taut silence.

"You still love her."

It wasn't a question, but Solo considered it all the same. It was strange to think of Hyacinth now as a woman he'd loved. He *had* loved her passionately, had longed for her when he was away, fighting. The letters he'd sent had been filled with such sentiments, his loneliness at being away from her, his desire and regard for her. Now, all he felt was grief and loss and guilt, his love overwhelmed by the force of more powerful emotions, by the way he'd let her down. How could he have let himself fall in love with Jemima, when he knew all he was guilty of? How could he have forgotten his promise to honour Barnaby's memory? He had been close to her brother too, had loved him as he would his own sibling, had fate gifted him such a thing. Barnaby had been impossible not to love, the kind of charming, good-natured fellow who never said a bad word about anyone and thought the best of everyone he met. If only Solo had never crossed his path, but Barnaby had admired him beyond reason, like a beloved older brother. He had begged his father to buy him a commission so that he might follow Solo to war. Hyacinth had pleaded for Solo to talk him out of it, and Solo had tried so hard to do so, all too aware the boy was not fit for such a life, but he'd failed. So, he promised Hyacinth he would keep him safe for her, and he'd failed to do that too. He'd wanted to die when he'd heard the news, had wished it had been him. He remembered the hatred in her eyes when he'd told her, and had hated himself far, far more.

"My feelings are irrelevant. I lost a man I regarded as dearly as my own brother and, in so doing, I failed her. I vowed never to marry as penance for that failure. She could not bear to look at me after what happened, and I could not blame her for that. I had offered for her, though, and it was my fault she could not go through with it. It seemed only right."

He dared to look back at Jemima, to see her staring at him with such pity in her eyes he had to look away.

"I'll pack my things," she said, her voice dull. "I'll need a little time to arrange a place to stay, but if you could give me until the end of the week...."

"What?" Solo spun around, disbelieving. "*No*. You cannot go, there is no need for you to go."

She gave a surprisingly bitter laugh and that he had made such a sound come from her made his heart contract. "Our agreement is at an end, my lord. I am of no use to you. I will not stay under false pretences."

"No, Jemima. I need you to stay. *Please*. I cannot... I need your friendship. Can you not give me that much?"

She looked up at him, tears streaming down her cheeks. "I could give you everything I have, if you would only let me."

Solo shook his head and then turned away as she tied her garter and got to her feet, putting her pelisse and bonnet back on.

"You'll stay?" he asked, hating the pleading in his voice but unable to stop it. He'd get on his knees and beg her if he must, pride be damned. "*Please*, Jemima, don't leave me alone here."

"Very well," she said, her voice dull, and then walked to the door and left, without another word.

Chapter 14

My Lord Marquess,

Thank you for your reply. Please do not regret for a moment your actions in exposing such cruelty. Any hurt I have suffered is merely to my pride and pales into insignificance when I consider what those people have endured. I should like to visit the mills one day and see all that has been accomplished there. I shall happily write to the excellent Mr Wheatcroft and discover what I may, for I notice that you still have not revealed the name of the anonymous benefactor who has done so much to restore the mills and the fortunes of all who work within them. Yet I feel certain I know who is responsible. Will you not confide the truth in me?

I am staying with my brother at present and intend to remain here for some weeks. His wife, one of my dearest friends, is awaiting the arrival of their first child and I have come to lend my support as best I may. As you can see, I am not so very far from Dern.

As the weather has been so fine of late, I've taken to walking around Hever Castle. The owner, Mr Waldo, is well known to my brother and has given us leave to visit the gardens whenever we desire. As it is barely a ten-minute walk from my brother's home, it has become my favourite destination on a sunny afternoon.

Please give my very kindest regards to Miss Barrington. I hope she is well and that I may have the pleasure to see her again. I am certain our paths will cross, sooner or later.

—Excerpt of a letter from Miss Matilda Hunt to The Most Honourable Lucian Barrington, Marquess of Montagu.

20th February 1815. Briar Cottage, Mitcham Village, Sussex.

"She's not here."

Solo felt his heart plummet to his boots at Mrs Attwood's terse comment. His shock and disappointment must have shown on his face, for the woman's expression softened just a tad.

"Oh, it's only for the day. She's gone to visit a friend over Edenbridge way."

He let out a shaky breath, only then realising his lungs had stopped working. He nodded at Mrs Attwood. "Thank you. Please tell her I called."

He handed her his card, which Mrs Attwood took from him with an impatient sigh, clearly irritated by such formality.

She folded her arms and gave him a hard look. "I don't much care for what's going on here. Don't understand it none, either."

Solo stiffened, glaring at the insolent creature. How dare she presume to judge him when he was trying to do the best by Jemima?

"I do not pay you to pass judgement upon me, madam. I'm certain there are higher powers to do the job quite adequately. I thank you."

The woman snorted and shook her head. "I don't suppose my notions of sin and morality are the same as most people's, I'll give you that, but I do know you've broken that girl's heart. How her spending her days weeping is supposed to do either of you a mite of good is beyond me, but I assume an educated man such as yourself would know better than I. Good day to you, my lord."

With no further ceremony, she slammed the door in his face.

He'd broken her heart.

The words were a weight in his chest, at once a burden and a comfort, for if he'd broken her heart his own had been torn to shreds. She had wept for him, for the pain he'd brought her. Solo turned on the spot, still standing on the doorstep of her cottage, unsure of what to do. He must leave, of course. He'd come to the front door this morning, and to be seen dithering there would do neither of them any good. Forcing one foot in front of the other, he returned the way he'd come, walking the long way around rather than using the hidden path through the garden. Though the day was sunny and bright, there was a cold wind. It chilled him, making his bones ache and his leg protest more than usual. All his aches and pains had seemed worse since he'd made his decision. Why was it that doing the right thing, the honourable thing, was bringing them both so much pain?

Cursing, Solo made his way back to the house. He would lose himself in his books. It had been his escape from the world ever since he'd returned here, too brittle with grief and guilt to cope with reality, with people and inconsequential chatter.

Yet, when he returned to his study, the first book that came to hand was *Undine*. He turned to the page where her husband, the knight, betrayed her by unthinkingly lamenting not having married a normal woman instead of a water nymph. Undine returned to the water, heartbroken. He gazed down at the beautiful illustrations but did not see them, seeing only the pain in Jemima's eyes when she had told him she loved him. Solo slammed the book shut, breathing hard. He would not regret it. He would not regret meeting her. She had brought him joy. For a brief moment he had known what it was to feel alive, part of the living world, to feel loved. He would not regret that. No matter the price.

***

Jemima regarded her friends and tried to find pleasure in their company. She had known that Matilda would be here, but Harriet and her brother Henry had come to visit, too. Harriet looked marvellous, decked out in a jaunty yellow carriage dress. It must have been chosen by her husband as it was indulgent and far more frivolous than anything Jemima had seen her wear before, or perhaps happiness had given her the confidence to dress with more flair. Her laughter filled the room as her brother teased her and Harriet returned the favour. It was so wonderful to see them, yet Jemima felt somehow removed from the gathering, like a ghost, not fully present.

Alice was glowing, plump and resplendent, reclining on an elegant chaise longue, propped up with silk cushions. Nate looked on, grinning, every bit the proud father-to-be. Happiness and love radiated from him, and it was so obviously returned that Jemima had to batter down a surge of jealousy. Despite telling herself she was every kind of fool imaginable, she could not help but daydream about Solo, about being his wife, carrying his child. Would he fret and fuss over her like that? Yes. She knew that he would. He had a kind and gentle heart, despite the violence he'd experienced in his career. Even the pain she felt now—the pain he was inflicting on them both—was imposed because he wanted to do what was right for her. Foolish man. How strange to wish he would let her ruin herself, but she didn't care much for anything else now. What was the point of being thought a lady when any joy had been taken from her life?

She wanted to share a life with him, and if she must leave respectable society behind for that, so be it. Now that both Minerva and Matilda knew and had not judged her harshly, she felt certain she would still have her friends, and that was all she truly cared about. If the rest of the world wanted to believe her a fallen woman, well, what did it matter? With a jolt, Jemima realised she had been staring into her teacup in silence and was being a poor guest. She forced herself to smile and attend the conversation.

"I swear it wasn't my fault," Henry was protesting as his sister rolled her eyes at him.

Harriet set down her teacup and levelled him with a look over the top of her spectacles.

"It's always your fault. I never met a man more likely to get into a daft scrape than you."

"Harry, that's not fair. I was only trying to help the wretched woman retrieve her cat and all I got was scratched to bits and attacked with an umbrella. I ask you, Nate, where's the gratitude? Women today don't appreciate a gentleman's efforts, I swear."

Nate looked up from the plate of biscuits he was perusing and shook his head. "Don't drag me into it. Alice is very fond of cats."

"So am I!" Henry retorted, though it was clear he was reconsidering.

"You were just trying to show off for her," Harriet said, not bothering to hide her amusement. "The cat was perfectly capable of getting itself out of the tree, but no…. You had to go playing the hero and climb up after it."

Henry flushed. "The blasted woman stood there, wringing her hands, tears in her eyes and all but wailing. What the devil was I supposed to do?"

Harriet gave a snort. "Tell her the foolish creature was quite all right and would be down presently."

"Well, I wish I had!" Henry folded his arms, indignation written all over his handsome face, a face Jemima now noticed bore several fine scratches. "The blasted animal ruined a cravat and one of my best shirts, and I'll likely be scarred for life!"

"Oh, do hush," Harriet said, shaking her head with all the concern one would expect from a sibling. "I can't believe you are still complaining. It was days ago."

Henry huffed and sat back with his arms folded over his chest. Jemima glanced over to see Matilda struggling not to laugh. She caught her eye, and Matilda grinned at her. The conversation returned to whether Nate and Alice's child would be a boy or a girl, and Matilda shifted closer.

"Are you well, Jemima?" she said, keeping her voice low. "You look pale today."

Jemima forced a smile and nodded. "A bit of a headache is all. I shall take a walk before the journey back home. I'm sure some fresh air is all I need."

Matilda studied her for a long moment but said nothing else on the subject, for which Jemima was grateful.

"I was right, by the way. Nate knew Miss Jackson, as she was then."

Jemima's head snapped around so fast it was a wonder she didn't strain something.

"He did?"

Matilda nodded and set down her cup and saucer. She leant towards Jemima, murmuring in her ear. "Ask him about her in private, before you leave. I'm sure he'll tell you more."

Jemima's heart jolted and it was all she could do to keep her hands still and her mouth closed, the desire to question Nate was so strong. What if the woman had been unworthy of Solo's affections? Then she could convince him that she did not deserve the vow he'd made, that she was punishing him out of cruelty? Though she felt herself to be a wretched friend, she was only too glad when the visit ended. She hung back as Henry and Harriet took their leave, Henry escorting his sister back to Holbrook House.

Matilda gave Jemima a hug before she turned to her sister-in-law. "Come along, Alice. I'll help you upstairs for your afternoon nap."

Alice laughed as Matilda hauled her off the chaise longue with some difficulty. "Everyone has become so bossy these past weeks. I swear, Tilda, you're as bad as Nate."

"Oh, this is nothing," Matilda said, winking at Jemima and Nate. "I can be far bossier than this. Just wait until the baby comes."

"I can vouch for that," Nate said, ducking as his sister took a swipe at him.

"Wretch," Matilda replied, though there was laughter in her eyes.

"Come, Miss Fernside," Nate said, giving her a courtly bow and then offering his arm. "Allow me to escort you for a short walk. Matilda said you wished for some fresh air before you left, so we shall take a turn about the garden."

Jemima gave Alice a fond hug goodbye and sent Matilda a look of gratitude before she took his arm and followed him outside.

"What a lovely garden," she said as they walked out into a large expanse of neatly tended ground broken up with large borders trimmed with formal topiary hedges.

"It doesn't look much at this time of the year, but come the spring, it will be a riot of colour. Alice loves flowers," he said, turning to grin at her. "She's been working hard with the head gardener, and I fully expect the place to be magical once she's done."

"It's lovely to see you both so happy." Jemima could not help the wistful sigh that accompanied her words, and she flushed a little as Nate turned his blue gaze upon her.

"We are happy. Happier than I deserve, no doubt. I'm sure your time will come too," he added, giving her a warm smile.

Jemima laughed a little but could not bring herself to say anything.

"You wanted to know about Hyacinth Jackson?"

She avoided Nate's enquiring glance, wondering exactly what Matilda had told him. "I do," she said.

To her relief he didn't question her, simply nodded.

"I've not see her much of late, but Hyacinth Jackson was, and is, a beauty. She had men falling over her the year of her come out, but Baron Rothborn won her hand. Of course, the war was raging, and he was forced to leave his fiancée to return to the fighting. She was a vivacious sort though and was still popular and much seen at social events in his absence."

"I'm sure Lord Rothborn would not have expected her to sit at home," Jemima said, striving to be fair when, in her heart, she wanted to hear the woman was a conniving temptress.

Nate looked at her and returned a sad smile. "No, from what I have heard of the fellow, I don't suppose he would have."

Jemima held her breath, wondering if Nate knew more than he was saying. "Matilda has told me this information is important to you"

She gave a jerky nod. "I love him," she said, and then flushed scarlet, wondering what on earth had made her blurt such a thing out. "Lord Rothborn, I mean. He loves me too, but he won't marry me because… because he made a vow and…" She snapped her mouth shut, aware she'd said too much. This was not her story to share. Jemima looked up as warm hands took hers and squeezed.

"There *were* rumours about her, about an affair. I saw them alone together myself, but… but that is not necessarily proof, though I always assumed… All I do know for certain is that man married her as soon as she was out of mourning."

"Oh."

Jemima's heart thudded, an odd sensation in her stomach. Was it coincidence, were the rumours just the *ton's* usual ill-natured gossip, or was there more to it? Nate had seen them together, after all.

"Miss Fernside?"

Jemima looked up to find Nate watching her with concern.

"Be careful what you do with this information. A man does not like to be made to look a fool."

Jemima nodded, her head buzzing. "Where does she reside now?"

Nate studied her for a long moment. "They have fallen on hard times. She likes to live lavishly, and her husband has taken to drinking and gambling, but has no talent for the game. I barred him from *Hunter's* two years ago. The last I heard Viscount Kline and his wife were renting rooms in Hans Town, but whether they are still there, I cannot say."

"Thank you," Jemima said.

He nodded, but did not look altogether happy about the information he'd given her. "Have a care, Miss Fernside. I found her to be a spiteful woman when she was young and wealthy. I do not know what kind of woman she is now, but in my experience time and reduced circumstances don't often improve people."

Jemima nodded, knowing this was a warning she ought to heed. "I understand, and I do thank you for everything."

Chapter 15

Dear Miss Hunt,

Thank you for asking after me. I am very well. I would like to see you too. ~~Can you come and visit me?~~ *I cannot ask you to come and visit me at Dern even though I want to. It isn't proper as Uncle isn't married. That seems silly.* ~~Can you marry my~~ *I have drawn you a picture of the horse, like the one in the gallery, except mine is pink. Mine also has ribbons. And it has a hat. Do you like it?*

Uncle Monty took me riding yesterday. My pony isn't pink, but she is very beautiful and very fast. She always beats Uncle Monty. I must go now, as I must do my lessons. I am learning French. I don't like French.

—Excerpt of a letter from Miss Phoebe Barrington to Miss Matilda Hunt.

22nd February 1815. Briar Cottage, Mitcham Village, Sussex.

"Oh, good morning, my lord."

Solo waited impatiently for Bessie to invite him in, but the girl just stood in the doorway, twisting her apron between her hands.

"Are you going to keep me waiting outside all morning, Bessie?" he asked, aware he sounded too stern, but his patience was wearing thin.

He needed to see Jemima. He had hoped she would call on him yesterday, once she'd learned he had come to her, but he'd waited all day to no avail. So, here he was again, desperate for just a few moments in the company of the woman who would willingly share his bed if only he would forget what honour meant and take everything she offered him.

"She's not here, my lord."

"The devil take it, where is she now?" he snapped, and then remembered his manners.

It was no business of his where Jemima had gone. He had rejected her as his lover. They were only to be friends. He did not wish for her to feel beholden to him. If she did, she might start flinging her clothes at him again. His body stirred with interest at the idea and he cursed himself for a scoundrel.

"Forgive me, Bessie, that was uncalled for," he said, trying to get a grip on his temper and his sanity, which seemed a dreadfully difficult thing to do these past few days.

"I-I don't rightly know, my lord. I'm sorry. I'll be sure to let her know you called, though. Good day to you."

There was something about the maid's demeanour that set alarm bells ringing. She was flushed and anxious, and clearly wanted him to leave. Solo caught the door and pushed it open again before he had to experience it slamming in his face once more. No doubt Bessie, who had always idolised him, now thought him a monster, just as Mrs Attwood did.

"Where has she gone, Bessie?" There was a warning note to his voice which no man under his command had ever heard with equanimity.

Bessie quailed a little, to the detriment of her apron, which was becoming a crumpled mess as she twisted it back and forth between her hands. "I don't know, my lord, truly I don't. Only that she's g-gone to London to see someone. Please, don't ask me more, for I don't know."

The poor girl looked so miserable that Solo did feel a monster. He could not fault her loyalty to her mistress if she knew more and, if she did not, shouting at her would not grant her the knowledge. He nodded.

"Thank you, Bessie. I'm sorry for my wretched temper but I… I worry for her," he added, knowing that sounded pathetic but wanting her to understand.

"I know, my lord," she said, offering him a sympathetic smile.

He turned as she closed the door on him and felt his temper flare once again as he saw the vicar, Mr Pemble, making his way up the path. It was obvious from the village gossip Mrs Norrell kept abreast of that the man was looking for a wife, and the idea that this dull, priggish fellow had more to offer Jemima than he did made Solo want to bellow with fury.

"She's not in," he said, knowing he sounded terse but quite unable to moderate his tone.

Besides, everyone knew he was a bad-tempered devil. It would hardly come as a surprise when half the village appeared to be scared to death of him.

"Ah, well, a pity," Mr Pemble said, attempting to give Solo a wide berth on the narrow path, but still heading towards the door. "I shall just leave my card and the book we spoke of during my last visit. She seemed so very interested, so I thought I would lend it to her. Good day to you, my lord."

The man gave Solo a very deferential bow, which did not improve his mood. There was nothing to be gained by staying and starting a silly row, which he felt quite able and willing to do, so he turned and made his way back to The Priory, still seething with irritation.

Why had she gone to London? Who was she seeing? From what she'd said, he knew none of her friends were in town at present. Even Miss Hunt, who seemed to be her closest friend, was here in Kent, so why…? He stopped in his tracks as he considered. Mr Briggs. Had she gone to see Mr Briggs?

The agreement drawn up between them had been a substantial one. Solo would provide her accommodation and pay all her bills as well as providing an allowance for pin money to spend as she saw fit. If, after five years, she wished to end their arrangement she was free to do so and would receive a large amount on which she could live comfortably, if not lavishly, for the remainder of her life. If she ended their agreement before five years, he had agreed to be generous, but had left that to Mr Briggs to make whatever arrangements necessary. He had supposed that, if she wanted to end things earlier, it would be because things had not gone well, and decided Mr Briggs would be best suited to handle the matter.

That Jemima might have gone to London to ask to be freed from their arrangement made his stomach twist into a knot. He ought to have spelled it out for her. He ought to have explained that he would give her anything, everything she wanted or needed. If she preferred to have no further financial dependency on him, he would sign over the cottage and a lump sum now, far more than he'd originally intended after the five years. Then she need never feel beholden again. Except she would, of course she would. So did that mean she would leave, that she would go away and start again somewhere else, but she'd promised, she'd told him she would stay.

He closed his eyes, leaning heavily on his cane as his leg throbbed, the pain echoing in the hollow chamber of his heart. How had he gotten so damn old? Surely, he wasn't an old man yet, still in his prime, but he felt the weight of the past years spent alone bearing down on him. For every year he had passed, isolated at The Priory, he believed he had aged a decade. With Jemima near, those years had tumbled away from him. He had awakened to each day with his soul growing lighter, the pain of old scars lessening, but if she were to leave….

No.

No, damn it. He had to make her stay.

***

22nd February 1815. Hans Place, Hans Town, London.

Jemima stared out of the hansom cab and felt her stomach clench as her nerve threatened to fail her. Hans Town was familiar. Before their finances had dwindled, she had lived here for a time with her aunt. It was a decent location, just respectable enough for those on the fringes of the *ton* to still be considered acceptable. What a comedown for a viscount and his lady, though, as the house she was looking at through the window was not one of nicer ones of the area.

"Are you sure about this, Jem, love?" Violet asked, her voice kindly and full of concern.

Jemima shook her head. Her palms were sweaty in her kid gloves, and she wanted nothing more than to tell the driver to take them back to the coaching inn where they'd taken a room for the night.

"No. Not in the least, but I must do something."

"Yes, love. I do understand. The silly fool is sacrificing both of you for his loyalty to a woman who's likely no better than she ought to be, but... but I should not like to see you hurt."

"But I am hurt, Violet." Jemima turned her gaze upon Mrs Attwood and knew she could not hide the pain in her eyes. "I cannot continue in this fashion. It will bring us both misery, I know it. He wants me to be his friend, but we are not friends and I do not think I can pretend that we are, when the truth is we are so much more than that. He will not let me love him unless he can return my feelings honourably. If he cannot marry me, I will lose him, and I will *not* lose him. Not if I can prevent it. I must fight for him. He has fought so many battles for his country, surely I can face this one little skirmish for him... for us."

"Well." Violet smiled, her eyes sparkling with tears and her voice a little thick, "when you put it like that…. To battle, Miss Fernside. We have a foe to vanquish!"

Whilst the sense of camaraderie with Violet at her side remained, any heroic spirit faded as Jemima dragged her unwilling feet towards the front door and knocked. Her heart was beating so hard and fast her head spun, and she felt increasingly ill. A man opened the door. He was too young to be a butler, so she suspected they had promoted a footman to the job, as he was far cheaper. The man showed them into a bright and elegant, if sparsely furnished, front parlour and took Jemima's card. A few moments later another man joined them.

He was tall and broad-shouldered, and must once have been a devilishly handsome fellow. His hair was thick and blond, but his face showed signs of dissipation, and his middle had become a little too thick for the coat he wore, which she suspected he could not do up. A rather garish waistcoat completed the ensemble, giving him a rakish appearance Jemima could not quite like.

"Miss Fernside." He greeted her warmly, making her regret her harsh assessment. "I am sorry, but my wife is indisposed this morning. We had a rather late night last night. May I be of service to you? I am a paltry offering, I'm certain, but I shall do my best."

"You are very kind, my lord," Jemima said, shaking her head, uncertain if she was relieved or disappointed. "I should not wish to trouble you."

"Oh, no trouble at all. It's not every day a fellow gets a visit from such charming callers, even if they were not intended for him."

He gave them the benefit of a dazzling smile and, for a moment, the dissipated exterior fell away, and she saw the handsome man he must have been. With a flash of anger, she remembered that this man may have stolen Solo's life. It was possible Lord Kline had carried on an affair with the woman Solo was in love with, whilst Solo risked his life for king and country over and again. This man had married and wasted his fortune on gambling, whilst Solo had returned with ghosts and scars to an empty house and heartbreak. Her anger fired her courage, made her brave enough to speak out.

"Very, well, my lord," she said, drawing in a deep breath, grateful for Violet's staunch if silent support at her side. "I should like to speak to you about Baron Rothborn."

The effect of her words was quite startling. The jovial smile fell away in an instant and the man seemed to age before her eyes.

"What about him?" he asked.

His voice was dull, and she got the sense that he had been waiting for something like this. Jemima hesitated. She had known what she would say to this man's wife, but now, to her husband, she wasn't sure how to begin. He stared at her, hands clenched, and she saw that he was sweating and anxious.

"Please, Miss Fernside, you came all this way with something to say, I beg you do not let your nerve fail you now," he said. He stood a little taller, squared his shoulders. "I have been waiting these many years for the man himself to call me out. I can only wonder why you are here and not him. I know damn well it isn't for lack of courage."

"He doesn't know," Jemima said, realising at once that her suspicions had been correct.

The viscount gave an incredulous laugh and sat down, as though his knees had given out. "Good God. How is that possible?"

Jemima stared at him, realising the man had lived in fear of such an outcome for years. "Since his return from the war, Lord Rothborn has become something of a recluse."

He stared at her, uncomprehending. "I know he doesn't mix in society much, but he was always such a popular chap. I assumed his friends still called upon him."

"No, I don't believe he has allowed anyone close in the past years. He lives alone, he sees no one, and no one see him."

"Yet, you are his friend, *Miss* Fernside?" There was a speculative gleam in his eyes and Jemima flushed, aware of the insinuation, even though there seemed no malice in the question.

"I am," she agreed, very aware of her rigid posture, of her gloved hands clasped demurely in her lap. "I live in the same village as Lord Rothborn and... and we have become friends."

There was a drawn out silence into which she blurted, "He is in love with me, and I with him, but he made a vow to your wife never to marry and... and I wish to ask her to release him from this vow, for he has done nothing wrong. I believe she knows this at heart."

Now she knew the truth, Jemima wanted to tell him his wife was a heartless, faithless jilt, but she suspected this would not come as a surprise to the man before her.

"A vow? What manner of vow?"

Jemima realised she was relieved to discover the viscount knew nothing of his wife's behaviour. For all he appeared to be a wastrel, there was something inherently likable about the man, and she did not wish for him to be a part of Solo's torment any more than he already was.

"You truly don't know?"

He gave a bitter laugh and shook his head. "There is a great deal I do not know about Hyacinth, I assure you."

Jemima nodded, aware of the bitterness of his words. "When Solo—Lord Rothborn—returned from the war to tell your wife her brother was dead, she blamed him for it. She told him she could never marry the man responsible for her brother's death. He took her words very much to heart, as he already blamed himself. Your wife broke his heart, my lord, by giving him this as a reason for jilting him, and as a penance he told her he would never marry, but... but it wasn't the reason she declined him, *was it,* Lord Kline?"

There was a taut silence during which Jemima held her breath, certain they would be thrown out onto the street at any moment.

"The bitch!"

Both she and Violet jumped at his outburst as the viscount surged to his feet.

"I'll bloody kill her!"

Jemima grabbed Violet's hand and the two women stared at each other in horror as Lord Kline ran from the room, his footsteps thundering through the house as he took the stairs two at a time.

"Oh, good heavens!" Jemima exclaimed, hurrying into the hallway where the young butler was dithering.

"Don't just stand there," she implored, as the fellow looked back at her with wide eyes. "*Do* something!"

"Not likely," he said, shaking his head. "More than my life's worth."

"But he said he would kill her!"

The butler snorted. "Aye, not for the first time neither, and I shouldn't blame him if he did."

Jemima was so taken aback by this that for a moment she did not notice the commotion at the top of the stairs, until there was a female shriek of indignation.

"Take your hands off me, you fiend!"

"Damned if I will, Hyacinth," the viscount shouted, towing his wife down the stairs in her nightgown. "You've got some explaining to do."

"Out, now," Violet muttered, grabbing Jemima's hand and heading for the front door.

"Stop them, Jones," the viscount yelled at the butler, who finally moved and stood before the door, blocking their escape.

There was something wild in the viscount's eyes as he dragged his wife before them. "You wanted answers, Miss Fernside. Well, I'd like a few of my own. So let's have them, Hyacinth. What did you tell Rothborn when you broke things off with him? Why does the poor devil believe himself responsible for your fool brother's death?"

Jemima clutched at Violet's hand, watching in abject horror as Lady Kline was thrust before them. She was clearly a beautiful woman, though there were dark circles under her eyes, and her black hair was a tangled mess beneath the lacy bed cap she wore. She glared at her husband, and then turned her attention to Jemima.

"Who wants to know?" she demanded, her sneer marring any beauty and making her look ugly indeed. "Who are you?"

Jemima gathered her courage. She was doing this for Solo, for their future. "I am Lord Rothborn's friend, and I ask you to release him from the promise he made you never to marry. To ask you to look into your heart, if indeed you have one, and to take away the guilt he lives with. I think you have made him suffer enough for something that we all know was not his fault."

Lady Kline snatched her arm from her husband's grip and walked towards Jemima, looking her up and down with contempt. "His *friend*? He must be desperate. I don't know you, so you're not of the *ton*. What are you, a dressmaker, a governess hoping to snare a title?"

Violet surged towards the woman. "Why you little cow—"

Jemima snatched at Violet's hand and shook her head at her before she could strike Lady Kline. She would fight her own battles. Putting her chin up, she stared back at the woman with defiance.

"My uncle was the Earl of Huntington."

It had been a long time since Jemima had used her uncle's name in such a way. He had not been a nice man, and she did not appreciate the association, but needs must.

"Aye, and one of her closest friends is the Duchess of Bedwin, so I'd watch your tongue," Violet added with relish.

Lady Kline gave a snort of disgust, though Jemima knew she could not be faulted for her lineage even though her branch of the family had faded into obscurity through lack of funds and bad marriages.

"What did you do, Hyacinth?" The viscount's voice was full of revulsion and Jemima was truly shocked by the hatred in his eyes as he looked upon his wife. "Lord Rothborn is a good man, one of the best I have ever known. God knows we treated him ill enough, but if what Miss Fernside says is true…. Hell and the devil, I knew you were a cold-hearted bitch, but this is something else. How could you?"

"Barnaby is dead!" she shrieked, flying at her husband in a flurry of lacy bed clothing. She hit him over and over, hysterical now as she screamed at him. "Rothborn promised me he'd keep him safe and he's dead, *dead*! He was the only good thing in my life! The only thing I loved."

The viscount took hold of his wife and gave her a hard shake. "He went to war, Hyacinth! Rothborn tried to stop him. How the devil he kept the fool alive as long as he did, I'll never know. You know he risked his own life more than once to save the bloody idiot because Barnaby told you so. Your brother was a good fellow, but he didn't have the brains he was born with. You know this, Hyacinth, you *know* it! Rothborn could not have saved him. So, not only did you cheat on the fellow while he was fighting for his country, you've saddled him with this guilt all these years? Shame on you."

He let go of her, as though he could not bear to touch her for a moment longer. He strode up and down the corridor, looking like a man on the edge of sanity as he clutched at his hair before turning back to his wife in fury.

"Rothborn was fighting for his own life as the army retreated, and you think him responsible for the fact your brother disobeyed a direct order to halt? I know what Rothborn told you, and I know what other men have told me. The man tried to protect you from the truth, but I shan't. Barnaby put himself and others at risk from his actions. It was a wonder he was the only one to die. Christ, if Rothborn had been there, he'd have been killed too, trying to stop the fool from playing the hero. There was nothing anyone could have done. You will write to Rothborn at once and tell him you beg his forgiveness. You will confess that you were unfaithful, and you can tell him I'll meet him anywhere at any time if he wishes for satisfaction. God knows I'd welcome a bullet to my brain if it meant I could be rid of you."

Lady Kline glared back at him. "I wish he *would* kill you. It would almost make it worthwhile to be free of you, but I won't do it! He still loves me, and I won't have you spoiling that. I should have married him. I wish I had! He was always the better man."

"Oh, but wife, you *will* do as I say this once."

Jemima and Violet stood staring in disbelief as this melodrama unfolded before them. If there was one thing Jemima was heartily glad of, it was that Solo had never married this woman. For all that he had suffered, a lifetime with a wife like this would have been far, far worse.

Violet tugged at her hand and Jemima nodded, edging towards the door. The butler had decided to play least in sight, which Jemima did not blame him for at all. She doubted he was paid well enough to endure such scenes. Husband and wife were still screaming at each other, but Lady Kline turned just as Jemima got her hand on the doorknob.

"How dare you come here, stirring up trouble? I'll make sure everyone knows you're his whore, *Miss* Fernside, and then we'll see what fancy friends you keep."

Jemima took a breath. She had known the risk she took in coming here, knowing from Nate the character of the woman she sought to deal with, and she had been prepared for that. Besides which, once she was ruined, Solo would have no need to keep protecting her reputation. It would be done. So she put up her chin and smiled at Lady Kline.

"I never doubted your riposte, madam, but you see, I am not like you, only faithful when the eyes of your betrothed were upon you. You could not keep your heart for one man, a man who was risking his life to keep you and your friends safe. I pity you for everything you cast aside, for you still don't understand the value of what you lost. I love Lord Rothborn, and I would endure anything to be with him. So, please do tell your vile tales to whomsoever you please, I don't give a damn."

Lady Kline looked like she'd been slapped, but the admiration in Lord Kline's eyes was enough to make Jemima blush.

"Well, well, lucky Rothborn. I do believe he will have the last laugh after all. What I wouldn't give to have married a woman like you."

Jemima watched in astonishment as Lord Kline gave her a deep and respectful bow.

"He is a lucky man, Miss Fernside, and you may rest assured I will do my damndest to make sure everyone knows that, no matter what this vile creature does."

Jemima inclined her head and left the house with as much dignity as she could manage, but, once outside the door, she discovered she was trembling hard. Violet hurried her down to the hansom cab they had paid to wait for them, and bundled her inside.

"Well, Jemima Fernside, I was never prouder in all my life," Violet said, staring at her in awe. "Who would have thought a little slip of a thing like you had so much gumption?"

Jemima gave a shaky laugh, and promptly burst into tears.

Chapter 16

Dear Robert,

I had the most fascinating chat with a Mr Gabriel Knight the other day. He has made significant investment in a proposed railway project, and I must say I was rather impressed with what he has in mind. I think it is just the sort of thing you would find of interest and I cannot help but believe there is a significant opportunity to be had here. I must inform you, however, that on investigation I discover the fellow is not a gentleman and has a dubious reputation as a rake and a libertine. Despite this, I believe his instinct for finance is not to be sneered at. All those who have worked with him report that he is scrupulous in his business dealings. At the risk of you thinking me vulgar, I must point out he's rich as Croesus from his own endeavours. He needs a man like you to help get this project off the ground, though, and I think it certainly worth your time to hear him out.

You did say you wished to renovate the property in Hampshire, and if it is in the shocking state, I suspect it must be, that will take a pretty penny to achieve.

—Excerpt of a letter from Lord Fitzwalter to his nephew, His Grace, The Duke of Bedwin.

24th February 1815. Mitcham Priory, Sussex.

"Oh, thank goodness," Mrs Norrell said on opening the door to Jemima. "Honestly, if it wasn't that I know he's suffering himself, I'd have clobbered him with the skillet by now, as God is my witness."

"Oh, dear," Jemima said, hurrying inside and handing over her pelisse and bonnet. "Bessie said he'd called twice and wasn't very happy."

"Serves him right," the housekeeper said in a low voice, shaking her head. "Blithering idiot."

On impulse, Jemima gave the woman a hug, touched by her words. She knew in what high regard Mrs Norrell held Solo.

"He's doing what he thinks is right, Martha. Protecting me."

Martha nodded and hugged her back.

"I know. I just wish he'd…." She sighed and made a helpless gesture. "He was happy for a little while there, and it was so good to see."

"I'm not giving up," Jemima said, though she was not looking forward to speaking to Solo. She wanted to set him free, but to do that, she had to tell him the truth.

Martha returned a warm smile. "I'm glad. He needs you. Go on in, you'll find him in his study. I think you must know the way by now, and it will be a nice surprise for him."

Jemima dithered in the grand entrance hall for a few moments after Martha had left her, gathering her courage before she could force herself to walk to Solo's study and knock.

To Bed the Baron

The terse command to come in did not make her feel better, but she opened the door and went in, and was gratified by the change in Solo's demeanour as he saw her.

"Jemima!"

He surged to his feet, and had crossed half the room before he checked himself and paused. Jemima forced herself not to be hurt by his actions, knowing his instinct had been to run to her and take her in his arms. He was trying to do right by her, she knew that.

"You look well, Miss Fernside," he said, and it was the hardest thing not to howl with frustration at his formality.

Well, he could be as formal as he wanted, Jemima was having none of it.

"Good morning to you, Solo. You do not look well, my love. Are you not sleeping?"

He let out a breath of frustration.

"You ought not—"

"Oh, piffle," she cried impatiently. "You do as you wish, Solo, but I won't pretend my feelings away, nor what has passed between us, certainly not when we are alone."

He frowned at her and she didn't know whether he wanted to change his mind or argue with her. In the end, he did neither.

"Where did you go?" he asked.

He looked pale and worried, and she hated how unhappy he was. Well, she would change that, she just had to be brave a little longer.

"Did you go to see Mr Briggs?" he demanded when she didn't respond at once.

Jemima stared at him, perplexed. Why on earth would he think...?

"Oh, Solo," she said sadly as she realised. Despite his disapproving glare, she walked straight up to him and took his hands. "Of course not. I promised to stay, did I not? I'm not giving up that easily, I'm afraid."

He let out a breath and squeezed her hands tight for a moment before releasing them. Her heart ached as he turned away and walked back to the window.

"I'm a selfish devil, I know that, but I'm glad all the same. More than I can say."

"You don't have a selfish bone in your body, Solo," Jemima said, feeling a wave of anger for all he had been forced to suffer. "But I have. That's why I'm here. I'm not prepared to live like this, as your friend, when we both know there is far more than friendship between us."

He swung around, panic in his eyes. "But you... you just said—"

"And I meant it." She spoke over him, forcing herself to get the words out, to reveal what she'd done. "I won't share you, though, Solo, and I am. I'm sharing you with ghosts and a burden of guilt which you do not deserve, and that needs to stop. Which is why I called upon Lady Kline."

The silence that fell upon the room was so charged all the hairs on the back of Jemima's neck stood on end.

"You did what?" His voice was barely audible, disbelieving, and Jemima put her chin up.

"I had a very interesting conversation with Lord and Lady Kline, Solo. Lord Kline was especially surprised to discover the promise you made his wife never to marry, bearing in mind he knows full well you were not responsible for her brother's death, and... and that he had been carrying on an affair with your fiancée for some months before you were injured."

Jemima could not breathe. She could only stare at Solo, and watch the impact her words had. He flinched as though she'd struck him, and then the colour leached from his face only to be swiftly replaced by a dull red flush.

"Get out."

He was breathing hard, though he didn't look at her, didn't move a muscle.

"Solo...."

"*Get out!*"

She had never heard him shout before, not like this, not with such rage.

Though her heart was slamming in her chest, tears prickling at her eyes, she stood her ground.

"No. I don't doubt you don't wish to hear this, and I am sorry for it, but I won't let you sacrifice our future at that awful woman's altar. Lord Kline has paid a heavy price for his betrayal. If you could see them, Solo, see what kind of creature—"

"Enough!"

Jemima closed her mouth, unable to stop the tears now, though she tried, clenching her jaw to hold onto some semblance of calm.

"You think this makes it better? You think I wish my memories tainted by... by salacious gossip?"

"It is not gossip! Her husband told me himself, she admitted to it!"

"I don't want to hear this...." Solo strode to the door, leaning heavily on his cane. "I had thought better of you, Miss Fernside, than to go about dragging up the past. You disappoint me."

He yanked the door open and walked through it, leaving her alone.

With fury and disbelief, Jemima charged after him.

"Dragging up the past?" she threw at him incredulously. "*Me?* The only place it's possible to be with you is in the past, because that is where you've buried yourself. The ghosts don't haunt you, Solo, you haunt them because you are too guilty to live or to love in the here and now. Well, the guilt is not yours to bear, so you must let it go or let it destroy you, but if you ignore the truth, I shall not stand around and watch you do it! I love you too much to see you do that to yourself."

She turned on her heel and ran for the front door, not bothering to call for Mrs Norrell to bring her coat and bonnet before she flung it open, tears streaming down her face. Too late, she saw Mrs Granger and her two daughters on the steps of The Priory. Had they heard what she'd said? Even if they had not, her tears and distress were telling enough. There was nothing to be done now. She had ruined everything, ruined herself for nothing, and all she could do now was endure the outcome. She ran past them and hurried home, slamming the cottage door and wishing she was a million miles away from this place and these people.

***

It took Solo precisely three minutes to realise he'd made an error in judgement, yet pride held him immobile. He didn't know what to think, how to feel, such were the tumult of emotions rioting through him.

He could not believe Jemima had taken matters into her own hands and gone to face Lord and Lady Kline all alone. A mixture of pride and mortification assailed him. That she would do such a thing for him touched his heart, yet his pride revolted at Lord and Lady Kline believing he had sent a woman on his behalf, or that they might think he had been pining away all these years for Hyacinth, when that was far from the truth. Yes, he'd had his heart broken, but it had long since mended. With the benefit of hindsight, he knew that he and Hyacinth would have been an ill match. She had always been lively and vivacious, and desperate to find entertainment at every moment of the day. He would have found that wearying soon enough, and he knew she would have found him dull.

Yet, to discover she had been unfaithful hurt him, for he had believed his memories of that time to be something lovely and untarnished, before the war had tainted everything, including him. To discover that too had been an illusion…. Depression threatened to drown him, to smother him with its weight, but he shook it off. He would have the truth, by God, and he'd show them he did not need a woman to stand for him. Relieved to have a purpose to occupy his mind, he called for his carriage to be readied at once, and found Mrs Norrell stomping away from the front door in an absolute fury.

"Well, I hope you're proud of yourself," she snapped, her anger so blatant that Solo took an involuntary step back.

"This is none of your business," he began, too impatient to do what he must to endure a lecture from his housekeeper, even if he suspected he deserved one.

Mrs Norrell made a sound of disgust. "Oh, well, that's all right, then, as it is none of the village's business, either, but everyone will know of your affair with Miss Fernside by teatime. You've ruined that girl, my lord, and you'd better make it right or you can expect to receive my notice by the end of the week."

With that, she stalked off, slamming the kitchen door with considerable force before he could ask what the devil she was on about.

Solo shook his head. He did not have time to deal with Mrs Norrell's tantrum. He would see Jemima on his return, once he had sorted things out for himself, and then…Then they would see what they could salvage from this sorry mess.

***

"No, you will not run away."

Violet crossed her arms over her chest and shook her head so vigorously that her curls bounced.

"B-But I've ruined everything," Jemima sobbed. "I ought not to have interfered. I've wounded his blessed pride and now he won't w-want to see me again and t-that awful w-woman, Mrs Granger, she saw—"

"Stuff and nonsense." Violet made an unladylike sound of contempt and poured two large glasses of brandy, pressing one firmly into Jemima's hand. "Drink that and listen up, my girl. Yes, that man has taken a blow to his pride and he's still smarting, but he'll come around soon enough. You knew full well he'd not be pleased to hear his fiancée had played him for a fool." She tsked and shook her head, giving Jemima a pitying look. "Silly goose. Of course he went off in a temper, but he'll come back again too, just you wait and see. I've been playing this game far more years than I like to contemplate, and I know what I'm about, so you just sit tight. This is no time for going off half-cocked and making the poor fellow go charging about the countryside looking for you, once he comes to his senses."

Jemima gave her nose a vigorous blow and took a sip of the brandy.

"You really think so?" she asked, hating the reedy, uncertain quality to her voice.

Violet rolled her eyes. "I do. Honestly, if only I'd known what I know now at your age," she lamented before sitting down and taking Jemima's hand. "You drink that and take yourself off for a nice nap, you look done in. Then we'll have a quiet evening and a good dinner, and you'll feel much more the thing. I'll get Bessie to put out your best dress and do your hair so you look like a queen, and you'll be ready to face the silly fellow when he comes running back to lay his heart at your feet."

Jemima frowned. No matter how much she wanted to believe Violet was right—it was true that she had a deal more experience of men, after all—she could not believe Solo would calm down so quickly, let alone forgive her with such ease. She'd been a fool to imagine she could manage his temper. She'd not seen it before this last encounter, not really. He'd been so terribly angry, and she regretted having brought him pain. It had been selfish of her too, for she was manoeuvring things so that he could marry her, and if he'd wanted to badly enough... still, there was no point in thinking of such things. Not now. The least she could do was face him one last time before she left, and she could not stay. Bessie had gone down to the village just hours after Jemima's scene with Solo, and had returned to confirm that the vile Mrs Granger had lost no time in spreading the gossip. By now, the whole of Mitcham Village would know that Jemima had fled The Priory in tears, with no hat nor coat, and it was obvious what they would make from that pretty scene. She had burned her boats and would only bring Solo the gossip he had tried so hard to avoid. She would have to leave, for both their sakes. Though she would have endured anything to be with him if he loved her and wanted her close, to be vilified without it... no, that was too much to endure.

***

24th February 1815. Lingfield Manor, Edenbridge, Kent.

"I'm so sorry I can't go with you," Alice lamented as she gazed at the sunny afternoon outside the parlour window. "But a waddle about the garden is all I can manage now. The idea of walking miles across the countryside carrying this...."

She looked down ruefully at her swollen belly, and Matilda laughed.

"Don't be silly. As much as I shall miss your company, I am perfectly content to go alone, but are you certain you do not wish me to stay? I will happily do so if you prefer."

Alice rolled her eyes. "Certainly not, I am going to finish my novel," she said, waving her copy of *Castle Rackrent* at Matilda defiantly.

Matilda snorted as she tied the ribbons on her bonnet. "You mean you will pretend to read two pages, and then have a nice little doze."

"Well, honestly, you are the worst kind of friend. How dare you see through my cunning plan!" Alice huffed and folded her arms, though her eyes danced with amusement.

"Your secret is safe with me," Matilda whispered, kissing the top of her friend's head and leaving her to put her feet up and nap in peace.

Matilda strode out, enjoying the tentative caress of the sun upon her face. The day was chilly, but that touch of warmth on her skin was like a balm after so many weeks of cold. It was a promise that spring was around the corner, a promise that was illustrated by a few intrepid daffodils, blooming early, enticed by the last few mild days and a bright blue sky. By the time she reached the gates to the beautiful gardens that surrounded Hever Castle, her cheeks were glowing, and she allowed herself to slow her steps and simply to enjoy her surroundings.

As she approached the castle itself, she noticed a very fine carriage drawn up outside with four magnificent grey horses. Her heart sped a little as she realised it was familiar.

"Miss Hunt!"

A childish squeal of delight rang out and, a moment later, Matilda laughed as she saw Phoebe Barrington running full pelt towards her.

"Phoebe, slow down!"

That voice had Matilda's head snapping up even as Miss Barrington barrelled into her, throwing her arms about Matilda. The impressive, romantically lovely castle that had stood for so many years might as well not have existed for all she could see of it. Montagu was there, immaculate and precise as always, and that was all she could focus on. His tall, lean figure commanded attention, the sun glinting on his pale golden hair. Angel or devil, she wondered. He was so beautiful her heart sang *angel* without a second thought, but she was not foolish enough to judge by appearances.

He is the kind of man who can do something quite unforgivable, and then beguile you into forgiving him.

His uncle had said that of him, had said his handsome face hid a sick and twisted nature. Matilda felt a shiver of misgiving but held Montagu's gaze. His eyes were guarded as they always were, hiding his thoughts, keeping the truth from her. Still she stared, unable to tear her eyes away as he watched her from across the courtyard. Matilda smiled, trusting her own instincts even though she had been wrong before, unable to stop herself from finding happiness in seeing him again, before returning her attention to Phoebe. The little girl stared up at her, clutching her about the waist, eyes bright with excitement. Her bonnet had fallen off her head and hung from her neck by the ribbons.

"Good afternoon, Miss Hunt. My uncle said he had a surprise for me, but I did not realise it was you. I am so happy it is."

Matilda laughed, watching surreptitiously as Montagu spoke a few words to the butler who had emerged from the castle.

"I rather think a visit to the castle was your surprise," she said, touched that Phoebe was so pleased to see her.

"Oh, pooh, who cares about a musty old castle? I'd much rather see you."

"You cannot argue with that, Miss Hunt."

Matilda tried in vain to stop her heart thrashing about in her chest like a landed fish as Montagu approached them. Though she knew this was dangerous, knew it was a terrible idea, whatever the truth of the man before her, she could not regret it. When she had mentioned her walks about the castle grounds, she had known full well what she was doing, so there was little point in lamenting the fact that Montagu had acted as she had known he would.

"I do not care to argue," she said, hardly able to hold his gaze she was suddenly so nervous. "I am flattered beyond reason, I assure you."

"Can we see the castle now, Uncle?" Phoebe demanded, tugging at his hand.

Montagu raised an eyebrow at his niece. "I am not a bell pull, child, so please desist your infernal yanking on my arm, and I thought you had proclaimed the castle musty and uninteresting?"

"Oh no, only in comparison to Miss Hunt," Phoebe replied with perfect gravity.

Matilda stifled a laugh as Montagu's lips twitched.

"I cannot fault your conclusion, Phoebe. She *is* far more interesting than a castle. Well, I suppose I might allow a young lady to visit the castle with me, but not a hoyden."

He flicked at her tumbled bonnet with a negligent hand, one eyebrow quirking.

Phoebe gave a long-suffering sigh and rammed her bonnet back on her head, redoing the bow with a scowl of concentration.

"There!" she said, folding her arms and glaring at Montagu.

Montagu returned a pained expression. "Well, I suppose it is an improvement, of sorts. I dare not hope for more. Come along."

Matilda watched, enchanted as Montagu held out his gloved hand and Phoebe took it, grinning at him with delight. Then Phoebe turned and held out her free hand to Matilda.

"Come along, Miss Hunt."

"Yes, Miss Hunt," Montagu replied, his cool gaze meeting Matilda's, the challenge in them clear. "Come along. I would not like you to miss the tour."

She took Phoebe's hand, feeling a burst of pure joy as the little girl's fingers curled about her own.

"Oh, this is perfect," Phoebe exclaimed, tugging both of them at once, hurrying them over the drawbridge and into the castle.

Matilda did not dare look at the marquess, did not dare consider the dangerous happiness uncoiling in her chest, or that she wanted to agree with Phoebe's words all too readily. It was perfect.

Chapter 17

Lady Helena Adolphus,

It seems that I must thank you for arranging the meeting with Lord Fitzwalter for me. From our conversation, I believe it was a success and he will speak to the duke. I am hopeful that your brother will recognise the extraordinary opportunity he is being offered.

I am in your debt.

—Excerpt of a letter from Mr Gabriel Knight to Lady Helena Adolphus.

24th February 1815. Hans Place, Hans Town, London.

Solo scowled at the settee before him as though it had done him a personal affront. When Mr Briggs had given him this address as the present residence of Lord and Lady Kline, he had already been shocked. The viscount, as Solo remembered him, had been a vastly wealthy, dashing young buck, exactly the kind of fellow he had expected to win Hyacinth's hand. That she had agreed to marry a mere baron had surprised no one more than him. At that time, Hyacinth had been the height of fashion, a lavishly dressed leader of society. So to come here now, and discover the furniture—what little there was of it—in dire need of updating....

He shook his head. That was none of his affair. All he wanted was to uncover what had been said here, what exactly Jemima had discovered. Impatience gnawed at him. Though he'd been informed that Lady Kline was in and would see him, he'd been kicking his heels for almost half an hour now. He had just resolved to seek out the butler and enquire if there was a problem when the door opened.

"Solo! Oh, my darling...."

Solo stiffened as Hyacinth flew across the room, throwing herself into his arms in a flurry of silk and lace. She clutched at his jacket, sobbing against his chest, and Solo stared down at her with alarm and consternation, not having the least idea what to do with her.

"Hyacinth," he said, after bearing the indignity for as long as he could. "Hyacinth, please. Whatever is the matter?"

He took hold of her wrists and gently pushed her away from him.

"Oh, how can you say that, my love? Does your heart not remember all that we were to each other?"

She stared up at him, her dark eyes soft and tearstained, her lovely face not so very different from how he remembered her. The seven years since they'd parted had been kind.

"You are a married woman now, Lady Kline," he said firmly, relieved to discover that his heart did not in fact remember, or at least, it remembered, but it no longer regretted.

Indeed, all he felt was a measure of distaste for such an alarming show of emotion over something that had ended a long time ago.

"Oh!" Hyacinth flounced away from him, holding her hands over her heart. "You are still angry with me, but I have suffered too, Solo. My sorrow would not allow me to marry you, but my heart...." She cast a look over her shoulder at him from under thick dark lashes. "My heart has ever been yours."

Solo watched her and discovered he felt very much like he was being treated to a performance. He remembered that coquettish look. It was one he'd often seen during their courtship, usually if she was being denied something she wanted. Yet he'd never viewed it so dispassionately before. How strange, that this woman who had made him wild with desire and jealousy now seemed only a stranger acting a part. Had she been acting then, too? Had none of it been real for her?

"It would seem there is a deal of debate about that fact," he said, finding himself amused by the flash of anger in her eyes.

It was quickly hidden, the heartbroken ingénue reappearing with startling speed, but he had seen, and he knew in that moment that all Jemima had told him had been true.

"Your little friend has been telling tales," she lamented, eyes cast down. "Have you forgotten me, thrown me over for that dull little creature, when I have loved you all these years?"

"Yes, I have forgotten you," Solo said, finding he was rather enjoying himself. "And she's not the least bit dull. In fact, she's rather extraordinary. I still cannot believe she came here all alone just to get me to see sense."

"Sense?" Hyacinth repeated, her indignation apparent. "You mean to say you can forget my brother, forget what you did? You broke your promise to me! He's dead, is he not?"

A stab of pain lanced through his chest at her words and Solo knew he would never be entirely free of the guilt he felt over Barnaby's death. It had not been his fault, though. The thought was a new one, one he had dared not consider before, too weighed down by depression to allow himself such a glimmer of hope. If he had not been injured, perhaps he could have saved Barnaby, but the injury had been unavoidable and what followed had been fate. Barnaby had ever been a romantic fool, too eager for glory to stop and think about his own safety, let alone that of his men.

Solo could see that now in a way he had not seen it before. He still hated that his career had ended too early, that the war had continued without him, and so many of his friends and colleagues had been lost, but it could not have been helped. It was not within his power to change any of that. Life dealt you the cards, and you had to play the game as best you could. He'd been sitting out for far too long, too afraid his cards had no value, his hand not worth the trouble of playing, but he'd been wrong, terribly wrong.

Suddenly, he was seized with the desire to see Jemima.

Hyacinth flew at him, her hands grasping the lapels of his coat. "Do you mean to stand there and tell me that means nothing to you? That *I* mean nothing to you?"

The door opened and Viscount Kline entered the room. He paused for a moment, taking in the picture before him.

"Hyacinth, put the poor man down. You're making a scene."

"Oh, you've not begun to see a scene," Hyacinth sneered at her husband, and the pretty mask she wore so well fell away.

Solo could see something cold and calculating that made him shiver. Once again, he took hold of her wrists, moving her away from him.

"I will never forget your brother, Hyacinth. Barnaby was my dear friend and I shall always mourn his loss, but I did not die that day, and I am tired of living as though I did. I came to tell you I bear neither of you any ill will for whatever passed between you whilst we were engaged, but neither do I feel the need to keep my vow to never marry."

"You faithless wretch!"

Lord Kline burst out laughing at his wife's heartfelt exclamation.

"Oh, ho, that's a good one, Hyacinth" he said, almost doubling over with mirth. "Give us the waterworks next. She's dashed good at them, Rothborn, just watch."

"I hate you!" his wife cried with passion, before turning to glare at Solo. "Both of you!"

She ran from the room in a flurry of skirts and lace, and Solo found himself alone with Viscount Kline. The humour on the man's face evaporated, and Solo hardly recognised the fellow he'd known. He looked older, weary and jaded. Would he have looked like that if he'd married Hyacinth?

"I shouldn't blame you if you called me out. I know I deserve it," Kline said, his expression bleak.

Solo shook his head, contemplating the scene he'd just witnessed. He suspected such scenes were not unusual in this house. "I think perhaps you've suffered enough."

Kline gave a bark of laughter, which might have been the least happy sound Solo had ever heard.

"You have no idea, but believe me when I tell you, you are a lucky man. Your Miss Fernside gave us what for, I can tell you. Held her head up like a duchess and told us what she thought of us. Didn't turn a hair when Hyacinth said she'd ruin her, either. My wife, the little darling, threatened to tell the entire *ton* Miss Fernside was your whore, and do you know what she said?"

Solo felt his blood run cold, realising just what Jemima had been subjected to here, and how he'd treated her by way of thanks.

The viscount kept talking, unaware of everything Solo was feeling. "She said she pitied Hyacinth for not understanding the value of what she'd lost, that she loved you and would endure anything to be with you. Miss Fernside looked Lady Kline in the eyes and invited her to tell her vile tales to whomsoever she pleased, because she didn't give a damn."

Solo felt his throat grow tight. She had said that she'd come here for him, and risked everything for him, and he had thrown it all back in her face. He looked up as the viscount approached him, his expression grave.

"I don't know what the past years have been like for you, Rothborn, but I know I'd swap with you in a heartbeat. If you have an ounce of sense, you'll forget you ever knew Hyacinth and marry your Miss Fernside before she can get away from you."

"Yes," Solo said, discovering his voice was a little unsteady. "Yes, I believe I shall do just that."

He held out his hand to the viscount, who looked rather surprised but shook it warmly.

"Thank you," Solo said, smiling and feeling as if a weight had been lifted from him for the first time in almost a decade.

"Don't thank me, the lord knows I deserve nothing more than perdition," Kline replied drily. "But I think you know well enough where your gratitude lies. Give Miss Fernside my kindest regards, Lord Rothborn. I am privileged to have met her."

***

24th February 1815. Hever Castle, Edenbridge, Kent.

"Why did Anne Boleyn get her head cut off?"

Matilda frowned at Phoebe, wondering how best to answer that question. Montagu was on the other side of what had been the Boleyn's private parlour in the west wing of the castle. The atmosphere was heavy with history and Matilda had a sudden surge of melancholy, imagining Anne Boleyn as a little girl much like Phoebe, running in and out of these rooms with no idea of what her future held in store.

"I'm not sure we will ever know for certain," she said, aware that Phoebe was a child, albeit a bright one. "But she played a dangerous game for high stakes. She became queen, but there was a dreadful price to pay for that. I do not know if she became greedy and plotted treason, as history would have us believe, or if a powerful man wronged her simply because he could."

"She was wronged. She became a pawn in Thomas Cromwell's game, and she died for it."

Matilda looked around at Montagu in surprise. "You know this?"

Montagu shook his head. "No. It is only my opinion, but there is evidence of a sort, if one cares to look for it."

"What evidence?" Matilda demanded, fascinated.

The marquess moved to the window and looked out. "A letter to Charles V from Eustace Chapuys. Chapuys told Charles that Cromwell had said *il se mist a fantasier et conspirer le dict affaire*, which has been translated as 'he set himself to devise and conspire the said affair,' suggesting that Cromwell plotted against Anne."

"Good heavens," Matilda said, her hand going involuntarily to her throat. "I had no idea."

Montagu shrugged. "It is only a theory." He looked up to see her clutching at her neck, and the ghost of a smile touched his lips. "I think you are safe from the axe, Miss Hunt."

She flushed and returned her attention to the painting she had been studying.

"I'm famished," Phoebe complained, whose enthusiasm for the castle was waning.

"You astonish me," Montagu replied, tweaking at the ribbons on the little girl's bonnet. "Anyone would think you did not consume enough to keep Wellington's army provisioned for a week when you broke your fast this morning."

Phoebe laughed and threw her arms about him, staring up beseechingly.

"Unnnncle..." she whined, drawing the word out.

Montagu tutted, though the warmth in those usually cold eyes was evident. "I believe Mrs Appleton may have provided a basket...."

Phoebe gave a yelp of delight and ran from the room before Montagu had even finished speaking. He sighed.

"She's delightful," Matilda said, unable to hide her smile.

Montagu winced, blond brows furrowing as Phoebe's footsteps thundered away from them, but he appeared pleased by the comment. "I think so, but I'm afraid I let her get away with murder. Heaven alone knows what kind of lady she'll grow up to be. I shall have to pay some poor fellow to marry her the moment she comes out. I shudder to contemplate it."

Matilda laughed, knowing he was joking even though she suspected he worried about such things more than a little. "I think she will be happy and confident, knowing she has the world at her feet and an uncle ready to slay dragons for her if needs be."

Montagu made a soft sound of amusement as he looked back out of the window. His expression was serious, though, and it occurred to her that she rarely saw him smile, let alone laugh. Those gentler expressions were seldom evident at all, but most often coaxed from him by his little niece. He was so rigidly controlled, never letting his guard fall. She knew it was rare for him to even bother with polite conversation, which she suspected he despised. Matilda believed she was one of the few people to whom he ever spoke candidly, and perhaps only because her opinion did not matter to the wider world. That was a lowering thought.

"And who slays your dragons, Miss Hunt?"

Matilda started at the question, remembering what she had said about Phoebe. Though she watched him closely, he did not turn back to her, his attention fixed on a spot in the far distance. There was no clue as to his feelings about the question, or the answer, yet he *had* asked.

"Myself, when I am able, but otherwise, my brother, I suppose. Where he can."

Montagu nodded, as if he'd assumed as much. He turned to face her, his gaze as uncompromisingly direct as it always was. "It is disheartening to know I am the dragon of the piece. I always fancied myself the hero in such stories when I was a boy. I would have seen myself as your knight in shining armour, I'm sure, but then the nonsense we believe as children rarely has any place in reality, does it?"

There was a cold edge to the words that troubled Matilda, and she could not help but wonder what kind of boy he had been.

My word, you should have seen him as a boy, the face of an angel. It was impossible to believe him capable of the slightest wrongdoing, or to refuse him anything, and so I didn't, and now you suffer the results of my foolishness.

His uncle's words came back to her and she pushed them away, unsettled. She would not judge him on another man's say so. Not even one who purported to be protecting her from danger. His uncle had not gained her trust, but to some extent Montagu had, a little at least.

"It is not nonsense to dream, my lord. Indeed, I believe the dreams we have as children are forgotten at our peril, for they are the hopes of our more innocent selves," Matilda replied, taken aback by the bitterness of his words. "It is only a danger when we forget the difference between dreams and reality."

The briefest flash of that elusive smile barely touched his lips and yet it stole her breath, all the more powerful for its exclusivity.

"I am always surprised to discover how romantic you are, Miss Hunt, even after all you have endured."

"Endured?" she exclaimed, flushing and turning away from him, unsettled by her reaction to the smile, to his words. "Hardly that. I am most fortunate, and have an abundance of friends and family who care for me. I am not a desperate case, I assure you."

Matilda busied herself with studying the fine craftsmanship of the carving in the intricate panelling, needing a moment to gather herself. She dared a glance back at him to see him tug at the cuffs of his shirt, first one, then the other, it seemed an oddly unconscious gesture from a man who seemed to never so much as arch an eyebrow without considering it first. He caught her watching him and stiffened. It was some time before he replied.

"And yet your dreams were stolen from you, first by your father, and then by me."

"You give yourself too much credit, I'm sure."

He did arch an eyebrow at that, every bit of his cool, aristocratic armour in evidence.

"*Really?*" he said, his incredulity blatant. "You've blamed me for your position many times before now. Rightly, I suppose. Have we rewritten history, or are you pretending it is no longer true?"

Matilda stared at him, confused, not knowing what she did mean, for he was correct. She had blamed him. He *was* to blame, and yet she knew now he could not have acted any other way. He could have been kinder certainly, he might have tried to mitigate the situation, but as he'd told her once, if he'd tried to protect her the people who had believed her innocent of wrongdoing might then have questioned it. For it would have been entirely out of character. Why would the cold Marquess of Montagu seek to protect her unless there had been an affair? It had taken her some time to see the truth behind those words, but there was truth all the same. No. He could not have done differently.

"No," she said. "Nothing has changed except my understanding of you. I ought not have been there that night, despite the wretched circumstances. I knew it then and I know it now. My father and my brother share their portion of blame, but I have long since forgiven them. You were needlessly cruel, but you owed me nothing and I assure you I did not expect you to marry me to make things right. I never have been and never will be the kind of woman you must wed."

She said it for her own benefit as much as because it was true, reminding herself of the gulf between them, and of the danger. As she watched his reaction to her words, he opened his mouth to speak and then stopped. His jaw was tight as he turned away from her, his face closed down. It seemed a long time before he spoke again, but she could not fill the void, conscious that he was on the verge of telling the truth, wanting desperately to hear it.

"I have tried these many months to get closer to you, to change your mind, to stop you from despising me, and now...."

Once again, he stopped, and she could sense the fierce tension within him, aware that he was warring with himself, with what he would let himself say. She longed for something that might reveal a glimmer of his true feelings. Suddenly she wanted to tell him she understood how difficult it was, but whatever battle had been fought, Matilda felt she had lost as he let out a breath and shook his head.

"We had best find Phoebe before she makes herself sick."

"Montagu...."

Before she could think better of it, Matilda had reached out and taken his hand. He stilled utterly, staring at her gloved fingers curved around his. Whatever she had been about to say she could not remember, the words dying in her throat, her attention consumed by the warmth of his hand as it permeated the fabric separating their skin. She ought never to have touched him. The air between them seemed to shimmer, like the haze that made the world shift and distort on an unusually hot day. She only realised she was holding her breath when he spoke, his hand firming around her own.

"I wish I had not stolen your dreams, Matilda," he said, his voice low, before lifting his silver gaze to hers. "But as they *are* lost to you, I give you fair warning, I will do all I can to replace them with my own."

"I know," she said, astonished she could speak at all when her breath was trapped in her lungs. He was so near, and her heart and body ached with the desire to close the gap between them. Fear licked at her senses as she realised just how dangerous this was.

"I dream of you."

"Don't," she said, suddenly terribly afraid, afraid not only of how little she really knew of this man, but of how much she might risk to discover more.

"I wish I could stop. Order me to stop, Miss Hunt," he demanded, his expression intent as he stared into her eyes. "I thought that I had begun this game, that I knew the rules, but I have forgotten how to play, or perhaps the rules are changing before I can learn the new ones. Is it you rewriting them, I wonder, or is it fate pulling our strings?"

Matilda shook her head, not knowing what to say, unable to believe he felt as out of control as she did whenever he was near.

"I am as helpless to stop it as I believe you are," he continued, as he took a step closer to her, the fraying edge to his words making her believe he meant it, as unlikely as that seemed.

He was always in control, never made a move, said a word without intent, and yet….

"I was a fool to tell you I would be here," Matilda exclaimed, knowing she had only made things a thousand times worse. If he was indeed playing outside the rules they had both known existed, then being alone with him was beyond dangerous. "There is no future for us and there is no point in pretending otherwise. It is foolish to dream of something that can never happen. It can only lead to misery."

"You just told me our dreams are not nonsense, that we must hold on to them," he countered, his grip on her hand growing tighter.

She shook her head, desperate now, needing to escape the desire in his eyes, the longing which echoed in her own heart. If she stayed any longer, she would reach for him.

"I said we should remember childish dreams, but not confuse them with reality."

"All days are nights to see till I see thee, and nights bright days when dreams do show me thee."

Matilda gave a startled laugh, a little hysterical at such romantic words, touched and dreadfully shaken. Her eyes filled with tears even though she knew she was a fool. He was closing the trap he had laid from the start, nothing more.

"Oh, a Shakespearean sonnet? *Truly*? You do not play fair, my lord." She tried to make the words light-hearted and amused, but they rang out nervous and agitated.

"If I play, I play to win."

"I am not a trophy to be put in a cabinet," she protested, trying to hold onto the indignation she felt, to find the will to tug her hand free of his, to put some distance between them, but she was caught in the silver of his gaze, trapped there with him.

"I would not confine you, Matilda. I would never keep you in a cage. I would set you free, if you would only let me."

"And what of your wife?" she demanded, remembering exactly what it was she was being offered here.

A flash of anger showed in his eyes and he shook his head. "My wife will know what is her affair, and what is not. Our kind do not marry for love. You *know* this. It is business, land and power and money. Do not pretend otherwise."

"Yet, you will go to her bed, she will have your children."

Yes, she thought, *remember that. Spell it out so there can be no mistake, no pretence of romance when it is nothing but a sordid deception.*

"Until I have my heirs, of course."

Cold words, no softening to remove the sting, simply the truth. Reality, not dreams.

Matilda nodded, glad for the reminder, the sharp sting of realism. She would rather die than know he spent his nights with another, see another woman have the children she ached for. Even if she could bear all of that for the chance to be with him, everyone knew his opinion of siring bastards. The Barringtons were known for their rigid morality, for despising those who sired children outside of the marriage bed. He would not willingly give her the babies she longed for, and if they arrived as babies were wont to do, she could not be certain he would acknowledge them. *If* he acknowledged them they'd have a chance in society, but if not... She tugged her hand free. "I should be getting back. Everyone will wonder where I have gone. Good afternoon, my lord."

"Matilda, don't go...."

She ignored his call, hurrying away from him, seeing nothing of her surroundings until she was outside, drawing in lungfuls of clean, cold air as if she could purge herself of heat and desire and foolish dreams.

"Miss Hunt, you aren't leaving?"

Matilda forced herself to appear calm, to put a smile on her face and hold her hands out to Phoebe. "Yes, dear. I had no idea I was to get such a lovely tour of the castle. I only came out for a walk, and my family will wonder where I am if I don't return soon."

The little girl's face fell, and Matilda felt her heart clench. They ought not to use Phoebe as chaperone. She ought not be involved in this dreadful game of cat and mouse, no matter how much Matilda wished to see her, wished to be her friend. She could so easily love this funny, endearing child, but there was no possibility for her to do that. While her Uncle Monty wanted to make Matilda his mistress, there could be no friendship between them and, if he ever succeeded, Phoebe would be lost to her. It would not be at all proper for her to know her uncle's paramour. Matilda battled away the tears that threatened and wiped a little smear of jam from the girl's mouth with a finger.

"Was it a nice cake?"

"Lovely," Phoebe said wistfully before giving Matilda a fierce hug. "Can I see you again?"

"I... I don't know," Matilda said, not wanting to deny her anything, but not wanting to lie. "Your uncle is a busy man, and I doubt I shall see him again for a while."

"I wish you could come and stay with us at Dern, and I don't care if I'm not supposed to say so." Phoebe stepped away from Matilda and folded her arms, her pretty face mutinous. "I *do* wish it. I want to invite you. I *am* inviting you and I shan't take it back, no matter if he scolds me for it. Uncle has invited lots of my friends to keep me company, but he has no friends, he's always alone. You don't want him to be alone all the time, do you, Miss Hunt? It can't be good for a person to be always by themselves?"

Phoebe reached out and took Matilda's hands, pleading in her eyes. Matilda stared back at her, speechless. How could she possibly answer?

"I'm afraid grown-ups have a lot of silly rules which are nonetheless very important, Phoebe," she said gently. "And as much as I would love to visit you, I really cannot do so. It would get me into a lot of trouble, you see. And I'm sure your uncle isn't always alone. I expect you have an army of servants, and no doubt he sees people after you have gone to bed. Just because you don't see them, does not mean he does not have visitors or go out to socialise. I have seen him many times in town, at parties and balls."

"Only if you will be there, I expect," Phoebe said dully. "You're right. Grown-ups are stupid. I'm sure you are both happier when you see each other. He looks forward to seeing you, I can tell, and... and you do like him, a little at least, don't you? He's really very kind, and not nearly so stern and proud as he seems. He hardly ever scolds me. Not properly, anyway."

It was the hardest thing to keep her heart in check, to remind herself that Phoebe was seeing the world through the eyes of a child. She did not understand, could not comprehend the truth, the complexities of the world and adult emotions. Yet Matilda's foolish heart yearned to believe and wanted so much to tell the girl that she liked her uncle very, very much, and she would visit in a heartbeat and ensure he was never alone again, if only she could.

"I'm certain he's the very best of uncles, and yes, I do like him, of course, but now I must go. Goodbye, Phoebe. Enjoy the rest of your outing."

With that she leaned in and kissed Phoebe's cheek before she straightened and walked away, and did not look back.

Chapter 18

To Mr Gabriel Knight,

You owe me a debt.

Oh, the possibilities.

—*Excerpt of a letter from Lady Helena Adolphus to Mr Gabriel Knight.*

24th February 1815. Briar Cottage, Mitcham Village, Sussex.

Jemima lifted her head from the pillow at the sound of a soft knock on her bedroom door. Her eyes were hot from crying, and her brain seemed full of cotton wool.

"Come in," she said, too listless to get up.

"Jem, dear, there's a Lady Helena and a Mrs de Beauvoir here to see you. Shall I tell them you're indisposed?"

"Minerva!" Jemima sat up so fast her head spun, and she clutched at the bed, closing her eyes.

"There now, that's what you get for not eating a bite after such an upset, nor even a sip of tea, silly goose," Violet scolded, clucking about her. "Do you wish to see the young ladies, then?"

"Yes. Oh, yes," Jemima said, wanting nothing more than to pour out her troubles to Minerva. She wasn't so certain about Helena, who had always rather intimidated her, but surely Minerva wouldn't have brought her here, knowing her situation, if she didn't believe Helena would be sympathetic to Jemima's predicament. "Help me tidy myself up, please, Violet."

Five minutes later, Violet had made her hair look somewhat less dishevelled, though there was little to be done with her complexion, which was pale and blotchy from crying, nor her eyes, which were red from the same cause. Her dress was crumpled too, but she did not wish to keep her friends waiting. They would understand soon enough, and forgive her for not looking her best.

The moment Jemima opened the door and saw Minerva's face fall at the sight of her, she knew it would be all right.

"Oh, Jem, whatever has happened?" she cried and opened her arms. Jemima fell into them and sobbed against Minerva's shoulder as Helena pressed a handkerchief into her hand. Jemima shot her an anxious glance, to which Helena returned a soft smile.

"I shouldn't be here if your situation bothered me, Jemima. I know we aren't close, but I should like to change that, if you'd allow me."

"You know, then?" Jemima said, sniffing and making use of the pretty handkerchief, which smelled faintly of lily of the valley.

Helena nodded. "Minerva explained a little, for which I hope you'll forgive her, but she only did because she knew I wouldn't give a damn. I don't give a snap of my fingers for what society thinks. I won't give up a friend for any reason if I don't wish to, and I don't wish to, Jemima."

Jemima gave a startled laugh and realised Minerva had been right. Helena was not the haughty, spoilt heiress she appeared on the surface. There was far more to her than that. Helena leaned in and hugged Jemima, so she was enveloped between her two friends, their support lending her the courage she'd been lacking since her dreadful row with Solo.

Mrs Attwood brought in tea, a large fruitcake and plates full of biscuits, with a pointed remark that Jemima had eaten nothing and would likely swoon if she didn't soon, before she left them alone. Minerva sat close to her, hugging her at intervals as Jemima told them as much as she felt she could of her sorry tale without embarrassing Solo or giving them a story which was not entirely hers to tell. Helena poured tea and gently plied her with dozens of tiny slices of cake until she'd likely eaten half a plum cake without even realising it.

"Lady Kline is a gilflirt and always has been," Helena said, making Jemima start, for she was certain she'd not mentioned any names. Helena just reached over and patted her hand. "I know far more than I ought to about a lot of things. My brother was not exactly a model of propriety before he met Prue, and he could be shockingly indiscreet with what he told me when he was foxed. Not that I ever let on," she said with a mischievous grin.

"I'll bet," Minerva said, chuckling.

Helena dimpled, putting her pretty nose in the air and feigning indignation. "I learned a great deal about men and the world from those late night talks with him. Even better, he never remembered a thing about it in the morning. I remember him telling me about Baron Rothborn, though. Robert liked him a good deal, I believe. He always said the fellow had a lucky escape from Hyacinth."

"He was right," Jemima said with a sigh.

"From what I've seen of her, I agree." Helena smiled at her curious glance. "I saw her a few weeks ago at a rout party. A dreadful dull affair it was," she added with a grimace. "Nonetheless, I do not think that excused the lady from flirting outrageously with a handsome military man in full view of her husband. She went out of her way to make a fool of the poor viscount."

"She clearly has a taste for uniforms," Jemima said, not much liking the cattiness of her words, but too wretched to take them back. "She liked Solo well enough until he lost his."

"Never mind her. Lord Rothborn is no fool, and he'll come to his senses soon enough," Helena said, with such a decisive tone that Jemima stared at her, almost able to believe what even Violet had not been able to convince her of.

"I believe Helena is right, Jemima," Minerva said, her expression more thoughtful. "Mrs Attwood did right to make you stay. She was also right that a man with as much pride as your baron seems to have would not take the news he'd been played a fool with equanimity. It must have been a shock to him to realise he'd wasted so many years on a woman who was not worth so much grief and guilt. How pitiful and ridiculous the poor man must have felt."

"Solo could never be pitiful or ridiculous," Jemima retorted with a flare of anger.

Minerva gave a soft laugh and reached over to squeeze her hand. "Of course not, Jem, but do you not think he must have felt it? You faced the woman on his behalf, you faced her with a truth I cannot help but wonder if he suspected but did not wish to confront. Perhaps it is easier to hide from the world under a blanket of guilt and grief than start over again, alone."

Jemima stared at her and then smiled. "Married life agrees with you, Mrs de Beauvoir. You are wiser than ever."

Minerva flushed even as she beamed with pleasure.

"It agrees with me admirably," she replied, looking very smug indeed.

"Oh, please don't," Helena wailed. "If I have to hear any more about her wonderful, brilliant, adorable husband, I shall cast up my accounts."

Minerva stuck her tongue out at Helena, who immediately retaliated in kind and three of them fell about laughing.

"I never realised what naughty children you two were," Jemima said, feeling a good deal better than she had, with even a little hope that they were right, and Solo would come back to her. After all, Mrs Attwood had said so too, and they both believed it.

"It's Minerva, she leads me astray," Helena said with a straight face.

Minerva choked on her cake so hard, Jemima was forced to slap her on the back.

"Lies," Minerva said, gasping and reaching for her tea. "All wicked lies."

Jemima looked from one to the other of them with affection, until her gaze fell on a large, battered hat box on the floor beside Minerva. "What's that?"

Minerva gave her a devilish look and reached for the box, taking off the lid and removing a man's top hat. It was still black and shiny, though the brim was a little worn. Unlike most hats, however, it was stuffed with lots of tiny folded slips of paper.

"Oh, no," Jemima said, her heart sinking. With a frown, she peered into the depths of the hat. "Are they breeding in there?" she demanded. "I'm certain we didn't write that many dares."

Minerva and Helena exchanged glances and Minerva bit her lip. "Well, Bonnie came around the other day, and it was cold and wet, and we were all dreadfully bored…"

Jemima groaned. "There's only me and Matilda to go. Matilda says she won't take one, Helena has already taken hers, and everyone else has done theirs."

Helena shrugged. "You never know when a young lady will need a challenge to change her life and her fortunes. One ought to be prepared."

"Are we going to start dragging them in off the streets now?" Jemima demanded.

"No, of course not." Minerva laughed and sighed wistfully at the hat, almost looking as though she wanted to take another. "But it seemed wrong to leave it empty with just a few lonely scraps of paper at the bottom. Besides, we had a great deal of fun thinking them up."

"Oh, I just bet you did." Jemima rolled her eyes and then threw up her hands as the two of them batted their eyelashes at her.

"Oh, very well. I'm in enough trouble, a little more won't hurt any. The entire village believes I'm a scarlet woman, which I am I suppose, and my protector has run away to London to see his lost love. How much worse could it get?"

"That's the spirit," Helena said, deadpan, at which Jemima could not help but laugh.

With due solemnity, Minerva shook the hat so that the dares rustled, and sighed as though in expectation of what was to come. They were all silent as Jemima reached her hand in. It was foolish for her heart to beat in such an extraordinary way, as if a silly dare could change anything. Still, she closed her fingers about one little scrap and pulled it free. She stared down at it for a long moment before she summoned the courage to unfold it.

"Well?" Helena and Minerva demanded in unison.

Jemima read the line and burst out laughing, and then found herself sobbing into Helena's mangled handkerchief again. Minerva plucked the paper from her fingers with a sigh and read it aloud.

"*Find something you want and stop at nothing to get it.* Well, what sensible advice."

Helena snorted. "I suppose that's one of yours. Still, I cannot deny the sentiment is a fine one. It's the sort of thing I might have written myself. Of course, one might decide one wanted the crown jewels, which could cause something of a furore."

Minerva wrinkled her nose at the idea. "We agreed from the outset, such silly notions were not to be countenanced, and I believe we both know that what Jemima wants is Lord Rothborn."

"Yes," Helena said, putting an arm about Jemima's shoulders. "Preferably on his knees begging for her forgiveness and promising her the world."

Jemima gave a stifled laugh. "Nothing of the sort," she protested, though if she were honest the idea found considerable favour in her heart.

She knew she would run into his arms at the first hint that he had reconsidered his hasty words, but still... an apology for railing at her so would be nice. The ladies looked up as Violet knocked and put her head around the door.

"Is everything all right? Should I have Bessie bring more tea?"

Jemima shook her head. "No, thank you, Violet and don't dither in the doorway, come in and meet my friends properly. Lady Helena, Minerva, this is my dear friend and companion, Mrs Violet Attwood. She's been wonderful to me, and I don't know what I should have done without her."

To Jemima's surprise, Violet positively glowed at her words and snatched up a handkerchief from the sleeve of her dress.

"Oh, now, stop that at once," she protested, dabbing at her eyes. "What will Lord Rothborn think if he returns and finds us bawling? We can't have the silly man thinking he's overset us all."

"Nor even Jemima," Helena said as she gave Jemima a critical once over.

Jemima flinched, knowing full well she looked a dreadful mess.

"You know, if you want to make a man fall to his knees and beg forgiveness, you must do better than that crumpled gown and... what *did* you do to your hair?"

"Oh, that's my fault, I never could do hair, but she was in such a rush to see you both she wouldn't wait for Bessie," Violet admitted. "And her ladyship is quite right, Jem, dear. I suspect we shall see Rothborn yet today, and it won't do for you to be looking as though you're pining away for him. A lady must have some pride."

Jemima looked between her friends and sighed. "Well, you are welcome to do whatever you will, but I tell you now, if you can find my pride hiding in a dark corner, do go and fetch it back, for I would fall at his feet if he arrived this moment, and that's the truth."

Minerva took her hand, her eyes full of sympathy. "I know just how you feel, but just as the tea and cake and a nice chat made you feel better, so will preparing yourself to see him again. No matter what happens, facing him in all your finery will give you courage."

Violet gave an approving nod. "I've always said a woman's best frock is her suit of armour. If you feel confident in your appearance, it follows through to everything else. Might seem silly, but it's true."

"You are a very sensible woman, Mrs Attwood," Helena replied, taking in Violet's elegant Pomona green morning dress with black velvet trim with obvious admiration. "Shall we send for Jemima's maid and see what we can do?"

"Yes, Lady Helena, let's do that."

"Oh, just Helena, please," Helena replied, waving away the honorific. "It so stuffy otherwise."

With this burgeoning friendship and happy accord between all parties, Jemima was borne back upstairs, and didn't dare utter the faintest protest.

***

It was full dark when Solo felt the carriage sway to a halt and he peered outside, frustrated to discover he was not greeted by the lights of The Priory, but The White Horse in Mitcham Village. A moment later the door opened, and his coach driver appeared, touching a finger to his hat apologetically.

"Blaise has thrown a shoe, my lord. I'm right sorry, but as we're passing through the village...."

Solo groaned but waved a hand at the fellow. "Fine, yes, of course. It makes sense. Tell Mr Carter I'll pay him double if he can do it in half his usual time. I need to get home."

"Right you are, my lord. Will you wait inside the inn?"

"Yes. I may as well," he said, climbing stiffly down from the carriage.

His leg was playing merry hell after too many hours of enforced stillness combined with being jolted over bad roads. A stiff drink was certainly in order, though having to wait still longer before he could see Jemima chafed his patience, which was already stretched too thin. If he wasn't likely to fall down a hole and break his ankle, he'd take his chances walking home in the dark, but he couldn't risk it. He was damned if he'd go back to being an invalid for months on end. It was hardly an inviting prospect for the young woman to whom he was desperate to propose. He might not be entirely whole, but a bit banged up around the edges was better than a broken-down crock, and so he'd best bide his time.

The interior of The White Horse was cosy and lively. Solo had been a regular visitor once upon a time, but he couldn't remember the last time he'd come in for a drink. Nothing had changed, though he thought perhaps there was an odd quality to the gazes trained upon him. The villagers had always treated him with respect—too much deference, in fact—since his return from the war. The people here seemed to think he'd won the battle of Sahagun single-handed for all the fuss they made about it, but now there was something else. A couple of fellows elbowed each other and chuckled, their conversation clearly ribald, though they kept their voices down.

"Good evening, my lord."

Solo looked up as George Adams, the proprietor, greeted him from behind the bar.

"Adams," Solo replied with a friendly nod. "A glass of your best brandy, if you would."

"Right away, my lord, and may I say it's a pleasure to see you back here."

"Thank you," Solo replied, frowning as the barmaid tugged the arm of another serving wench, the two of them giggling and casting him considering glances.

Solo accepted his drink and sipped it, uncomfortably aware that he was the topic of conversation, not that anyone spoke loud enough for him to hear. Some of the eyes upon him were amused, admiring even, others… were not.

The vicar, Mr Pemble, who had so solicitously left a book for Jemima a few days earlier, was definitely glaring at him.

"Mr Adams," Solo said carefully, when the man came to refill his glass. "Is there a note pinned to my back inviting people to kick me?"

Mr Adams flushed a surprisingly bright red for such a large barrel of a man. "Er… no, my lord, not that I know of."

"Then do, I beg you, enlighten me as to what the excitement is. My presence seems to have stirred a pot I was unaware existed."

Solo's words were polite enough but held an edge that no man had ever heard without giving him the answer he'd demanded. Mr Adam's flush deepened before settling into a sickly green.

"I-I-I," the man stammered. "I'm sure I couldn't say, my lord."

"Devil take you," Solo muttered and turned around, one elbow still upon the bar as he addressed the rest of those present. "Mr Adams seems unable to explain to me what it is everyone is finding so damned fascinating about my presence tonight, so I'll have it from the horse's mouth, shall I?"

A deathly silence filled the room and Solo felt that no one moved so much as an inch as he stared from one man to the next.

Finally, Mr Pemble got to his feet, his face screwed up with disgust as he looked at Solo. "It pains me to speak so to someone we have all long held in such high regard, but I cannot overlook the actions of a man who brings the entire village into disrepute."

"Disrepute?" Solo repeated, his voice dangerously low. "You'd best explain yourself damned quick, sir. I should not like to demand satisfaction from a man of God, but slander is not something I will tolerate from anyone."

Mr Pemble blanched, seeming to shrink a couple of inches before Solo's cold gaze. Still, he put up his chin.

"Do you deny it, then? Deny what Mrs Granger and her daughters heard? What they saw with their own eyes? Your... *doxy*... running from your house in tears, no coat nor hat? Not only do you bring such a lewd woman into our village and install her as if she is a gentlewoman, passing her off among your neighbours as one to whom we should owe our friendship, but are you so wicked as to send her fleeing from you in fear?"

Solo felt for a moment as if he'd been doused in iced water. It did not last long as a wave of red-hot anger surged through him. He cast his cane to the floor and crossed the distance between Mr Pemble and himself in three large strides, quite numb to the pain in his leg now. He picked the unfortunate clergyman up by his cravat and hauled him against the wall where the fellow dangled, squirming on tiptoes while Solo tried to restrain himself from doing him an injury.

"My *doxy*?" he growled through his teeth. "You dare speak of a lady so, filthy little worm? Miss Fernside is everything she appears to be, and if I am lucky enough to have given a decent account of myself, I am hopeful that the lady will soon by *my wife*, not that I, nor any man, can claim to deserve her, you *pestilent arse*!"

Solo let go his grasp on the clergyman's cravat and made no attempt to halt his consequent thud to the ground. The fellow remained there, whimpering as Solo turned to regard the rest of the inn, all of whom were staring at him with wide eyes and rapt attention.

"Any other questions?" he asked, not bothering to raise his voice. He had no need to; you could have heard a pin drop in the next village. Every man shook his head, never taking their eyes from him. "The next man or woman who dares breathe another vile lie disparaging Miss Fernside will answer to me in person to explain themselves, and you may invite Mrs Granger to attend me on the morrow in my office, at nine sharp, to do just that. Good evening to you."

Solo returned to the bar, where Mr Adams had already retrieved his cane and handed it to him with a deferential nod.

"Adams," Solo said, his voice still terse as he bade the fellow goodbye and stalked out of the inn.

Chapter 19

Miss Hunt,

I write in the full expectation you will throw this missive on the fire unopened but, for Phoebe's sake I must take the chance. Since your rather abrupt leave-taking this afternoon, I have heard nothing from Phoebe but demands that I should allow you to visit her. She tells me she has invited you and refuses to accept that there is nothing I can do to make you come here. I have never seen her become so passionately angry with me, as if it is I that keeps you from her. She has now gone to bed fully resolved never to speak to me again. Whilst I have understood for some time that a woman has the power to upset my peace of mind, I had never realised a small girl could do it so thoroughly.

I know, of course, that you cannot come here without risking your reputation, and you have made it abundantly clear this is more important to you than any other aspect of your life, but I shall not speak of that. It so happens that I have business which takes me to town soon, and if you could find a friend or friends to accompany you, you might visit Dern and Phoebe with no one to condemn you for doing so. The housekeeper is used to giving tours of the place when I am not in residence and I will ensure she welcomes you and makes you at home. If you could find it in your heart to remain at Dern for a day or two, I believe Phoebe may forgive me – in time – for disappointing her so.

You have my word of honour that I will keep away for the duration of your visit

—Excerpt of a letter from The Most Honourable, Lucian Barrington, Marquess of Montagu to Miss Matilda Hunt.

Close to midnight, still the 24th February 1815. Briar Cottage, Mitcham Village, Sussex.

By the time the carriage drew up outside Briar cottage, Solo was beside himself with impatience. Thanking heaven that the lights were still on in the parlour; he didn't bother pretending that finding the place in darkness would have made a jot of difference. He would see Jemima this night if he had to rouse the entire cottage, The Priory, the village and the dead too, if it came to it. So it was in this uncompromising frame of mind that he raised his fist to pound upon the door, only to have it open magically before him. There stood Bessie, arms folded over her chest, staring up at him and looking a very long way from impressed.

Oh, how the mighty had fallen.

Finding himself discomfited by Bessie's uncompromising gaze, Solo cleared his throat.

"I would see Miss Fernside... please, Bessie," he added as her eyes narrowed.

"Why? You come to shout at her some more for telling you the truth?"

Solo stiffened. Mrs Norrell might rail at him on occasion but he was quite unused to being spoken to so by a maid of all people, and yet he knew that Bessie was protecting Jemima, that she was cross with him for the same reason he wanted to cut out his own heart, and he could not fault her for her loyalty.

"No," he said, leaning heavily on his cane as his leg throbbed and fretted with complaints after a day which had taxed it sorely. "Only to beg forgiveness, Bessie, if you would allow me to."

As if he'd rubbed a lamp and summoned a genie, Bessie's expression softened, her eyes full of the admiration he'd taken for granted ever since he'd known her.

"Ah, well, now… that's different. Come along inside out of the cold, my lord. That's it, give me your coat and hat, and let me know if I can bring you a bite of supper or something once you've got everything settled between you."

Solo felt his throat tighten ridiculously at the maid's swift change in demeanour, and even though he knew he ought not lower himself to ask her, he found he didn't care a damn about propriety and what a gentleman ought to do.

"Will she let me settle things between us, Bessie?" he asked, hating the uncertainty in his voice.

Bessie paused, looking up at him, her gaze intent once more. "If your intentions are good and… and *honourable*," she said, putting her chin up, challenge glinting in her eyes, "I reckon she might."

Solo let out a breath of relief. "They are, Bessie, I promise you."

Bessie flashed a swift grin at him. "Well, then, what you waitin' for? You'd best go and ask her what you came here for. You'll find her in the front parlour."

Solo did not need telling twice and strode directly to the door, flinging it open without so much as a knock. Jemima was standing by the fire and whirled around as the door flew open, her grey eyes wide. The dress she wore was a deep pink shot silk which glinted garnet red as she moved. The firelight burnished her hair, turning the blonde to shades of gold and bronze, and Solo wondered how his heart could keep up the ridiculous pace it had set, but it only seemed to thrash about harder and faster as he considered what a fool he'd been. Yes, he'd been a fool for ever loving Hyacinth, but that was nothing compared to how he had behaved that morning. Had it only been hours ago? He felt he'd endured a lifetime in the moments between then and now. He could only pray that Bessie was correct, that he had not broken Jemima's trust in him utterly, that he still had a chance for forgiveness.

"My love," was all he managed, the words snagging in his throat, but it seemed to be all that was required as she crossed the room at a run and flung herself into his arms.

"Forgive me," he begged, enclosing her in his arms. "I was a damned, bloody fool and I knew it within moments of you leaving me. You were right, right about all of it. I think that's why I was so bloody angry. You forced me to face the truth. I *was* haunting the damn place, hiding from life, from the possibility of being hurt again, but I'm done hiding, Jemima. I want to live...I want to live with you by my side, with no shame for what I have done, no regrets for what you have been forced into."

He moved away from her, determined to do this as it ought to be done, to ensure she had no doubt of his intentions. Awkwardly, he got to his knees.

"Oh, no... Solo, get up, your poor leg!" Jemima protested, blushing and crying as she realised what he meant to do.

"Do stop fussing, love," he said, grinning at her. "A fellow likes to do a thing properly, though you may need to help me up again."

He chuckled as she stared down at him, her eyes glittering with unshed tears, one hand covering her mouth. He took the other one, bearing it to his lips and pressing a kiss to her knuckles.

"Jemima, if I have achieved anything at all these past weeks, I hope I may have made my feelings clear, but as I've made such a spectacular mess of everything, I can't have any faith in that, so I must spell it out to you. I love you. I believe I may have loved you from the first moment I saw you in Hatchard's, attacking that poor old fellow and his defenceless book."

She stifled an unsteady giggle, but Solo ploughed manfully on.

"Despite your many attempts to seduce me, I have somehow kept myself *reasonably* pure, although my every thought of you has been nothing less than wickedness and decadence, and torture to endure. The truth is that I will be a wreck of a man without you. I need you. I need your love, your kindness and your good sense, your scolding when I'm bad-tempered, your laughter and all your smiles. I need you in my bed and by my side, always and forever. Please, darling Jem, make me the happiest of men and say that you'll marry me."

In hindsight, he wasn't sure she actually gave him an answer, just dropped to her knees and flung her arms about his neck with such enthusiasm he fell backwards, narrowly missing bashing his brains out on the leg of the sideboard. Undaunted, he grabbed the back of her neck and pulled her mouth down to his, kissing her with all that was in his heart and finding that poor, traumatised organ soar as she returned his kisses in kind, holding nothing back.

Breathless, he rolled her over and gazed down at her.

"Was that a yes?" he asked, a trifle unsteady after such turmoil.

"Of course it was a yes," she said, blinking at him, her eyes full of laughter. "Though you quite took the wind out of my sails, you know. I spent the entire evening working up to such a splendid scold for you with so many fine set downs, and now it's all gone to waste."

"Save them," he counselled gravely, stroking her cheek with his thumb and not bothering to hide the adoration she must be able to see in his eyes. "I look forward to them. No one has ever scolded me like you do, and I adore it."

"Nonsense," she said, huffing. "Mrs Norrell has it down to a fine art."

Solo shrugged. "Perhaps, but it's not the same, though I suppose in a strange way it is. She's known me since the day I was born, and she scolds me because she cares. I know you do too, and it is the strangest thing to realise, but I have needed to hear someone get cross and rail at me when I'm being an idiot because they love me and they know I can do better, *be* better."

Jemima shook her head, holding his face between her hands. "No, not for that, only because I know you could be happier, and I intend to prove it to you."

"I intend to let you," Solo replied, and kissed her again. With a bit of help he got his protesting leg working again and got to his feet, settling in a chair by the fire and taking a great deal of pleasure in tugging Jemima into his lap. There was a deal more kissing and sighing which strained all his good intentions to their limits, but he endured. When he finally stopped for breath and looked up, his gaze fell upon a slightly shabby top hat sitting on the small round table to the side of the chair. Peering down at it with a frown, he noticed it was full of bits of paper.

"What is that?"

Jemima grinned. "That might take some time to explain."

It did, as she interspersed her story with kisses which he was only too happy to return, alongside caresses that were in danger of getting out of hand if he didn't leave soon. Somehow, he kept himself in check, and she finished her tale.

"So, you took a dare?"

She nodded. "Though I was not so brave as the others. They practically had to force me, and in truth my dare was very easy to accomplish."

"What was it?" he asked, wondering how she could possibly think she wasn't brave.

"Find something you want and stop at nothing to get it. Though," she added thoughtfully, "to be fair, I wanted you from the outset, and I suppose I did stop at nothing, not even that frightful Lady Kline, so...."

"So you did not need a dare, my love. You are without a doubt the bravest woman I have ever met. It was you who returned my courage to me, Jem. No one else. Only you."

She sighed happily, kissed him again, and then began to giggle.

"What?"

Solo frowned as she shook her head and tried to rearrange her face into something less amused, but her luscious lips would not play along and kept turning up at the corners, making him want to kiss them again, so he did, but he did not stop her giggling.

"How is a fellow supposed to concentrate on kissing you thoroughly when you keep sniggering so?" he complained.

"Oh, I do beg your pardon," she said, pressing her lips together with her fingers as though that might keep her laughter contained. "It's only something Lady Helena said, and... and...."

"Tell me."

She shook her head.

"Jem," he said, his voice stern.

"Oh, well... it's only that, when she heard my dare, Helena said that what I wanted most was you, preferably on your knees begging for my forgiveness and promising me the world."

"Oh, is that all?" Solo replied placidly. "Then, I should say you have completed your dare with success."

"Yes," she agreed, and kissed him again.

It was the hardest thing to leave her. Though he longed to take her to bed, he was not about to make love to her for the first time in the tiny cottage with Bessie and Mrs Attwood too close for comfort. Dragging her through the gardens in the dead of night was not an option either and, besides which, he'd determined to do this all properly. He would kill any scandal by behaving with the utmost propriety and Mr Pemble—damn his eyes—would marry them and eat crow in the process if he didn't want his living to go to someone a deal more charitable. Solo was well respected by the bishop, an association he would not hesitate to use if his wife was not treated to the respect she deserved. He was mollified and yet further tortured when Jemima protested him leaving, and worse still, not taking her with him.

"But what does it matter now?" she demanded. Her indignation when he told her she would walk the aisle, if not completely innocent, then at least virginal in fact, was a balm to his own desires, knowing she would miss him and chafe at his absence just as badly. "Everyone at The Priory knows I have spent the night in your bed and—"

"And *I* will know," he said, pressing a finger to her lips before she could tempt him beyond sanity. "Spare a thought for my eternal soul, would you?"

"Piffle," she muttered, folding her arms. "You don't believe that any more than I do."

"I believe that I love you, Jem, and that I wish you to walk down the aisle with your head held high before the Mrs Grangers of this world. Which is another good reason you must be here and not at The Priory in the morning. I had a little set to in the village earlier, and she ought to be calling on me with an apology on her lips at nine sharp, at which point she will come here and repeat the process. I beg you will remember your position as Baroness Rothborn and be as haughty as a queen, or you'll never recover from it. A spiteful tattle monger like that needs a firm hand, or she'll get even further out of line."

"What kind of set to?"

The gleam of interest in her eyes made Solo grin and so he recounted his evening's work in the bar, earning himself a shocked squeal of delight as she heard of how he'd treated Mr Pemble.

"Oh, the poor man," she said, trying and failing to school her face into one of sympathy for the odious cretin. "One ought not find amusement in such things when, really, he had the right of it."

"Devil take him, he most certainly did not!" Solo retorted, furious all over again. "He called you a doxy and said I'd brought the village into disrepute. *Disrepute!*"

Jemima soothed his fury away by kissing him until he could barely remember his own name, never mind whatever it was he'd been upset about, and so it was close to dawn before he could finally tear himself from her and return to The Priory.

Chapter 20

My dear friend,

I am writing to tell you I am going to be married…

—*Excerpt of a letter from Miss Jemima Fernside, copied to each of the Peculiar Ladies.*

25th February 1815. Briar Cottage, Mitcham Village, Sussex.

Jemima listened to Mrs Granger's stilted apology in silence, her face utterly expressionless. This was less to do with punishing Mrs Granger for being a vile tattle monger, and more because Violet was glaring at the woman with such fierce dislike that Jemima had to work hard to keep her own countenance impassive. Like Solo, Violet believed she should crush such behaviour before it had the temerity to raise its head again, but Mrs Granger looked so miserable and flustered by the end of her apology that Jemima could not help but feel a little sorry for her.

"Thank you for your words, Mrs Granger," she said carefully. "I believe all of us have been guilty of jumping to conclusions at one time or another. It was not astonishing for you to believe the worst of the situation, but I hope that you have learned it was nothing but a foolish argument and my own nerves getting the better of me. I'm afraid everything has happened so quickly, and my change in circumstance is so dramatic that I became a little overwrought."

At this point, Jemima resisted the urge to cross her fingers and prayed she would not go straight to hell for telling such an outright plumper when the woman had been spot-on in her estimation. That she ought to have a deal more Christian charity in her heart, and mind her own business, was enough reason for Jemima to have enjoyed making her squirm, but she did not want an enemy in the village, and so she continued with that in mind.

"Lord Rothborn has gone this day to Doctor's Commons to obtain a common licence so that we may be married the day after tomorrow. There will be a wedding breakfast at The Priory, and the village will be invited to the celebrations... I do hope that you and your daughters will join us?"

The relief on the woman's face was so intense it was almost comical.

"Oh, *yes,* my lady. *Thank* you! I should not miss it for the world. It's been an age since there were any celebrations at The Priory. Oh, I remember the balls and parties when I was a young woman—too many moons ago now—but we have often reminisced and said that it's such a shame for the young people that such entertainments have been lost to them."

"I am not a lady quite yet, Mrs Granger, just Miss Fernside, but yes, I can imagine it must be a loss to the society of the village. Lord Rothborn is not much of a one for socialising, but I think perhaps I might persuade him to give the occasional ball. Perhaps a garden party in the summer? It is a shame that the beautiful gardens about The Priory are not enjoyed by more people. What do you think?"

Violet sniffed with displeasure at the woman being offered such an invitation, but Mrs Granger positively glowed at having her opinion sought, and Jemima decided she knew just how to keep the lady on side and her tongue quiet—relatively so, at least.

"You let her off far too lightly," Violet complained as Bessie came in to clear the tea things, once Mrs Granger had taken her leave.

"She's too tender-hearted, that's the trouble," Bessie said with a sigh.

"Oh, I believe facing Solo to explain herself this morning will live in her memory for many years to come," Jemima said with a smile. "There was no need to make the poor woman into a pariah. I think she'll defend my honour to anyone who'll listen, now I have her onside. For I may decide not to invite her lovely daughters to the splendid events that I have planned at The Priory."

Bessie gave a chuckle. "Sneaky, that is. Perhaps not as tender-hearted as I'd believed."

"No, indeed," Jemima replied with a haughty sniff. "Lady Rothborn will be a force to be reckoned with."

"Oooh, you looked just like Lady Helena when you did that," Violet exclaimed with a laugh.

"I should think so, I've been taking note of how she does it," Jemima said with a grin. "She seems so terribly cold and aloof and aristocratic, and yet underneath she's an absolute dear."

"I liked her very much," Violet said, reaching for a sugar biscuit before Bessie could snatch them away. "Will she come to the wedding, do you think?"

Jemima nodded. "I think so, if she can. I wrote invitations to everyone this morning, but as it's such short notice I don't imagine most of them will be able to come. Only those who live close at hand."

"Well, it will be a nice surprise to see who makes it and, speaking of the happy day, we must arrange for you to be well dressed. Come along and let us see what can be contrived for a wedding gown, fit for Lady Rothborn."

***

27th February 1815. Briar Cottage, Mitcham Village, Sussex.

"Oh, miss, *miss!*"

Jemima turned from her position before the full-length mirror as Bessie thundered up the stairs, squealing with excitement.

"Whatever is the matter, Bessie?" she exclaimed as the maid almost fell through the bedroom door.

"Look!" the breathless creature shrieked, holding out a large, square leather box.

"Oh, my," Violet breathed, one hand going to rest upon her plump bosom. "That's jewellery, that is."

"It just arrived from The Priory, with this note, miss."

As Jemima took the note from Bessie, she felt her heart give a little flutter of excitement, not that the poor thing had done anything but flutter since she'd awoken at dawn. Today she would marry Solomon Weston, Baron Rothborn, and she felt certain she must be caught in the loveliest of dreams, for life could not possibly be this wonderful. Except it appeared it was, and she must get used to it. With fingers that were not entirely steady, she broke the seal upon the note.

My darling Jem,

Mrs Norrell tells me I am on no account allowed to see you before the wedding, an idiotic state of affairs and one that has thrown me into a frightful sulk. As you are not here to scold me, I am making the most of it and terrorising the staff. There is a fair chance they will murder me before the ceremony.

I had hoped to give you this gift in person, but I feel certain that you would like to wear it today and so I must be noble and sacrifice my own happiness to forgo that pleasure. You see what an admirably selfless and gallant man you are marrying. I hope you consider yourself fortunate.

Of course the truth is that there is no one in the world more fortunate than I, my dearest love, and I am counting the minutes until we are wed—as are the staff—I feel my life is starting over a fresh, that there is a clean page set before me, and I cannot wait to see what we shall make of it together.

In anticipation of all that is to come,

Yours ever,

Solo x

"Oh, no, don't cry!" Violet exclaimed, flapping a handkerchief at Jemima. "You are not going to get married all red-eyed and sniffy, madam!"

"I'm n-not crying," Jemima protested, choking a little. "I'm l-laughing *and* crying."

"Well, stop it at once!" Violet's fierce protest was rather diminished by the fact she was dabbing at her own eyes too.

"Oh, open the box, miss!" Bessie pleaded, shoving the large, flat leather case into Jemima's hands, making her gather herself enough to concentrate on opening the tiny gold clasp holding it closed.

The clasp sprang open and Jemima lifted the lid, and all three of them gasped.

"Oh, my stars!" said Violet.

"Lawks!" Bessie cried, grabbing Jemima's arm with excitement.

"Good heavens." Jemima stared at the parure set in awe.

Diamonds and pearls set in rose gold sparkled in the bright morning sunlight, stealing her breath. There was a necklace so fine it looked to Jemima fit for a queen. There were also two bracelets and drop earrings, as well as a brooch.

"Oh, put them on me, put them on!" Jemima said, as Bessie and Violet laughed with delight at her excitement.

"Oh, and there's this, too," Bessie said, taking a silk-wrapped parcel from the pocket on her apron. "Lord, what a hen wit I am! I nearly forgot, I was so excited by the box."

Jemima undid the velvet ribbon holding the parcel closed as Bessie fixed the necklace at the nape of her neck.

"Oh, look! Matching hair clips!"

By the time Violet and Bessie had fussed about her hair, the jewellery was in place, and her dress was arranged to their satisfaction, it was time to leave.

"Oh, Jem, you do look lovely," Violet said, proving that she wouldn't make it to the church before she started weeping again.

"Like a princess," Bessie said with a happy sigh, clutching her arms about herself. A sharp knock at the front door had Bessie scuttling downstairs. "That'll be the carriage!" she shrieked happily.

Taking advantage of the moment, Violet stepped forward and gave her a careful hug, ensuring she did not mess the bride's hair or wrinkle her dress. "I'm so happy for you, Jemima. It couldn't have happened to a nicer young woman."

"Thank you, Violet, for everything, and you know the cottage is yours for as long as you wish to stay here. I arranged it all with Solo."

"Oh, Jemima," Violet said, wide-eyed. "That's so… so very kind of you." Then she blushed, such an unusual reaction from Violet that Jemima wondered what she was hiding.

"Violet?"

Violet cleared her throat. "Well, it's only that... it might not be for so very long. You know those walks I take sometimes in the afternoon? Well, Major Hawkins has been joining me and, if I'm not very much mistaken, I think he might be asking me a question very soon."

"Oh, Violet!" Jemima exclaimed in delight, giving her a fierce hug.

"Stop it, you'll muss your dress!" Violet cried, though she was laughing all the same.

"Now tell me truthfully." Jemima made her face as stern as she could manage, wagging a finger at Violet. "Was it the peapod wine?"

"Oh!" Violet said, giving her a playful tap. "Stop it, you wicked girl. We're neither of us spring chickens, but no peapod wine was necessary, I assure you."

Laughing delightedly, Jemima followed Violet downstairs, only to be hustled into the parlour by Bessie, who was wide-eyed with awe and clutching at her apron. Not terribly surprising, when Jemima entered to discover the Duke and Duchess of Bedwin awaiting her.

"Prue!" she exclaimed, rushing to hug her friend, who beamed happily.

"Darling, you look magnificent," Prue said, making Jemima turn in a circle so she could admire her fully. "Now, we shan't stop, but I wanted to ask who was going to give you away, because Robert is getting very good at it, and I want to offer his services if you should like them."

"I'm very cheap," the duke replied, giving an astonished Jemima a wink. "I'm thinking of hiring myself out."

"Oh, hush, Robert." Prue rolled her eyes. "This is only the third time I've offered your services, after all, but it has to be said that there's nothing like having a duke give you away to lend one countenance. You see, Helena told us of the horrid gossip in the village, and I thought this would be an excellent way of shutting them all up."

"Oh, my," Jemima said, staring at Bedwin, who looked magnificent and very ducal indeed.

"That's a yes!" Prue said, clapping her hands with glee. "Now then, Robert, you take Jemima in our carriage. I shall go with Mrs Attwood, if the lady doesn't mind, that is?" Prue asked, holding out her hand to an astonished Violet. "I'm Prunella Adolphus, pleased to meet you. There, introductions done. Shall we go?"

Jemima gave a startled laugh as Prue led the way, her burgeoning stomach preceding her amid a stately swish of expensive fabric.

"My word." Violet stared after her in awe, uncharacteristically speechless.

"Such a managing creature, she is. I always knew she'd make an admirable duchess," Bedwin said fondly, before offering Jemima his arm. "Shall we?"

***

Solo tugged at his cravat. It had seemed fine when he left the house, but he was certain it had shrunk in the meantime. The blasted thing was choking him. He turned to the man standing beside him in front of the church. "Have you got the ring?"

Inigo sighed. "You've asked me that three times. I assure you the answer hasn't changed."

Solo scowled at him. "You're supposed to put my mind at rest and be a tower of support."

"You have a cane, lean on that," Inigo suggested, grinning at him.

"I don't remember you being quite so sanguine the morning of your wedding," Solo grumbled. "In fact, you stuttered and stammered the entire way through the ceremony."

Inigo snorted. "Yes, you great clod pole, and now you know why. It's terrifying."

Solo could not disagree. Standing now in the chilly environs of St Martin's Church, a building so ancient it had been mentioned in the Domesday Book, marriage seemed a terribly solemn and weighty deed to be contemplating. A shiver of apprehension thrilled down his spine as he panicked about exactly what he had to offer a bright, vivacious young woman like Jemima. Would she grow bored with him? Would she find him dull in a few years? Would she...?

His increasingly alarming musings were halted as Inigo elbowed him with some force. Solo looked up.

"She's here," Inigo hissed through his teeth.

Solo swung around and any doubts flew out of the window. His breath snagged in his throat as he caught his first glimpse of his bride. She wore a gown of white muslin embroidered all over with yellow flowers, and no veil, her lovely face the most glorious thing he'd ever seen. The smile she bestowed on him as their eyes met, so full of joy and anticipation, not only vanquished his fears but made him forget everyone and everything. If not for Inigo grabbing hold of his arm, he'd have marched up the aisle and taken her hand himself, quite ruining the splendid entrance she'd made on the arm of the Duke of Bedwin.

Well, that was a surprise. Though Jemima had mentioned she was friends with the duchess, Solo had never imagined she was on such intimate terms with her. Tearing his eyes from his beautiful bride and squelching a tiny surge of jealousy at the magnificent picture she made with the duke, Solo looked at the congregation and grinned. The villagers' eyes were on stalks, but in the front rows he saw a number of women whom he suspected were members of the Peculiar Ladies Jemima had spoken of with such affection and esteem. They too were beaming at Jemima, dabbing at their eyes and full of joy for their friend. As the duke bore his beloved closer, Solo felt his chest ache with happiness and pride.

"Rothborn," the duke said, looking very pleased with himself. "I believe this lovely creature belongs to you."

Solo found his throat too tight to reply, a situation he hoped he could resolve before he made even more of a muck of the ceremony than Inigo had. So he just smiled, nodded at the duke, and took Jemima's hand, feeling the tension that had beset him all morning fall away as her fingers curled around his own. She stared up at him, and he saw all his hopes and dreams reflected in her eyes. With a brief squeeze of her fingers, Solo decided he wanted the ceremony over and done as quickly as possible, and turned back to face the vicar.

Mr Pemble blanched a little and cleared his throat, and it soon became apparent that it would not be the groom who would stutter through this service.

***

"I need another handkerchief," Matilda lamented, looking at the mangled mess she'd made of the spare one she'd brought with her. "Two usually suffices, but Lord Rothborn looked so utterly spellbound, and Jemima was so very... *oh!*" she said, waving a hand as her voice trembled.

Helena sighed, watching as the newly married couple exited the church into the sunlight beyond.

"I know," she said wistfully, wondering if she would look upon the man she eventually wed with such adoration. "He looked terribly dashing and heroic in his uniform. All that scarlet and gold, and I don't think I've ever seen so many medals."

"Me either," Matilda agreed.

"Will you stay for the wedding breakfast?" Helena asked as she got to her feet, being careful to collect her reticule, as she was far too prone to leaving the dratted thing behind.

"I'd like to, but Alice needs to get back. She tires easily now."

Helena smiled, hopeful that she should have a companion for the journey back to her uncle's house, as Prue and Robert planned to stay at the estate in Hampshire for a few weeks while Prue was still fit enough to travel.

"Should you like me to give you a lift home then, so you can stay? We shall practically go past Alice's front door anyway, so it's no trouble."

"Oh, yes, thank you. I should like that, if Alice doesn't need me."

Matilda went away to speak with Alice and, having been assured that she could do perfectly well without her sister-in-law for a whole afternoon, Matilda returned to accept Helena's proposal.

"Excellent," Helena replied, tilting her face to enjoy the sunshine as they walked arm in arm back to The Priory. They'd dispensed with the carriages as it was only a short distance and the day too glorious to miss. "Will you stay in Kent for a while yet?"

Matilda nodded. "For as long as Alice wishes me to, and...."

She hesitated and bit her lip, and Helena's curiosity was immediately roused.

"And?" she pressed.

Matilda sighed and glanced sideways at her. "May I rely on your discretion?"

"Oh!" Helena said with a delighted, if quiet, squeal of excitement. "An intrigue! I knew it! *Oh*," she said again, staring at Matilda as she realised what she was most likely to have to be discreet about. "It's Montagu, isn't it?"

Matilda flushed, confirming this supposition without saying a word. "Not entirely, no," she said, sounding a little flustered. "But indirectly, yes, yes, it is."

"Well?" Helena demanded, delighted to be asked to share such a confidence with Matilda, whom she'd always admired.

Though Helena was the daughter of a duke and duchess, she often felt that Matilda carried herself with far more grace and nobility than she would ever manage. Helena always felt she was playing a part, whereas Matilda seemed to come by it naturally, as if she'd been born to it.

"Well," Matilda began, and then laughed at the obvious excitement she must be able to see in Helena's expression. "Well, the thing is, I have met his niece three times now. She's a dear little girl, about eight years old, I believe, and she is insistent that I come and visit her at Dern. Indeed I believe she has pestered poor Montagu to such an extent that he has agreed to vacate the premises so that I might visit the girl without fear for my reputation, but... I shall need a friend to lend me countenance and...."

"Yes!" Helena said before Matilda could finish another word of her explanation. "I've always wanted to see Dern. It's terribly ancient and full of secrets. Did you know the word Dern come from the Saxon *dierne,* and it even means concealed, secret, dark or hidden?"

Matilda stared at her in astonishment, and Helena flushed.

"Well, it does," she said a little defensively. "I like the history of old buildings, and I get bored a lot."

"Well," Matilda replied, laughing now. "Then I shall have the perfect companion for my visit, and I can well imagine you get bored. I've never known a woman less able to sit still for five minutes together. I'm only astonished you made it through the ceremony without fidgeting."

"I can behave," Helena retorted, sticking her nose in the air like the duke's daughter she was, before slanting Matilda a mischievous look. "When I feel like it," she added with a grin.

The two women laughed together, and carried on chattering in perfect accord, all the way back to The Priory.

***

Jemima had never smiled nor laughed so much in her entire life. Her cheeks ached, but she was so happy she felt she might burst with the effort of trying to contain it, so she didn't.

Not only was it the happiest day of her life because she had married Solo, but she was overjoyed to see so many of her friends had joined her. Harriet and her husband, the Earl of St Clair, as well as Harriet's brother Henry had come. To her astonishment and delight, Jemima discovered they had also brought Kitty and her husband Luke, who had come for a brief visit and happened to be staying with them. Aashini and Lord Cavendish had also come. Matilda had arrived, carefully helping a heavily pregnant Alice, with her anxious husband Nate on her other side. Alice and Nate left immediately after the wedding, but Jemima was more than touched by Alice's insistence on being there for the ceremony. Bonnie and her husband Jerome had come, bringing Minerva with them too, and Jemima felt her cup was most certainly overflowing. The only person who'd not made it was Ruth and, as she would not even have received the invitation yet, since she was out in the wilds of the Highlands of Scotland, there was no point in lamenting that fact. The only other person missing was Jemima's aunt, who would have been beside herself with pride over the presence of so many noble families, and in raptures about Jemima being given away by a duke, of all people. Jemima smiled to herself, though, certain that her aunt was looking down on her and feeling very pleased indeed.

She turned, gazing once more upon her husband, resplendent in full military dress uniform, and felt herself to be the luckiest woman who ever lived.

***

"You're happy?"

Jemima turned to her husband. What little remained of a very fine wedding breakfast was being ignored now. The voices of the assembled company rose in chatter and laughter as old friends caught up with news and the villagers relaxed and enjoyed all the benefits of an event at The Priory, which they had lamented losing for so long.

"Well, that's a foolish question," she said, leaning into him. "But no, I'm not merely happy, I'm beside myself with joy. I feel like one of those Montgolfier balloons that might fly away into the sky at any moment."

"Well," Solo replied, his expression grave. "I suspect too much champagne—the bubbles, you know—but you may rest assured I shall keep a tight hold on you, wife. I have plans that I do not intend thwarted by anyone, least of all you floating off into the blue."

Jemima stifled an unladylike snort of amusement. "I've only had three glasses of champagne," she retorted with as much dignity as she could manage, but she felt the bubbles *had* gone to her head.

She'd been too excited to eat anything all day, and the delicious drink on an empty stomach was making her feel giddy and silly. She beamed at Solo and tilted her head up towards him for a kiss. He rewarded her, briefly, but when he drew back his gaze was dark and hot and the giddy feeling intensified as it mingled with anticipation.

"Time to leave," he said, his voice as decisive as she'd ever heard it. "If we don't go now, I'm likely to ravish you on the table in full view of the assembled company, and Mrs Granger will believe she's been vindicated."

"Oh, well, we can't have that," Jemima said, torn between laughter and blushes and finding both were necessary. "Not after we've worked so hard to make her see how perfectly perfect I am," she added, batting her eyelashes at Solo and attempting to look innocent and guileless.

"Do that again once we're alone and see where it gets you, wife." Solo chuckled and grabbed her by the hand.

They left the celebration amid shouts of encouragement and much laughter and good wishes, some of which made Jemima's blushes scorch her cheeks. Not that she minded. It was wonderful to see everyone was enjoying the day and celebrating their happiness, and a few good-natured ribald comments could not spoil that.

"Thank heavens," Solo said in relief, once he'd pulled her into the quiet of his bedroom, far from the revelry and closed the door firmly on the outside world. "I've been longing for this moment since... God, Jemima, for all my life, it seems."

"Well, then," Jemima said, moving into his arms and sighing with pleasure as they closed around her. "We'd better not keep you waiting another moment, had we?"

They both had to wait rather longer than they wished to, as getting Solo out of his dress uniform took a little longer than anticipated, nervous fingers fumbling over the gold brocade and stiff buttons on his coat for far too long.

"I love this gown," Solo said, once he'd been stripped down to his small clothes and could concentrate on disrobing his wife. "Get it off at once."

Jemima giggled as he muttered and cursed over the number of buttons and layers of petticoats, but eventually only her shift remained.

"Is that the last layer?" he demanded, sounding impatient, though amusement and warmth filled his eyes.

"Why don't you find out?" she teased, running away from him and leaping onto the bed.

"Well, that's nice, running away from a wounded soldier," Solo huffed, watching her go. "What if I'm too feeble to chase you, my wicked bride?"

Wondering how she dared, Jemima knelt up in the middle of the bed and tugged the chemise over her head, throwing it to one side.

"Too feeble?" she repeated plaintively, pressing the back of her hand dramatically to her forehead. "Oh, woe is me," she sighed, and pretended to swoon against the pillows.

She cracked her eyes open a moment later as the mattress dipped, and squealed as Solo tugged her down the bed, settling between her thighs as he lay over her.

"I thought you were old and feeble?" she said, giggling and shrieking as he tickled her.

"Feeble? Me? My lady, I believe you must be thinking of someone else."

Solo moved against her, his arousal caressing her intimately and making her breath catch in her throat.

"Oh!" she exclaimed, winding her arms about his neck. "I believe you are right my lord. Not in the least feeble, *oh…* do that again."

Solo chuckled and indulged her and Jemima gave herself over to him, to his care, trusting in him utterly as he kissed and caressed, and made her body sing. Though they had only been intimate a few times she had missed this fiercely, missed his touch, his mouth, the feel of his body close to hers. That she could enjoy it now, enjoy him, with no more lingering feelings of guilt, was beyond anything she had dreamed of.

"So, so beautiful," he murmured, kissing his way down her stomach. "I have dreamt of this every night since you were last here, my darling girl. If I'm honest I've dreamed of it much of every day too."

Jemima gasped as he parted her legs, still moving inexorably down her body. Though he had touched her intimately before, very intimately, surely, he did not intend... he could not be thinking....

Her breath caught in her throat, her mind growing hazy and dim as she realised, *yes,* yes he really did intend to touch her there... with his *mouth.* Her disbelief and shock evaporated as pleasure undid every knot of apprehension until she was languid and pliant beneath him, her entire being shrinking, the world diminished to the place his mouth was intent on pleasuring. Little by little that languor dissipated, to be replaced by a simmering tension. Her body bowed, arching towards him, demanding more as sounds of desperation were torn from her. She clutched at his dark hair, holding him in place, pleading with him as the shimmering light beckoned her. His mouth was hot, burning against her intimate flesh, his tongue lapping, teasing gently until his fingers joined the equation. They slid easily inside her liquid heat, first one, then another, until she bucked and cried out, dissolving under his touch in a rush of sensation that left her gasping and spent, bright lights still dancing behind her eyes like fireworks.

She could have remained there, blissful in her lazy stupor, except her husband had other ideas, and she gasped anew as he moved back between her thighs. His hard member pushed at her, nudging inside the place where his fingers had slid so easily. The dimensions were somewhat different, however, and Jemima tensed at the strange invasion.

"Jem, darling," Solo said, his voice sounding oddly husky. "Look at me."

She did, smiling as she focused upon his beloved face and feeling the tension fall away at once, remembering that she was loved, cherished, and that he would never hurt her if he could help it.

"I love you," he said, and she made a soft sound of surprise as he thrust inside her, once, hard, and held her as she caught her breath, staring up at him with wide eyes. "Sorry," he said, an apology in his eyes. "I'm sorry. Does it…?"

"No," she said at once, shaking her head as the pain had been fleeting, had already been forgotten as she held tight to him, relishing his heat and his strength, the power within him that had seen him through so many challenges and trials and triumphed over every one of them. "I love you too."

He let out a breath of relief and Jemima clung to him as he lost himself in pleasure, in her. Somewhat to her surprise, his enjoyment of her was every bit as arousing as his undivided attention. The softly muttered curses and groans fired her blood as his body thrust harder and faster, quickening that gathering feeling at her core, bringing back the desperate need that had made her cry out like a mad woman and demand more and faster and *now*.

"Oh God," he moaned, his hands clutching at her bottom so hard she expected to see the imprints in the morning, tilting her hips just so. "Oh, Christ, Jem, yes…."

He shuddered and jerked violently, such primitive sounds ripped from him as he spent inside her that she was overwhelmed, overcome by his reaction to her and followed in his wake, gasping and laughing and clinging to him as another mad surge of joy tumbled her over the edge into bliss.

It was some time before either of them could find anything sensible to say, not that they cared. It was enough to lie in each other's arms, contemplating fate and luck and happily ever afters that were worth every moment of waiting.

"How many children shall we have?" he asked, tracing a lazy circle round and round one breast as he contemplated the question.

Jemima shifted so that she could look up at him. "How many do you want to have?"

He grinned then. "I don't mind. As many as we're blessed with, but I want to try for at least a dozen."

"Good heavens!" Jemima said, a little alarmed. "You're not serious?"

"No," he agreed, tumbling her onto her back. "I just want an excuse to keep you in my bed as often as possible."

Jemima laughed. "Foolish man. We're married, we don't need an excuse."

"Hmmm, just as well," he murmured, nuzzling her neck. "Though I have heard rumours of balls and garden parties, and I fear I may not keep you here as often as I might like."

"Oh," Jemima said, serious at once. "But I shan't arrange anything you don't like or approve of, Solo. I know you don't much like society and—"

He pressed a finger to her lips before she could explain any further.

"I shall look forward to seeing the old place come alive again. It's been standing too long all alone with only me to haunt the ghosts. I want the place to ring with laughter and music, and for it to be brought to life the way you have brought me to life." He hesitated and then gave her a rueful smile. "Though perhaps not *all* the time."

Jemima laughed and reached up to press a kiss to his mouth. "Of course not all the time. I want you all to myself, you foolish man, but a garden party in the summer, and perhaps a Christmas ball, would not be too much for you to endure, I think?"

He grinned and waggled his eyebrows at her like a theatrical villain. "So long as I can drag you into the bushes and have my wicked way with you at the garden party, and debauch you under the mistletoe at the Christmas ball, I shall look forward to it."

"I promise, you may," Jemima said solemnly, drawing a cross over her heart.

"Excellent," Solo replied, as though they'd reached an important agreement. "In the meantime, however, I think we ought to get in some more practice."

And, as Jemima could find no fault whatsoever with this idea, they did.

Girls who dare— *Inside every wallflower is the beating heart of a lioness, a passionate individual willing to risk all for their dream, if only they can find the courage to begin. When these overlooked girls make a pact to change their lives, anything can happen.*

Eleven girls – Eleven dares in a hat. Twelve passionate stories. Who will dare to risk it all?

Next in the series

To Ride with the Knight
Girls Who Dare, Book 10

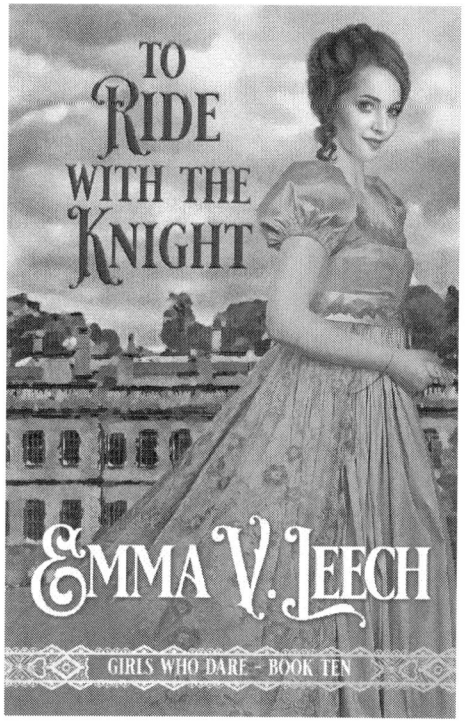

A reckless beauty...

Lady Helena Adolphus is no stranger to scandal. Her brother may be a duke, but his black reputation once threatened her own chances of making a good match. Now returned to the bosom of the ton, Helena is feted and courted as much for her loveliness and wild green eyes as for her hefty dowry. Yet the eligible bachelors leave her cold and respectability is deadly dull. There is only one man who makes her pulse leap, and she knows she'd be a fool to pursue him.

A ruthless man…

Gabriel Knight understands desperation. Born into poverty and raised in a foundling home, Gabriel used every opportunity to claw his way out of the gutter. Now one of the wealthiest men in England, wicked Knight is dismayed to discover his success has not bought him happiness. Restless and bored, he blames his ennui on the pompous aristocrats he despises, those who still close doors in his face.

An imprudent affair …

Though Helena is aware of Gabriel's animosity for the ton that shuns him, the sinful man tempts her beyond all reason. He is out to ruin her, and she knows it, but her stupid pride won't let her back down from each scandalous challenge he sets her.

As the heat of attraction flares hotter between them, the risk of getting burned only makes riding with the Knight ever more enticing.

Available May 29, 2020. Pre-Order your copy here: [To Ride with the Knight](#)

Want more Emma?

If you enjoyed this book, please support this indie author and take a moment to leave a few words in a review. *Thank you!*

To be kept informed of special offers and free deals (which I do regularly) follow me on *https://www.bookbub.com/authors/emma-v-leech*

To find out more and to get news and sneak peeks of the first chapter of upcoming works, go to my website and sign up for the newsletter.
http://www.emmavleech.com/

Come and join the fans in my Facebook group for news, info and exciting discussion...

Emmas Book Club

Or Follow me here......

http://viewauthor.at/EmmaVLeechAmazon
Emma's Twitter page

About Me!

I started this incredible journey way back in 2010 with The Key to Erebus but didn't summon the courage to hit publish until October 2012. For anyone who's done it, you'll know publishing your first title is a terribly scary thing! I still get butterflies on the morning a new title releases but the terror has subsided at least. Now I just live in dread of the day my daughters are old enough to read them.

The horror! (On both sides I suspect.)

2017 marked the year that I made my first foray into Historical Romance and the world of the Regency Romance, and my word what a year! I was delighted by the response to this series and can't wait to add more titles. Paranormal Romance readers need not despair however as there is much more to come there too. Writing has become an addiction and as soon as one book is over I'm hugely excited to start the next so you can expect plenty more in the future.

As many of my works reflect I am greatly influenced by the beautiful French countryside in which I live. I've been here in the South West for the past twenty years though I was born and raised in

England. My three gorgeous girls are all bilingual and the youngest who is only six, is showing signs of following in my footsteps after producing *The Lonely Princess* all by herself.

I'm told book two is coming soon ...

She's keeping me on my toes, so I'd better get cracking!

KEEP READING TO DISCOVER MY OTHER BOOKS!

Other Works by Emma V. Leech

(For those of you who have read The French Fae Legend series, please remember that chronologically The Heart of Arima precedes The Dark Prince)

Girls Who Dare

To Dare a Duke

To Steal A Kiss

To Break the Rules

To Follow her Heart

To Wager with Love

To Dance with a Devil

To Winter at Wildsyde

To Experiment with Desire

To Bed the Baron

To Ride with the Knight (May 29, 2020)

To Hunt the Hunter (July 3, 2020)

Rogues & Gentlemen

The Rogue

The Earl's Temptation

Scandal's Daughter

The Devil May Care

Nearly Ruining Mr. Russell

One Wicked Winter

To Tame a Savage Heart

Persuading Patience

The Last Man in London

Flaming June

Charity and the Devil

A Slight Indiscretion

The Corinthian Duke

The Blackest of Hearts

Duke and Duplicity

The Scent of Scandal

The Rogue and The Earl's Temptation Box set

Melting Miss Wynter

The Winter Bride (A R&G Novella)

The Regency Romance Mysteries

Dying for a Duke

A Dog in a Doublet

The Rum and the Fox

The French Vampire Legend

The Key to Erebus

The Heart of Arima

The Fires of Tartarus

The Boxset (The Key to Erebus, The Heart of Arima)

The Son of Darkness (October 31, 2020)

The French Fae Legend

FANTASY ROMANCE
THE FRENCH FAE LEGEND
EMMA V. LEECH

"I had no idea about the beautiful world I was going to step into. A delightful combination of romance, mystery, adventure and fantasy. Emma has created an 'other world' so tangible and relatable, it feels almost real - at least I'm hoping." ***** Amazon Customer

The Dark Prince

The Dark Heart

The Dark Deceit

The Darkest Night

Short Stories: A Dark Collection.

Stand Alone

The Book Lover (a paranormal novella)

Audio Books!

Don't have time to read but still need your romance fix? The wait is over...

By popular demand, get your favourite Emma V Leech Regency Romance books on audio at Audible as performed by the incomparable Philip Battley and Gerard Marzilli. Several titles available and more added each month!

Click the links to choose your favourite and start listening now.

Rogues & Gentlemen

The Rogue

The Earl's Tempation

Scandal's Daughter

The Devil May Care

Nearly Ruining Mr Russell

One Wicked Winter

To Tame a Savage Heart

Persuading Patience

The Last Man in London
Flaming June
The Winter Bride, a novella

Girls Who Dare
To Dare a Duke
To Steal A Kiss
To Break the Rules
To Follow her Heart (coming soon)

The Regency Romance Mysteries
Dying for a Duke
A Dog in a Doublet (coming soon)

The French Vampire Legend
The Key to Erebus (coming soon)

Also check out Emma's regency romance series, Rogues & Gentlemen. Available now!

The Rogue
Rogues & Gentlemen Book 1

1815

Along the wild and untamed coast of Cornwall, smuggling is not only a way of life, but a means of survival.

Henrietta Morton knows well to look the other way when the free trading 'gentlemen' are at work. Yet when a notorious pirate, known as The Rogue, bursts in on her in the village shop, she takes things one step further.

Bewitched by a pair of wicked blue eyes, in a moment of insanity she hides the handsome fugitive from the local Militia. Her reward is a kiss that she just cannot forget. But in his haste to escape with his life, her pirate drops a letter, inadvertently giving

Henri incriminating information about the man she just helped free.

When her father gives her hand in marriage to a wealthy and villainous nobleman in return for the payment of his debts, Henri becomes desperate.

Blackmailing a pirate may be her only hope for freedom.

Read for free on Kindle Unlimited

The Rogue

Interested in a Regency Romance with a twist?

Dying for a Duke
The Regency Romance Mysteries Book 1

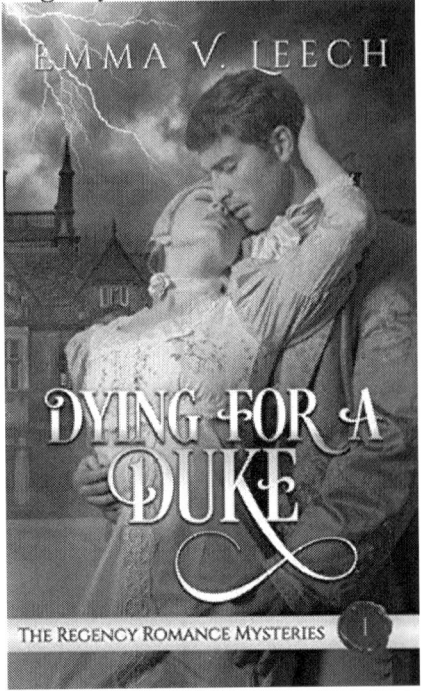

Straight-laced, imperious and morally rigid, Benedict Rutland - the darkly handsome Earl of Rothay - gained his title too young. Responsible for a large family of younger siblings that his frivolous parents have brought to bankruptcy, his youth was spent clawing back the family fortunes.

Now a man in his prime and financially secure he is betrothed to a strict, sensible and cool-headed woman who will never upset the balance of his life or disturb his emotions ...

But then Miss Skeffington-Fox arrives.

Brought up solely by her rake of a step-father, Benedict is scandalised by everything about the dashing Miss.

But as family members in line for the dukedom begin to die at an alarming rate, all fingers point at Benedict, and Miss Skeffington-Fox may be the only one who can save him.

FREE to read on Amazon Kindle Unlimited.. Dying for a Duke

Lose yourself in Emma's paranormal world with The French Vampire Legend series…..

The Key to Erebus
The French Vampire Legend Book 1

The truth can kill you.

Taken away as a small child, from a life where vampires, the Fae, and other mythical creatures are real and treacherous, the beautiful young witch, Jéhenne Corbeaux is totally unprepared when she returns to rural France to live with her eccentric Grandmother.

Thrown headlong into a world she knows nothing about she seeks to learn the truth about herself, uncovering secrets more shocking than anything she could ever have imagined and finding that she is by no means powerless to protect the ones she loves.

Despite her Gran's dire warnings, she is inexorably drawn to the dark and terrifying figure of Corvus, an ancient vampire and master of the vast Albinus family.

Jéhenne is about to find her answers and discover that, not only is Corvus far more dangerous than she could ever imagine, but that he holds much more than the key to her heart ...

FREE to read on Kindle Unlimited The Key to Erebus

Check out Emma's exciting fantasy series with hailed by Kirkus Reviews as "An enchanting fantasy with a likable heroine, romantic intrigue, and clever narrative flourishes."

The Dark Prince
The French Fae Legend Book 1

*Two Fae Princes
One Human Woman
And a world ready to tear them all apart*

Laen Braed is Prince of the Dark fae, with a temper and reputation to match his black eyes, and a heart that despises the human race. When he is sent back through the forbidden gates between realms to retrieve an ancient fae artifact, he returns home with far more than he bargained for.

Corin Albrecht, the most powerful Elven Prince ever born. His golden eyes are rumoured to be a gift from the gods, and destiny is calling him. With a love for the human world that runs deep, his friendship with Laen is being torn apart by his prejudices.

Océane DeBeauvoir is an artist and bookbinder who has always relied on her lively imagination to get her through an unhappy and uneventful life. A jewelled dagger put on display at a nearby museum hits the headlines with speculation of another race, the Fae. But the discovery also inspires Océane to create an extraordinary piece of art that cannot be confined to the pages of a book.

With two powerful men vying for her attention and their friendship stretched to the breaking point, the only question that remains...who is truly The Dark Prince.

The man of your dreams is coming...or is it your nightmares he visits? Find out in Book One of The French Fae Legend.

Available now to read for FREE *on Kindle Unlimited.*

The Dark Prince

Acknowledgements

Thanks, of course, to my wonderful editor Kezia Cole.

To Victoria Cooper for all your hard work, amazing artwork and above all your unending patience!!! Thank you so much. You are amazing!

To my BFF, PA, personal cheerleader and bringer of chocolate, Varsi Appel, for moral support, confidence boosting and for reading my work more times than I have. I love you loads!

A huge thank you to all of Emma's Book Club members! You guys are the best!

I'm always so happy to hear from you so do email or message me :)

emmavleech@orange.fr

To my husband Pat and my family ... For always being proud of me.